Call It Chemistry

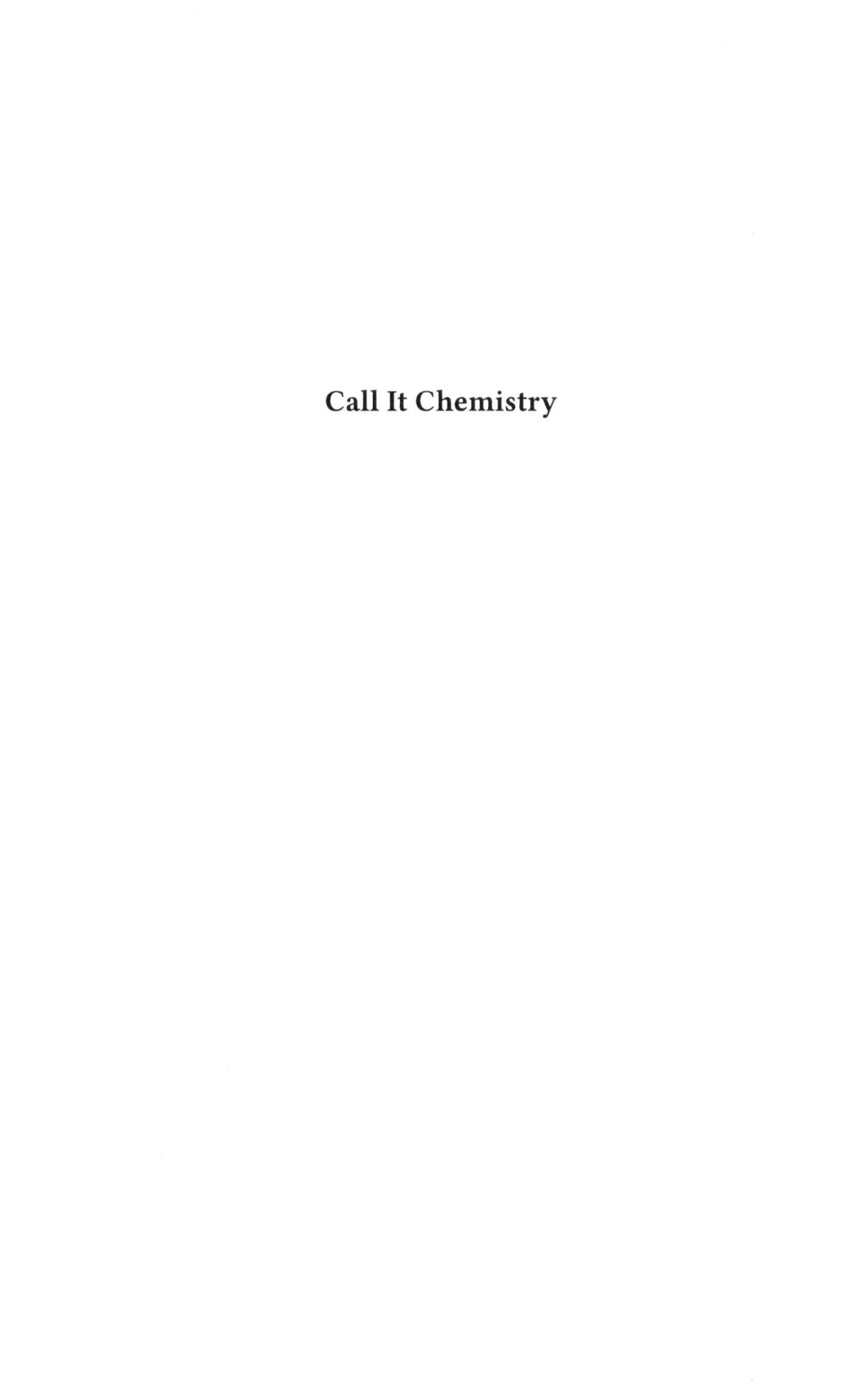

Call It Chemistry

Golden Grove Series Book 1

D.J. Van Oss

Copyright (C) 2019 D.J. Van Oss
Layout design and Copyright (C) 2019 by Next Chapter
Published 2019 by Liaison – A Next Chapter Imprint
Cover art by Cover Mint
This book is a work of fiction. Names, characters, places, and incidents are the product of the author's imagination or are used fictitiously. Any resemblance to actual events, locales, or persons, living or dead, is purely coincidental.
All rights reserved. No part of this book may be reproduced or transmitted in any form or by any means, electronic or mechanical, including photocopying, recording, or by any information storage and retrieval system, without the author's permission.

Chapter One

Twelve Years Ago
Golden Grove High

The day of the Nitrovex Scholarship Fair was clear, bright, and perfect. An omen if there ever was one.

Katie was doing a few last-minute checks on her project to make sure it sparkled. She didn't want to take any chances on something being out of balance. The judging was starting in only thirty minutes, and everything needed to be perfect if she was going to win.

She stepped back, put her hands on her hips and smiled.

Perfect and unavoidably grand. Her entry was a large mobile made of intricate glass pieces, each turning on its own gleaming silver wire. The slightest breeze moved the pieces like multicolored snowflakes in slow motion. It was brave, it was bold, it was her masterpiece. If she said so herself.

She stole a glance at Peter, one table over, bent over and fiddling with some tube on his project. His wavy black hair flopped over his blue eyes, and her heart did a flip, sticking the landing. She sighed. *Steady.*

She scanned the room, eying the other entries. It was the usual. Kenny Terpstra and his Tesla coil, which she was pretty sure his dad had built for him for their sixth-grade science fair. Looked like Ronny Sharp had taken some tadpoles from the creek, stuck them in his sister's blue wading pool and called it "The Miracle of Life." Down the row, Lisa Banks was trying to coerce some white mice through a maze, but they seemed more interested in crawling up her arm.

Katie grinned internally. The competition was thin this year. So much the better for her.

She had given up trying to convince her parents that art was her passion. But today was her best chance to show them she could make more than something they would stick on the refrigerator door or display on the back of a dusty bookshelf.

The annual Nitrovex Scholarship Fair was the brightest hope for many of Golden Grove's seniors who wanted to go to college. Funded by John Wells, the always upbeat founder of the local chemical plant where Katie's parents were chemical engineers, first prize was such a big gift that for some students it determined where you could afford to go to college.

That wasn't as true for Katie. Her parents were happy to send her to pretty much any decent school. As long as it wasn't the Mason School of Art in Chicago that she'd had her eye on since eighth grade. No, that wouldn't be "practical" and she needed to think about a "career."

She had begged them to the point where they had finally given her one hope. If she won the Nitrovex scholarship for her art project, they'd pay the difference.

She could already see herself in Chicago next fall, immersed in a world of endless creativity along with hundreds of other students just like her, laughing, sharing ideas. No more condescending comments like, "That's nice, but what do you really want to do with your life?" They would understand there.

She already knew she was going to start calling herself "Kate." She might even cut her hair short, like Audrey Tautou in *Amélie*.

But first, she had to win.

She went back to her work, admiring the glint of the fragile glass as it slowly rotated. Even under the stark, buzzing fluorescent lights of the noisy gym, her mobile was beautiful. *Just think what it would look like in a real art gallery.*

The local yokels might not get it, but Mr. Wells's wife, Mary, who she knew was an art connoisseur, would be sure to recognize her talent. And she was a judge this year.

And it was high time a project of culture and refinement got noticed. Who cared about the sex lives of tadpoles or a catapult made from Popsicle sticks that could chuck an orange across a room?

The only downside was that Peter had a project in the running, too. And if she won, that meant he would lose. But it wasn't like he was going to have a hard time getting into any college he wanted. He got straight As in everything.

She chanced another glance at his project, and she had to admit, it looked impressive. She wasn't exactly sure what it was supposed to be, but it had the requisite metal tubes, wires, and hoses sticking out of it. A little wisp of steam or something floated up from one of the connections. The corners of her mouth drooped. It looked like he was her competition.

She'd begun working on *her* project in early summer, right after school had ended. But, she'd told Peter, she had a problem. A problem she had to admit she'd created only to get his help. How to balance the glass in her intricate mobile. It was just science-y enough to get his attention and get him into her basement where she was working on it.

It had all been going so well. They were starting to connect again, sharing thoughts, dreams about the future after high school, occasionally "accidentally" touching hands. And then…

A hard frown creased Katie's face.

She moved in.

July 5, when she and Peter had been picking up bottle-rocket sticks from their yards after the neighborhood fireworks the night before, an orange and white U-Haul had pulled in front of the Proctor's old house across the street. Not the usual pull-behind trailer U-Haul but the big job, the semi. They watched all afternoon as it poured out furniture—nice-looking furniture, too, and a pool table and a ping pong table and a big-screen TV.

And then a light blue minivan pulled up. Illinois license plates. Cook County. She knew from her parents that meant Chicago and big-city sophistication and culture. The side door rolled open automatically and out stepped Miss Hair Toss, Miss Perfect Teeth, slow-motion, like she was auditioning for a movie.

Penny Fitch. Short shorts and a Tiffany watch. Katie could almost see Peter's blue eyes widen behind his glasses, lopsided smile on his face.

And that was it. It was clear. She needed to save him. Save him from this usurper, this new (obviously rich) girl from the city who had flounced in like she owned the place.

All summer long, Kate gagged when she heard, "Hi, Peter! Hey, Peter! What's up, Peter?" And then when senior year started, it got worse. Peter and Penny's lockers were only three feet apart. Katie's was on a different floor. Then at lunch, Penny would sit on the opposite side of Peter, battling her eyelashes and asking him for help with her chemistry homework.

Penny was ruining everything.

Peter couldn't see her like Katie could. He was too nice. That was always his weakness, too nice, to a fault. But Katie could see what was going on. Penny thought she knew him, that just because she was cute and liked science and was in cross country with him, she could pick him right up, like some sort of adorable puppy.

And how cute and giggly she acted around him. "Penny and Peter, two peas in a pod. It almost rhymes!" Kate heard her say at lunch once.

Barf. *No, it doesn't, you moron.*

All her cooing and tittering and hair tosses. Penny Fitch, the wispy witch. And when Katie was really mad, she used another word besides witch. Not out loud, of course, because *she* was still a nice girl.

But the thought that unnerved her most, the one she never dared entertain for more than a few seconds, was what if Peter was only being nice to Katie, too? What if all the time they'd spent together, growing up, sharing pecan pie shakes at Ray's Diner, was all just him being nice? What if she wasn't special?

No, that was negative thinking, and she squelched it.

It was her mission to protect Peter from this new girl.

Phase One: Keep him busy through the summer. That meant ramping up the need for advice on her Scholarship Fair project, pool parties with Peter at her friend's house (without Penny, of course), and anything she could think of to keep the witch at bay.

Phase Two, which commenced after school started, was harder: Katie made sure, whenever she could, that Penny never got a private word in with Peter, inserting herself into their conversations or making sure that one of her friends (none of who liked the new girl, either) did likewise. But there was still the proximity issue at home. Penny didn't live right next door (Katie still had that advantage), but she was close enough. Too close, judging by the smiles and waves she saw them exchanging and the runs they took together every so often.

That gave rise to Phase Three, the final and trickiest phase of all: the upcoming Homecoming Dance.

She had been dropping hints like lead feathers since late in the summer: *Is homecoming early again this year, Peter?... What's the theme for homecoming again, Peter?... What do you think of this homecoming dress I found online, Peter?*

Even for a boy, he seemed to be dense about getting the hint.

She hadn't gone to a Homecoming Dance until last year when Brian McDermott had asked her. Nice enough guy, but he wore too much aftershave and sweated when they slow danced. It had taken three days for the Brut to wash off her hands. Peter always smelled clean, like Ivory soap. At least that's what the Clarks used for soap in their guest bathroom the last time she'd been over there.

It was the final phase, her way of getting Peter off the starting line. If they could just go to homecoming together, then they could see what it was like to be a couple. Take the photo together under the flowered arch, smiling, she in the pink chiffon dress she'd already picked out online, him in his tux rented from Maxwell's downtown, complete with a pink tie to match her dress. He'd see the photo every day on his refrigerator where she knew his mom would stick it under a magnet.

Confidence flowed through her. She knew him. He was a science geek—he just needed to see something in action, see the quantifiable results, and then he would know they should be together.

It would be as factual as a chemical reaction, undeniable. Look at the charts and numbers, Peter! See the graph?

It wasn't a perfect plan, but it was a good one, and it was going to work. She had a feeling, some inner voice telling her, *This is it. He'll see it, he'll see me, and he'll know. We should be together.*

College? They could figure that out later. Long-distance relationships worked all the time, right? Once the Scholarship Fair was over, plan "Get Peter to Homecoming" would be launched fully into action.

As someone walked by behind her table in the gym, she caught a whiff of something sickly sweet and overpowering. Her jaw clenched as she turned her head and wrinkled her nose. The perfect teeth, perfect long black hair, and perfect clothes. The Wispy Witch was here.

She watched Penny sidle over to Peter, start talking to him, laugh, and then—yup, there it was, the perfect hair toss. She had a bet with her friends that Penny perfected her hair toss and simultaneous tittery laugh by practicing in the mirror.

Katie's eyes narrowed. Penny had her own project two tables over from Peter's, and there she was, hovering around Peter like a lovesick butterfly. She had a dozen other boys she could have glommed on to. Why didn't she pour her poison on them?

Oh, that's right. He's too nice to her. Peter was always too nice.

Katie watched as he followed Penny to her table, where he twisted some insignificant knob on her insignificant pile of whatever her project was. Some box with a hat and a…Who cares? She probably had her dad buy it online, anyway.

Well, she could shoot a life-sized Saturn rocket with bells on it through the roof for all the good it would do her today.

Katie went back to her adjusting a few pieces of her sculpture. The multicolored glass of the elaborate mobile twirled slowly, each piece reflecting shards of light. She'd already been getting admiring glances from students and even some of the teachers. She had a feeling.

This was her year.

Chapter Two

Present Day

A burst of fire puffed out of a test tube bubbling over a Bunsen burner. It roiled towards the ceiling in a mini-mushroom cloud before it evaporated. The stunned class let out a combined "Whoa…"

Peter Clark stepped back and turned off his torch. "And that's why we wear our goggles. So, can anyone tell me what the three products of combustion are?"

His classroom of high school students shifted in their seats, some looking at their phones, all avoiding eye contact with him. He picked up the heavy organic chemistry book from his desk, held it between his fingers, and dropped it.

The thud echoed like a cannon, and all heads shot up.

"The correct answer is fuel, oxygen, and heat." He moved to the whiteboard at the front of the room and began drawing with a red marker. "Oxygen is already in the air, and the heat is from the burner, which leaves the fuel. So, add anhydrous sodium acetate and sodium hydroxide and you get a combustible substance called methane. Otherwise known as cow farts."

A few titters rippled through the room.

He put down the marker, wiped his hands on his jeans, and glanced at the clock. "Okay, we still have a few more minutes, so I wanted to remind you about the test coming up next Thursday."

A chorus of groans rolled over the class.

"Yeah, yeah, I know, another test. I'm cruel and inhuman. But we wouldn't have to do the test early if some nameless bunch of knuckleheads hadn't nominated me for this teacher award thing."

The groans turned back to titters and smiles. Someone shouted out, "Go, Mr. C!" punctuated by a whistle. The class laughed.

"Yes, thanks so much. So, that being the case, I'll be in Des Moines next week on Friday. But don't worry, Mr. Potter has agreed to teach the class while I'm wasting my time at some awards banquet."

"Do you get to wear a tux?" Nick Norton shouted from the back row.

Peter smiled. He did love his class. "On a teacher's salary? You've got to be kidding me."

The class laughed again.

"Again, the more you study now, the less you'll end up having to cram on the last night—"

A tone blared through the classroom speaker, signaling the period was over. Students immediately began grabbing backpacks and books.

"Don't forget," he called out above the shuffling noise, "we're going to start working on gas laws and kinetic theory on Monday. Read through the experiment on page eighty-one." He tapped the side of his head. "And don't forgot your goggles!"

As students hustled out of his classroom, Peter moved to the whiteboard and began erasing the day's lesson, hoping at least one of the bleary-eyed kids in his Intro to Chemistry class had learned the difference between combustion and burning. This was the last class of the day, and even though most of them were good kids, they couldn't wait to get out the door and have school over with for the weekend.

It wasn't like many of them were going to be using much chemistry once they left high school. He wondered again what it would be like to teach at a small college or even a university. Some place where the students actually wanted to be there instead of home gaming, road tripping to the mall, or glued to their cell phones.

Oh, there were a few of the mathletes who got it, maybe even loved chemistry like he did, but he felt like he was running out of ways to make it interesting. Maybe if he dropped watermelons from the school roof to demonstrate kinetic theory…

"Ready?" Lucius Potter called from the doorway. "Pie shake's calling my name."

Lucius was tall, angular, and the oldest teacher at Golden Grove High. Considered by students and their parents as much a permanent a fixture as the deadly meat loaf in the lunchroom, he had just celebrated his forty-first year teaching every science class in existence. He stood with his long arms folded across his black wool vest, black thick-rimmed glasses and thick gray mustache giving him a professorial look that belied his playful nature.

Generations of Golden Grove students adored Lucius Potter, many having gone on to be doctors, scientists, or teachers themselves, like Peter.

"Just about ready." Peter moved to his desk, tapped a few keys on his laptop to shut it down, then closed the lid. "I'll do grades tomorrow at home."

Every Friday after school he and Lucius had pie shakes at Ray's Diner downtown, then gabbed about science and life. Mostly life, since they'd done science all week at school. Today the topic would almost certainly be the herd of hilarious beards that were cropping up around town for the competition on Sunday.

He grabbed his coat. Summer was definitely gone and the fall Iowa air could get pretty crisp later in the day.

Lucius entered the room, glancing around. He still seemed to marvel at the bright, clean sheen of the new high school building, built only a few years ago. Peter had to admit it was a huge improvement over the musty old brick building where he'd had to attend class.

He filled his briefcase with work for next week. "Got big plans for the weekend?"

Lucius shrugged as he came over to Peter's desk. "Nothing much. You? Going to the beard contest Sunday?"

"No, thank you. They're starting to creep me out, all those spider-faced guys popping up around the square. What is it with the weird conventions in this town?" This summer it had been the "Larry Convention" when the town filled up with three hundred guys all named Larry. "Besides, I need to get ahead on these lab grades since I've got that Des Moines thing next weekend. Wish they'd just send me the plaque or whatever so I didn't have to leave work. Some of these kids are on the edge as it is."

Luscious leaned against the desk. "Maybe you're pushing them too hard."

Peter could tell it was a goad. He put his pencil down. "Like you did me?"

"You didn't need pushing. You *wanted* to spend more time in the lab. 'Extra Credit Clark,' remember?"

"Not like I had much else to do around here."

"Oh, I think you had some other options. Still might," he added under his breath.

Peter wasn't sure exactly what that meant, but let it go.

"Besides," Lucius continued, "you deserve this award."

Peter nodded, but it was a suspicious nod. "I still think you put them up to it.

"The students? It was their idea actually. They're the ones that nominated you last spring."

Peter gave a sniff. "I don't suppose it comes with a raise?"

Lucius chuckled. "Not likely. But speaking of which." He put his briefcase on the edge of the desk and pulled out a manila envelope, then extracted a glossy page. "There is something I'd like you to take a look at." He pushed a brochure in front of Peter.

He scanned it, then looked up. "The Dixon School? That's in the Chicago suburbs, right?"

"It is. Taught there myself once. Just a few summer prep-courses, filling in for a colleague."

"Really? You never told me that."

Lucius shrugged. "It was a long time ago. We used chisels and rocks instead of pencils."

Peter turned the brochure over. Dixon was a private high school. It was old, prestigious, and expensive. "So, what's this about?"

Lucius leaned over and pointed to the bottom where a printed sticker had been attached. "Position's open there. They're looking for a new chemistry teacher for the upper grades."

"So?"

"Well, in case you haven't noticed, you're a chemistry teacher."

Peter sighed. "Lucius, this is way out of my league." He put the brochure down. "Besides, I have a job."

Lucius gestured at the row of windows to the left of Peter's desk. "Yes, with a lovely view of a utility shed and a rusty green dumpster."

Peter shrugged. "I don't know. I've kind of grown fond of knowing Roger will be dumping moldy tater tots outside my window at one-thirty every day. It gives me a calming sense of stability."

"I suppose it would be hard to leave that behind."

"Exactly. It's like you always tell me. 'If you ain't where you're at, you're no place.'"

Lucius pointed at his chest. "I say that?"

"Yup."

The older man rubbed his chin. "I think I stole that from an episode of *M*A*S*H*." He sat down on the edge of Peter's desk, seeming to grow serious. "Peter, you know I normally don't try to interfere in your life—"

Peter gave two short chuckles. "Since when?"

"Okay. But this opportunity at Dixon is a particularly good one. With your master's, your experience, and especially now that you've gotten this award, you're perfect for the job."

"I don't know…"

"They think so, too."

"They? They who?"

Lucius avoided his gaze. "I took the liberty of contacting that old colleague. He's now the school's principal. I told him about you, and they're interested."

"You didn't."

"Yes, and they want to set up an interview with you. If you're interested."

"I'm not."

This time, Lucius looked him right in the eyes. Peter hated it when his friend did that. It usually meant he was going to end up doing exactly what Lucius wanted. "Just do an interview. What can it hurt? Maybe I'll drop some hints around here that you're being headhunted. Might get you that raise."

Peter chuckled again. A raise might be nice, but…He shook his head. "I don't have time to go to Des Moines next week, much less all the way to Chicago."

"It's four hours from here. Not on the moon. At least say you'll think about it."

Peter knew once Lucius got something in his head he wouldn't let it go. "I'll think about it." But he knew he wouldn't.

Apparently, Lucius did too, because Lucius pulled out the magazine rolled under his arm and flipped it open.

Peter shook his head when he saw the cover. *Chemical Quarterly*. Out of the frying pan…"Who is it this time?"

"Whatever do you mean?" Lucius shut off the lights and headed into the hallway, scanning the journal's table of contents. "Say, here's something interesting."

"I'm sure." Peter closed and locked his classroom door. *Here it comes.*

"An article by Jeremy Von Hornig. What's that, his third article in the past five years?"

"You're the one that's counting."

"He was in your master's program too, wasn't he?"

Peter sighed. "I had to tutor him through our thermodynamics final. He set off the automatic sprinklers in the lab because he left a burner on all night."

"And here he is with an article in a national journal."

"Lucius, you're doing it again. I'm fine where I am. I like my job."

"Just making sure you know there are more possibilities beyond teaching in Golden Grove."

"I'm well aware. Besides, it's worked for you."

His friend nodded, jutting out his lower jaw. "True."

"And you never regretted it, right?"

"Teaching? No, not teaching."

Peter pointed to the journal. "Besides, these things are mostly just for status."

"True. Have you checked at Nitrovex lately?" Lucius persisted. "There are plenty of good chemists doing great work there."

"Are you trying to get rid of me?" Peter shook his head.

"Nope. Just heard they're really expanding their overseas operations."

"Heard that too." Peter always kept an eye on happenings at Nitrovex. What self-respecting chemistry grad wouldn't? But the thought of some cush job in Europe didn't appeal to him.

"I know John Wells pretty well. I'd be happy to put in a good word for you."

As they neared the front entrance, Peter waved back at a passing student. "Thanks, but no. Maybe someday. But right now, my—"

"—students need me too much," Lucius finished for him. "Yes, I know. Just remember, you're not as indispensable as you might think you are."

"Please…" Peter drew out the word and added a dramatic wave of his arm. "You're talking to the Science Teacher of the Year."

"My apologies, good sir," Lucius responded.

"Besides, Nitrovex does mostly organic chem. I'm more of a biochem guy." Peter pushed through the double front doors. "Believe me, I'm fine where I am." He pulled his car keys from his pocket. "Meet you at Ray's?"

Lucius looked as if he were going to say something, then just nodded. "Sure thing."

Outside, Peter found his blue Camry and unlocked it with the key fob. *I'm fine where I am.*

But exactly where was that? Trapped in his hometown's only high school, teaching the few students who cared enough to be actually interested in the difference between a mole and a molecule? Stuck in the same small town he'd grown up in? Left in the dust by people he'd gone to college with who've gone on to prestigious, big-paying jobs at companies like Nitrovex?

He looked at the cover of the journal. Was Lucius right? Was it time to move on, and up?

He opened the driver's side door and got in, dumping his briefcase and the stack of folders and papers on the passenger seat. The brochure from Dixon slid onto the floor, and he picked it up.

The place looked like a college campus, with laughing students walking among huge trees to stately old buildings. It did sound like a good opportunity. And he did have the qualifications. In fact, with his masters, he was probably over-qualified to teach at Golden Grove.

Maybe he did deserve a more prestigious job. How many more D's from disinterested students was he going to have to endure? Nothing against Lucius, but did Peter want to spend his whole life in Golden Grove? He'd never left, except for college and grad school.

If it hadn't been for his dad…

No, he wasn't going to go down that path again. But it wouldn't hurt to do some thinking. He could probably swing at least one interview, just to kick the tires, so to speak. He started his car, shifted it into reverse.

Besides, it was Chicago. It might have a lot to offer…

No, Peter, don't go there. It had been, what? Twelve years? Yeah, twelve years since he'd ruined her life.

Whenever he thought of it, he always told himself it was just high school. That place so far away, the place everyone was supposed to leave behind and move on from to bigger and better things, away from the embarrassing haircuts and the dropped lunch-room trays and the drama. But he knew that it was much more for some. For Katie Brady, the Scholarship Fair had been everything, all her hopes in one fragile basket.

And Peter had been the one to kick that basket over, scattering her hopes across the gym floor.

* * *

Twelve Years Ago
Golden Grove High

Peter's project for the Scholarship Fair was a chemical propulsion rocket. He didn't care much about winning the scholarship money. He just didn't want to disappoint his favorite science teacher, Mr. Potter.

He ventured a glance at Katie, who was wiping a smudge from her mobile at the table near his. B before C, Brady and then Clark. All through grade school, middle school, high school, even if they'd wanted to avoid each other, the alphabet wouldn't let them. Which was fine with him.

He'd always liked Katie, not just because she was his neighbor and they'd grown up together. Katie was...different. He felt so at ease with her. He felt...connected in some way. And at the same time, he felt flustered when he had to talk with her. Chemical reactions in the brain was what an online article said about it.

So, when she'd asked him to check a few things on her project at the beginning of summer, he thought maybe this was a chance for them to find out. Was there something more?

They'd always been friends—always would be friends, probably. But they'd grown up. She'd grown up, for sure.

He wasn't sure at first if he should have those feelings for her, but that lasted all of about three seconds when he'd seen her, outside, washing her dad's car in shorts and a tank top. Summer after their freshman year, June 8, his birthday. From then on he'd made a point of being home on Sunday afternoons, car-washing day. Felt a little guilty at first, but she was just, well...

Okay, the word was beautiful. Not only body beautiful, although a freckled, sudsy girl in a red tank top unquestionably fit that definition. Not drop-dead, over-the-top, unattainable six-foot-tall model beautiful. But it was more than that, and it unnerved his reliable scientific mind why he couldn't put his finger on it.

Like an atom or a molecule, it was there. It was there, somewhere, in how she cocked her head and smiled, the sprinkle of freckles around her nose, the perfume she started wearing—what was it called? *Lucky You?*

He liked the way she smelled. It wasn't like they spent a lot of time on her project. They spent half their time in her basement just talking, drinking Dr. Pepper out of bottles from the old machine the Brady's had there. She'd fiddle with her wire and glass bits. He'd give a few suggestions when she asked, mostly about balancing the weights, but that was it.

He just… *Admit it, Peter. You just wanted to spend time with her.*

A teacher was announcing something from the stage PA system. Judging was starting from the front tables and working its way back. He figured he'd have another fifteen minutes before they got to him. He checked the plastic tube that fed from the oxidizer tank to the base of his experiment and made sure it was snug in the fitting.

Katie had worked really hard on her mobile, and, even though he was no artist, he knew it was very good. Nitrovex might be all about chemicals, but that didn't mean they only picked the techy stuff. In fact, the owner's wife was an artist, and she was one of the judges today.

He stole another glance at her table. She seemed pretty confident. And she should be. Deep down, he hoped she would win. Even in middle school, she'd dreamed of going to art school, but he knew her parents weren't too big on the idea. A scholarship might be just the thing to change their minds.

He tested another connection and then stopped. The judges were a row behind and two tables back, working their way towards the front of the gym. Four serious-looking adults armed with clipboards. He swallowed, then stepped back. He knew his project was ready, and if he kept fiddling with it he might break something.

"Well, Mr. Clark, everything's looking good, I see."

Peter looked up to see the smiling, mustached face of his favorite teacher. "Thanks, Mr. Potter. I just checked all the connections. I think it'll work."

Mr. Potter gave him a small clap on the back. "Oh, it'll work fine." His teacher touched a tube and checked a connection. "Have to say, it's pretty ingenious. Chemical reactions as a propulsion device. I wouldn't be surprised if there were some practical uses for this type of thing."

Peter knew Mr. Potter was just being supportive, but he felt a swell of pride, anyway. The teacher gave him a wink and moved down the aisle.

He felt a sharp poke in his ribs. "Hey, Peter," a light voice said directly behind his ear.

He twisted in surprise, catching his hip on the edge of the table. A spare pipe from his project rolled off the edge of the table and clanged onto the gym floor. Everyone in the vicinity jumped, especially Katie, who moved between him and her sculpture.

"Geez, Penny, watch it," he said.

It was Penny Fitch, his new neighbor who'd moved in over the summer. Although Peter liked her—she always had a smile, and she liked science—she could get a little annoying at times. A lot of the guys were after her he knew. Petite with long black hair and blue eyes, a nice combination. Then he wrinkled his nose. She always wore so much perfume she smelled like the candle section down at Bailey's Variety. As pretty as she might be, she wasn't really his type.

He stole a glance at Katie, who was looking the other way.

"Sorry," Penny said. Smiling, she flicked back her hair and angled her head, like she was a model about to be photographed. Why did some girls do that? "So, Petey, what's this thing do? Looks impressive." She touched the plastic tube that led to the large, silver, metal casing that was the main propellant tank.

Peter touched her hand to stop her. "Hey, careful. You'll set it off."

She took her hand back. "Oops. Sorry again."

He shrugged. "It's okay." He glanced to the right. "They're going to judge in a few minutes. After that, you can touch it all you want."

Penny gave him a quizzical look. He felt his face flushing beet red. He tried to think of something, anything to say to get rid of her, but his brain had vapor locked. *Idiot.*

"Okay," she said after what seemed like an hour. She jerked her head in the direction of the next table. "You think she has a chance?"

Peter welcomed the changed topic. "Katie? Sure, she does. She's got as much chance as anybody else here. More, probably."

"If she does, she should thank you for all your help."

"Oh, I hardly did anything. She did all the real work."

Penny nodded, unconvinced. "Well, I hope you win."

"Oh. Thanks. You too."

"I'll come check you out later," she said, then turned with another hair flip and began to walk away. "Good luck," she called back with another smile at him before she narrowed her eyes at Katie's sculpture.

"Thanks," he managed to say. He suddenly wished he hadn't told Penny about Katie asking for his help. Maybe he shouldn't have said anything about her on those runs. He knew the rule about outside help, but that meant parents or an expert, right? Another student was probably okay, as long as they didn't contribute too much.

He stole a glance to the right. Katie was staring at him, lips pressed together in a hard line. Her eyes looked like they could cut through steel, and they were directed squarely at his forehead.

She quickly turned away, straightening something on her table.

Was she mad at him?

He didn't have time to find out. The judges were at her table.

The next twenty minutes were a blur of joy and crashing pain.

Chapter Three

Present Day

The yellow VW Bug crunched to a stop on the gravel beside the sign perched at the entrance to the town. Kate shut the engine shut off.

A quaint wood and brick sign proclaimed "Welcome to Golden Grove, Home of the Griffins."

She gazed through the windshield, down at the town, still familiar after all the years. The silver water tower peeking above the trees, the red roof of the fire station, the tops of the trees just beginning to turn various yellows and oranges in the fall Sunday sun. Not much seemed to have changed from this vantage point. Actually beautiful, if you were only visiting one of the picturesque shops and bakeries downtown, or looking down from the limestone bluffs at the slow-rolling Mississippi.

Maybe for some people, the Nitrovex workers, the shop owners, the Golden Grove "lifers," it was fine. But not for her. The bigger city had always been her dream, her escape, even before high school had chewed her up and spit her out.

She gripped the steering wheel and blew out some air. Okay, just in and out of town, then back to Chicago. No one from high school needed to know she was even here. She could handle a few days. She'd be out at the chemical plant most of the time, anyway.

She turned the key in the ignition and the car purred back to life.

Fifteen minutes later, she parked the Bug on the brick-lined curb in front of the familiar yard. She turned it off, then waited a moment, hands in her lap, listening, gazing out the side window she'd rolled down on her way into town.

It was quiet, the usual small-town Sunday silence, with just a few birds chirping and a car passing and disappearing a block or so away. In the distance was the rush of the grain elevator, a sound she'd forgotten about but knew meant fall was in full swing.

She noticed the maple tree that used to shade the front curb by the driveway was gone, but the huge elm that showered bright green leaves onto the driveway each fall was still near the front door. The bushes there were larger but still well trimmed.

The house had been painted. It was no longer the familiar pale yellow she remembered but a mixture of light green with white and yellow trim. A variety of potted plants were placed neatly on either side of the front steps, which led to an expansive porch lined with wicker chairs and supported with round white Corinthian columns.

The old porch swing was hanging there where she used to play dolls or read. Or play battleship with Peter. She smiled, remembering. Not all of it was bad. Then she glanced at the familiar house next door, and her smile faded.

She sighed, resisting an urge to just put the car in drive and head back to Chicago. The memories of this place were starting to close in on her like some giant hand. Even the air seemed familiar and stiff, as if the town itself had recognized her, remembered her, was telling her again how she didn't belong here anymore.

Sorry, Danni. Couldn't do it. Find someone else to spearhead the Nitrovex campaign.

No. There was too much of her career future riding on this assignment to consider bailing just because of some old high-school ghosts.

Carrying her light bag, she hustled up the narrow walk to the front door, stealing glances sideways. She felt like an infiltrator, a spy in her own childhood yard. She paused at the front door, feeling strange having to ring the doorbell to her own home. The familiar old *ding-dong* was followed by the sound of muffled footsteps.

Carol Harding's instantly recognizable cherubic face peeked through the lace-curtained window to the side of the door. Short and slightly stocky with short gray hair, she pulled the inside door open and beamed a motherly smile. "Katie!" she said, pushing past the screen door, arms outstretched.

"Hi, Carol." Kate dropped her bag, grinning as she hugged the woman who had practically been a surrogate mother to her when she was a teen.

The older woman released her, holding her at arms' length. "My goodness, you look so pretty."

Kate felt her cheeks turning pink. "Thanks."

Carol waved her hand. "Well, come in, come in."

As Kate grabbed her bag and entered the front hallway, the smell of fresh pine, home-baked bread, and apple-scented candles greeted her. It wasn't the smell of her house as she remembered it, but the difference seemed strangely comforting. Not the sterile house of two chemical engineers she'd remembered growing up.

A small orange tabby cat appeared from nowhere and began wending its way around her leg.

She frowned. "Sparky?"

Carol laughed. "Not quite. Son of Sparky, actually. That's Tommy." The cat gave another swipe around Kate's leg and then disappeared into another room. "Sparky ran away a few years ago. Never quite got the hang of the new house, I guess."

"Oh." Kate felt an unexpected pang. For a cat who'd hissed and acted like she had no business invading his space at the orchard. "You never found him?"

Carol shook her head. "No. I keep hoping he'll come back. Half expect him to show up with a dead mouse on the porch some morning. But, he's probably long gone by now."

Carol wiped her hands on an apron as she moved into what was once the house's drawing room, where visitors used to wait. It was a cozy, faded oak-trimmed room with the same light rose-colored wallpaper Kate had convinced her mother to hang when she was ten. *Still works*, she thought.

"So, how was your trip?" Carol asked as she sat in an old velvet-cushioned chair next to a round marble-topped lamp stand.

Kate put her bag down by the chair opposite her friend and sat. "Fine. Not as long as I remember."

"Well, perceptions change with time. You haven't been back for a while, remember?"

Kate gave a small smile. Was that a gentle dig directed at her? "Work keeps me busy. Climbing the corporate ladder and all."

She glanced around the well-appointed room, sprinkled with reading material and tasteful antiques. She recognized some of the items from Carol's orchard house. "The house looks great."

Carol returned a smile. "Well, it keeps me busy. Lots to dust. Between this, the Community Center, and my sewing group, I never have a lack of anything to do."

Kate remembered Carol's sewing hobby. "Do you still get together with your sewing buddies?"

"Oh, yes—weekly, here at the house. There's twelve of us now." She smiled impishly. "We call ourselves the Thread Heads."

Kate laughed. "Well, as long as you're staying out of trouble."

Carol's eyebrows arched giving her face an innocent look. "Oh, we do. Most of the time." She leaned forward. "Oh, Katie. It's so good to see you."

"You too, Carol." It really was.

Carol straightened a doily on the table. "From what your mother says, it sounds like you're doing very well."

"Pretty well."

"And you're going to do some work out at Nitrovex?"

"That's the plan. My company does corporate branding makeovers." She thought she'd better explain. "That means we talk to companies and find out what they're about, then come up with new logos, letterhead, slogans, that sort of thing. It's kind of like when you get a makeover."

Carol smiled. "Haven't had one of those in a while."

"With your natural beauty? You don't need one."

That got a dismissive hand wave. "Oh, shush. Well, with that kind of buttering up I'm sure you'll do just fine at your job."

Kate sighed. "I hope so. It's my first crack at a big account. Nitrovex has grown a lot." Not that she knew much about what the company actually made, despite her parents once working there. She could count the times she'd visited them on two hands. That and a mind-numbing field trip for eighth grade science were the only times she'd set foot in the place.

"Yes, John Wells has done wonders with that company. Always had a good head on his shoulders."

Kate arched her eyebrows. "Carol. Are you shopping around?"

Her friend caught her tone. "Oh, you. Behave. John's just an old friend. His wife passed away just a few years ago."

"Oh." She hadn't seen that in any of the Nitrovex materials. She'd liked Mrs. Wells, despite what happened at the Scholarship Fair. "You have any…other friends?" she probed. "Does Wally the mailman still deliver here?"

"If you mean male friends, then yes, of course, I'm acquainted with some of the men around here." Carol fussed with a button on her sleeve. "And, yes, Wally is still around and no, he's not my type. I hope you didn't come here just to grill me about my love life."

"Really?" Kate said, ignoring her. She crossed her arms, enjoying this little teasing session. "So, who is your type these days? Jock? Policeman? Painter? Scientist?"

"Let's talk about you," Carol said quickly. "Boyfriend?"

Kate interlaced her fingers across her knee. "Nope. I'm as free as you are, apparently."

"Good. I mean, that's nice." Carol seemed to be distracted by something outside the side window. Then she stood. "Here. Let's get your bag upstairs. I figured you'd want your old room?"

Oh, geez, her old room. Kate could still picture the dopey sunflower curtains she'd begged her parents for and the "My Little Pony" mural she'd plastered on the slanted ceiling. Lovely. She picked up her bag. "I guess so."

"I painted it last fall. Hope that's okay?"

Kate shrugged. Starlight Pony gone? Good riddance. "It's your house. Besides, everything changes sometime, right?"

Carol was already heading for the stairs near the front door. "Oh, I think you'll find a few things in the neighborhood you still like. Why don't we go for a stroll after you settle in?"

* * *

"So, why the walk all over downtown?" Peter asked. "A new exercise program for your knee?"

Lucius looked up from his watch. "Hmm? Oh, just need to get some screws from the hardware store."

Peter tilted his head. "Uh…the hardware store is the other way. And it's closed. Sunday, remember?"

Lucius took in a deep breath of air and slapped his chest like a lumberjack. "But it's such a beautiful day. Let's take in the sights."

The sights? In Golden Grove? The only sight around this weekend was the herd of crazy bearded guys roaming the streets.

Lucius was looking at his watch again. He was walking at a snail's pace, looking up and down the block.

"You okay? Your knee hurting?" Peter finally asked.

Lucius rubbed his right knee. "Now that you mention it, it is a little sore. Mind if we sit on a bench for a while?"

His older friend headed for a glossy green bench under one of the trees that lined Broadway, one of the four streets on the town square. A man sat on one end of the bench, legs crossed, calmly reading a paper, apparently unaware that his absurd beard appeared to be attacking his face.

"Okay…" Peter said. It wasn't like he was in a rush. The only other thing on today's agenda was grading papers, not his favorite, and the scenery downtown might be amusing with all the beards.

Lucius sat, then bounced right back up again and started walking back the way they had just come.

"Hey? Hello?" Peter called, starting to get worried as he followed. "I thought you wanted to sit."

Lucius gave him a quizzical look as he hurried on. "What's that?" He was clearly acting strangely. Early-onset Alzheimer's? Missed medication?

Lucius shook his head. "Oh. I thought I'd get some…glue. From the Stop-n-Pop."

Glue? Maybe that was it. Lucius had been sniffing glue. Dr. Lucius Potter was a glue-huffer.

Peter jogged to catch up. For a sixty-four-year-old, glue-sniffing Alzheimer's sufferer, Lucius could sure move fast when he wanted to.

* * *

Kate was struggling to keep up with Carol's pace. "Tell me again why we needed to come to the square?"

Carol was chugging along like a pint-sized freight train. "Oh, it's such a beautiful day for a walk."

A walk maybe. Kate hadn't planned on a run though. She also hadn't planned on a flat tire on her car. She'd gone out to move it into Carol's driveway and noticed that the left front tire was on the ground. Must have hit something on the way into town. She'd tried not to see it as an omen for her visit.

A jaunt downtown wasn't what she had planned for the afternoon either. Or ever. he air was cool, but she was sweating. The last thing she wanted was some local to recognize her and then have to lie about how great it was to be back in good ol' Golden Grove.

Jinx. A woman walking a tiny dog was approaching them, smiling in recognition.

"Carol! Hi," the woman said as she approached, then turned her attention to Kate. "Is that Katie Brady?"

Oh, geez. It was happening. "Hi," Kate said, totally not recognizing the woman with whom she was shaking hands. The dog was sniffing her ankle, his wet nose tickling.

"Francine Butler?" the woman said, still holding her hand. "I was your Sunday school teacher, in grade school."

"Oh, yes, of course," Kate said, plastering on a smile. "Mrs. Butler. How could I forget?"

"We're just on our way uptown to Ray's," Carol offered.

We are? This was news to Kate.

"Oh, I won't keep you then," Francine said. "Nice to see you again, Katie. Take care." She trotted on, pulling her dog, who was extremely interested in the smell of a stop-sign post.

One down, and hopefully no more to go, Kate thought.

"Let's go," Carol said, already marching on. "I have a craving for a pie shake."

They were moving through the business district of downtown. The Accidental Florist flower shop, Betty's Beads & More. A make-your-own candle shop? That was new.

Ah, Golden Grove, smiling, happy tourist trap. Nestled along the limestone bluffs of the Mississippi, so safe and secure. The only crime in the last month was probably someone littering their Vander Zee's-cruller wrapper on the pristine grass of town square.

No, the thievery here was much more subtle. Dreams, hopes, dignity. *Love.* She shook off the thought.

Carol was still scooting along the sidewalk, with Kate stuck to her heels. The trees here were huge, most already turning to golds, reds, and burgundies. Quite a difference from her neighborhood in Chicago, where all the trees were kept wrapped in iron cages. Blue sky peeked through the towering maples that lined Washington, one of the main roads that led downtown to the city square.

"I don't want to be late," Carol was saying.

"Late? For a shake?" She skipped forward a few steps to catch up. She wondered where Carol got all this energy.

"The lines might be long." Carol plowed forward.

Lines? At Ray's Diner? She imagined a herd of senior citizens lined up outside Ray's, clamoring to get their pie shakes and coffee.

They had reached the downtown square where most of the Golden Grove businesses were located. The square was clean, simple, and achingly picturesque. Even so, Kate kept her head low, not wanting to risk more recognition.

Carol suddenly slowed and starting waving furiously as if she had spotted someone. Kate almost bumped into her backside and had to grab her shoulders to avoid tripping over her. Ahead, she saw Ray's, green-striped awning and all. And no lines.

"Sorry," Carol apologized, tugging her along "Wow, look at those men's beards."

Kate swiveled to look in the opposite direction. Two guys were approaching, chatting. One with a beard that looked as if it had been caught in a wind tunnel full of egg beaters, the other shaped as a bird's nest with…were those real eggs? Egg Beater was carrying a trophy, beaming. "You've got to be kidding me," Kate said.

"I know," Carol said. "The windmill is much nicer."

Kate frowned. *He gets a trophy for basically sticking his face in a fan, and I got squat for designing a work of actual art. Put another check in the "life isn't fair" column.*

* * *

"Okay, we're here." Peter had his hand on the worn brass handle of Ray's Diner, waiting for Lucius, who now seemed to be less interested in a pie shake than waving at someone down the street.

Peter moved to see who it was, but Lucius turned and caught him by the arm. "Let's look at the menu before we go in," he said, almost shoving Peter over to the angled window where a faded yellow menu was posted.

"Lucius, this menu is the same one that was in the window when I was in high school. It's probably the same one that was there when *you* were high school."

Lucius shrugged, and then a hand tapped him from behind. "Well, hello there, Carol," he said a little too loudly. "What a surprise. Fancy meeting you here."

Pete smiled at his next-door neighbor Carol Harding, and then noticed the younger woman behind her. She was looking to the side at a cluster of the bearded guys. A heart-sparking flash of recognition went off in his head.

The same wavy red-gold hair. The scent in the breeze…what was it called again…the perfume? Lucky You?

All the memories came crashing. She was bright and beautiful, late afternoon sun catching her hair, splashing it with gold. It was her.

Katie.

* * *

A hand touched Kate's arm. Surprised, she whirled and fairly bumped into a man with smiling, brilliant blue eyes. Her head felt suddenly woozy; her knees buzzed. Her knees hadn't buzzed since high school.

All the years melted.

"Hi, Katie Brady," Peter Clark said.

Carol was beaming. "What a happy coincidence."

"Well, Miss Brady, what brings you back to our fair city?" the older man with Peter asked.

It took her an instant to place the name with the face. A few years older, but…

"Just business, Mr. Potter. Good to see you, and make it Kate, please." She tried not to look at Peter. Okay, just keep it cool. She could kill Carol later in the privacy of her old home. She extended her hand. "Good to see you too, Peter."

His hand was warm, strong. The breeze shifted. He smelled like, so help her, fresh sunlight. Now her knees were vibrating.

"Isn't this wonderful?" Carol looked like she was going to explode with smugness. "Two old friends reunited after so long." Then a crafty look crept over her face. "Lucius? Isn't this dress in Bernadine's lovely? Let me show you." She pointed to the mannequin in the window of the store next door.

"Dress?" Lucius was staring back at her blankly. Carol nudged him with her elbow and comprehension dawned. "Oh. Yes, of course. Is that the dress you were telling me about? The other day? The one you wanted to wear. Wear to church, that is. Once you bought it."

Carol grabbed his hand and fairly yanked him toward the store's window. "Wouldn't you like to look at it more closely?" She dragged him inside the store. "You too go ahead to Ray's without out us."

With a ding, the door shut.

Kate was alone with Peter.

"Um, nothing against Mrs. Harding," he finally said, "but I don't think she's going to be wearing that dress to church." He nodded at the short, skin-tight black dress the mannequin in the window was barely wearing. "Not unless she buys two and stitches them together."

Kate turned back around, still not wanting to make eye contact. "Well, Carol does like to sew."

An awkward silence followed.

"Look, Katie, I'm sorry. This wasn't my idea."

She nodded. "I know." What to say? You made my knees buzz, you jerk. Goodbye?

She could just feel two pairs of spying geriatric eyes watching them from inside Bernadine's. "They are a pair, aren't they?" She looked at Peter, really for the first time, and smiled.

"They are that."

Kate was still trying to process it all. This "happenstance" meeting, Peter, his eyes. His eyes.

"How are you, Katie?"

She winced slightly at hearing him use the old name. "I go by Kate now."

He nodded. "Right. Got it. Traveling incognito in your old town."

She scrunched the corner of her mouth. "Kind of."

He rubbed his wonderfully stubbled chin. "Well, then, we should come up with a good fake last name for you. How about Humperdinck?"

"I believe that was the name of your gerbil. No new last names necessary. Just trying to remain as anonymous as I can while I'm here."

"Kate Anonymous—got it."

Now the nervousness returned. She suddenly found a license plate on a nearby car very interesting. "I'm surprised you recognized me."

"Well, c'mon Katie—Kate. I'm not going to forget you." He smiled—a disarming, crooked smile, and folded his hands in front of him. "You look great, by the way."

Kate felt her face warm slightly. She narrowed her eyes even as her heart missed a beat. "Well, thanks. And look at you," she said, trying to deflect the attention. "All grown up."

He spread his arms. "Guess so. I'm pretty sure I've stopped growing—at least up, anyway."

"You look well. Fit, I mean." *Fit?* She sounded like his doctor.

He nodded. "Running, probably. I'm one of the coaches of the cross-country team, so that keeps me going. At least into late fall."

This was turning into an actual conversation. Is that what she wanted? Maybe if she got it over with, she'd be done. She could go on with her work, not worry about having to talk to him again while she was here. That could work out okay.

"Um, so...what do you do here, exactly?" As if she didn't already know.

He sighed. "Well, believe it or not, I teach chemistry at the high school."

"Really? I bet you're one of the favorites."

"Oh, I don't know about that." He stuck his hands in his pockets.

The "aw shucks" routine, but it worked for him. Kate cleared her throat. Another pair of bearded men came out of Ray's, brushing past them. One had a beard sculpted into a parrot sitting on his shoulder. The other looked like he was being swallowed by an angry octopus.

"So," she said, trying to ignore the weird interruption. "You've just stayed in good old Golden Grove?"

"Guess so." His smile went faint.

She didn't say anything for a moment, just watching his eyes. Was that it, then? Had they done their conversational duty?

"So, have you had dinner?"

Dinner? "I was supposed to have a shake. With Carol, before she disappeared."

He nodded. "Me, too. With Lucius." He shifted his weight. "So, look. They obviously think we're supposed to do some old-friend catching up, right?"

"Appears do."

"So, I say, why don't we humor them, have a greasy burger or a pie shake, shake hands, and say how great it was to see each other again? Then we can tell them we did our duty and they'll get off our backs."

It was reasonable, it was sound. It might even be painless. "Lead the way," she said with a wave.

He pulled open the heavy oak door for her. "After you."

She stepped inside. "So, do you still get a free lunch if there isn't any grease on the check?" she asked.

"Yup."

"Let me guess—never had a free lunch?"

"Nope." He smiled, and the door closed behind them.

Chapter Four

Ray's Diner, was a typical small town cafe. Still sporting chrome napkin holders, brick-red vinyl seats, and a counter with a row of classic round seats, its old-school greasy-spoon appearance contradicted the good food which the owner, Raymond Chow, had served there for the last thirty years.

It was the town hot spot for the locals, especially the crew of old retired men who gathered there every morning to drink coffee and chew on the latest farm reports, gossip, and argue desperately about politics. Raymond's unique pie shakes—a combination of a slice of pie blended into a milkshake—were legendary and drew repeat customers from miles around.

Peter followed Kate in. He half hoped the place would be empty. He was already embarrassed enough by Lucius and Carol's shenanigans. And then he'd put her on the spot by actually asking her to go through with the charade.

But she'd said yes.

And here she was, sauntering through Ray's like she'd never left, her wavy hair even more golden than he'd remembered, and longer, dancing down her back.

But she had left. Remember?

"Hey, professor!" a stubby man in a flannel shirt called out. He ambled out from behind the counter wiping his hands on a red-and-white striped towel.

Peter saw Kate glance at him. Peter just smiled and waved. "Hey, Ray. Usual booth?"

"Sure." Ray gave Kate the once over as he grabbed a couple of glasses of water from the counter. "Who's your lady friend today?"

"Today?" Katie turned to look at Peter with arched eyebrows.

"Oh, yeah," Ray continued with a sly grin. "Watch out for this one, miss. Town's most eligible bachelor."

Peter shook his head. "Ray now's not—"

"I'm just teasin', miss," Ray interrupted with a wink at Kate. He set the waters down, then went to retrieve some menus from behind the counter as she slid into the opposite side of the booth.

Peter wiped his sweaty palms on his jeans. It was one thing for Ray to tease, but he hadn't seen Katie—*Kate*—since high school graduation. And that was from a distance. After the debacle at the Scholarship Fair, it had been perfunctory hellos and hi's in the hallway, but that had been it. It was like she'd gone into some kind of shell. And then, not more than a few weeks after graduation, she was gone.

And he hadn't seen her since.

"So, how long have you lived in Chicago?" he asked, already knowing the answer but hoping to break the ice.

"About eight years." Kate took a sip from her water. "Five at the company I'm with now. We do marketing and branding for corporations. I used to do mostly graphic design, but I've been running a few bigger campaigns the last few years."

He already knew that, too. Every year or so—or was it more?—he'd be in his office, reeling from another mind-numbing round of budget requests or a particularly bad parent-teacher conference, and he'd google her, find her on her company website directory. All professional and sparkly and clean, confident smile set on her face. Kate Brady, along with the dozen or so young, good-looking grinning guys next to her on the directory page, their hipster glasses almost shouting how cool they were.

She wasn't married. He knew that, too. Small-town gossip reached deep and far, even when you'd been gone a dozen years.

Ray arrived with two well-worn plastic menus. "Here you go, folks. Just give me a wave when you're ready."

Peter passed one of the menus to Kate. He noticed her expensive running watch. Her stylish sweater, leggings, and riding boots made her look like she belonged in a downtown Chicago Starbucks instead of an Iowa diner. "Sounds like you're doing well."

She shrugged. "Well enough, I guess." Now she was studying the ice in her glass as she stirred it.

Don't let it get awkward, don't let it get awkward...

"Do you enjoy your job?"

"I do. And you?"

"Yes." Didn't he? "It's the new high school, now. Out on the edge of town. Where the old drive-in used to be?"

She nodded. "Oh, yeah. Where all the cool kids used to hang out? I remember. Last time I was there was probably grade school."

He nodded. "Me, too. We probably spent more time there jumping our bikes over the humps between the rows than watching movies." He paused. How much did she want to remember? "I still remember watching *Independence Day* there on the hood of your mom's Buick."

Kate wrinkled her nose. "Was that the one where the creepy alien tentacle thing squishes the guy against the window and makes him talk?"

"Oh, sorry. Yeah, I forgot how much you hated that scene." That was when she'd grabbed his arm, and he'd suddenly felt all grown-up, like a man. *A girl grabbed my arm for protection!* The thought made his stomach twirl a little, even now.

"Well, it has been a long time." She suddenly sat up straight. "I won't be in town long. I'm here to bid on a branding makeover for Nitrovex. You know, brochures, marketing materials, logo updates, website makeover, the whole deal. I have a meeting out at the headquarters tomorrow."

Today and tomorrow? That was all? "Wow, that's awesome, Kate. Hometown girl made good."

She smiled, but it was more of a grimace. "Something like that, I guess." She went back to studying her menu. "Wow, has this menu changed at all?"

"Doubt it."

"I still remember this line art drawing of the pig in the chef's hat." She pointed at the menu, smiling to herself. "I called him Porky."

"Yeah, I'm not sure why he even brings them over anymore. I've pretty much got the whole thing memorized."

She closed her menu. "To be honest, I'm not really hungry. How about I just get coffee?"

"Oh." Oh, as in, *Oh, you'd really rather be on Mars than here with me.* That oh. "Sure." He motioned at Ray. "Ray? Two coffees."

Ray arrived in a few seconds with a pair of green-rimmed mugs and a coffee pot. "Sure you don't want a tenderloin? Burger? Special is roast beef sandwich."

"No thanks. We're good." Peter said.

After Ray poured, then left, Kate took a sip, still silent.

"So, you're…" He glanced at her ring finger. "You're here for only a couple days?"

She nodded. "I've got my first meeting with Mr. Wells tomorrow."

"Which one? John Wells or his jet-setting grandson?"

"I didn't know there was a jet-setting grandson."

Peter nodded. "Corey Steele."

Her brow furrowed. "Sounds like a superhero's secret identity. From Golden Grove?"

Peter shook his head. "He grew up in Chicago, I think. He's John's daughter's son. He's head of their international group now. Causes a stir whenever he's in town. Rich. Good looking. Last year, they tried to recruit him for one of those fancy bachelor shows."

She rolled her eyes. "Great. Just what I need. A pampered jetsetter sticking in his two cents."

Good. Correct response. "Actually, I hear he's a pretty nice guy, considering. He's probably out of town, anyway. I think he spends most of his time overseas."

"I'm more interested in Mr. Wells. *John*," she said. "I'll need to get a lot of the back story of Nitrovex from him." She paused. "It's my first big test, this job. Truth is, I'm actually a little nervous."

"I'm sure you'll do fine." Peter wrapped his fingers around his own cup. "It all sounds very exciting, like you've found your niche in Chicago."

Man, her hair was pretty. A weaving of red and gold. Gold. Yes. Gold. Periodic symbol, Au. Atomic number, 79. Relative atomic mass, 196.96—

"Okay, ready for a pie shake?" It was Ray, next to the table, towel in hand.

Kate's face told the story.

"Ray, I think we're ready for the check," Peter said.

"Sure, you got it," Ray said and ambled away.

"Let me pick up the check," Kate said. "I have an expense account."

"Nope. You're the guest. Besides, I have a tab here." The joke fell flat.

She nodded, not quite smiling.

The silence was deadly. Twelve years of deadly.

She checked her watch as if it had bitten her. "Look, sorry to run—"

He began sliding out of the booth, thankful for the escape himself. "No, no, I'm sure you've got a lot of things to take care of."

They were both standing now, face to face, wordless. A glass clinked in the kitchen.

"Thanks for the coffee," she said.

"You're welcome. Good luck tomorrow." He stuck out his hand instinctively. She took it, her fingers warm, soft, electric for a moment before he released them.

Her face dropped, then rose. "Good to see you again, Peter."

He nodded. "You too."

He was still standing, still staring forward, hearing the ding of the door as she pushed through.

He suddenly wondered if this was the last time he'd see her. He had a feeling like something delicate and precious and just dropped from his hands and smashed on the concrete, and it was gone forever.

Ray came up, wiping a glass with a towel. "Nice girl. Date?" he asked.

Peter paused. "No. Just an old friend."

Chapter Five

Kate let herself in the front door with the key Carol had provided and found her host unloading the dishwasher in the kitchen. She snuck up behind her. "Need any help?" Kate said loudly.

Carol dropped a metal mixing bowl that clanged to the linoleum and wobbled under the table. She clutched her chest as she whirled around. "What in the world?"

Kate stood with her arms folded. "I thought since you were *such* a great help to me today, I'd return the favor."

Carol smiled weakly. "It was no problem at all." Her face wrinkled in confusion. "What did I help with?"

Kate put her hands on her hips. "As a matter of fact, a lot, as it turns out. You reminded me of the reasons why I live in a big city."

Carol pretended to straighten a loose lock of hair. "I'm still not sure—"

Kate gave an exasperated sigh. "You and Lucius and your little matchmaking scheme."

Carol kneeled down to retrieve the bowl under the table. "Well, I don't see the harm in two old friends catching up with each other."

"And I don't need someone shoving an old high school crush down my throat..." She stopped, put her hand to her head. "I'm sorry, Carol. I didn't mean that."

Her friend gave her a swat on the arm on the way to the sink. "Oh yes, you did. Don't worry. I've been called a busybody before."

Kate managed a smile. "I doubt that." Carol was one of the kindest, sweetest people she'd ever known. Her heart was always in the right place. It was her brain that got a little ornery at times.

"Not to mention that on the way home I was accosted by my high school math teacher, a woman who says she was the friend of my mother's hairdresser, and Denny Anderson, who's now apparently a police officer. All of whom remembered good old Katie Brady. You'd think this town put out wanted posters of anyone who's ever left here."

"Oh, it's just a friendly town. You know that." Carol put the bowl on the counter then moved to the table and sat.

Kate followed suit, pulling out her phone. Better check email, make sure nothing had changed for tomorrow.

"So," Carol ventured. "How was Ray's?" She pretended to rub a spot off the table.

"We just had coffee."

"Oh. How was Peter?"

"Fine, I guess."

"Oh. Did you have a pie shake? Lucius says Peter's favorite is pecan pie."

Kate sighed. She knew her friend would never drop this, so she might as well get it over with. "Carol, if I give you ten minutes to talk about my coffee with Peter will you promise to never bring him up again?"

"Fine."

"Good. Coffee was fine. Peter looks fine."

Carol gave a sly smile. "Yes he does, doesn't he?"

Kate made a face. "You know what I mean. He looks…content, I guess. He seems to like being here. Teaching, I mean."

"He does. And from what Lucius tells me, he's very good. His students love him. Did he tell you he just got voted State Science Teacher of the Year? Youngest one ever."

That caught her. "Really? Wow…no. But I guess he's not one to blow his own horn."

"No, he isn't. Just another one of his many fine qualities."

Kate shook her head. "I know what you and your partner in crime, Lucius, are trying to do, but before you get too far into the matchmaking, I'm letting you know now. High school was a long time ago. I was just a kid, and so was Peter, and that's all. Everyone needs to grow up sooner or later."

"Well, there's growing up, and there's growing up."

What was that supposed to mean?

Carol stood and wandered to the window. "I just thought, since it was just high school like you said, you know..." She was suddenly very interested in a ceramic cow flower pot in the windowsill.

"No, I don't know."

She turned. "Oh, Katie. I saw how upset you were that day after the fair. And I don't think it was just because of..." She waved her hand, apparently unable to say the words.

"Because Peter ratted on me and then destroyed my project?" Kate finished for her.

"You know very well it was an accident."

"The rocket, maybe. But him turning me in, taking Penny Fitch's side. That was no accident." Kate slumped back down in her chair. "I'm sorry. Can we talk about something else, please?"

"That's all right. I understand. Old feelings sometimes make us angry."

"I'm not angry." She nodded. "Actually, you know what? He did me a favor."

Carol cocked her head as she took a chair opposite her near the window. "How's that?"

She gestured with her hand. "Well, if I had gotten that scholarship, I probably would have gone to art school, right? Just to spend four years making pots out of cow flops or splashing together existential paintings depicting the tragedy of the disappearing Brazilian rainforest."

"But I thought you loved art."

"I do. I mean, I did, but where does that get you? Working at a Burger King while trying to guilt your relatives into buying your paintings every Christmas?" She shook her head. "No, not getting that scholarship was the best thing that ever happened to me. It got me to think practically, to *do* something practical, something useful."

"I suppose you seem to be doing well."

"I am. And if I don't botch this deal with Nitrovex, I'll be doing even better."

"I'm sorry, Kate. I shouldn't have brought it up."

Kate rubbed her forehead. "No, it's okay. It's fine."

"You want some tea? I've got some great peppermint decaf."

Kate nodded, a slight smile wavering on her face at her friends' peace offering. "Sure, thanks."

Carol returned the smile, then pushed through the kitchen door.

Kate took in a deep breath. *I would have won that fair.* What if I *had* won?

But you did, remember?

She rubbed her temples with her palms. The tension of this job. It was so much like that day, watching the judges analyzing her project, trying to read their faces, waiting for the results. All the work, all that summer, the hours in the basement. With money and college on the line.

* * *

Twelve Years Ago
Golden Grove High

Katie watched one of the Scholarship Fair judges, Mr. Riley—the history teacher and a football coach—circle her mobile. Eyes moving up and down, face expressionless, hand poised over his clipboard.

C'mon, smile. I will you to smile, you jock. It's art! It's not some stupid football.

He looked at his clipboard, wrote something, then looked back at the mobile, pointing out something to another judge. The thread of a smile creased his face.

Yes! If she could win over the football coach, that was a good sign.

Mrs. Wells was circling the project, nodding, smiling, gesturing. She was a lock, she had to be.

The other two were writing in their notebooks, talking in low voices to each other. One was Mrs. Wrath, the head librarian at the public library. Guess her fellow judges figured she was smart because she worked around a lot of books.

The final judge was a man in a tweed coat with those patches on the elbows. He was from the college, but she wasn't sure what he taught. He was smiling, but then he'd been smiling his way through the whole room. Katie frowned. Unreadable, that one. Then he laughed at something Mrs. Wrath said.

Laughing? Bad laughing or good laughing? C'mon, people's lives were at stake here. Didn't they know she wanted to look like Amélie and wear floppy flannel shirts in a grungy coffee shop next year?

Her heart was already clunking along like a nervous engine. Then she saw Peter watching her, and it about pounded out of her chest. Stupid, sympathetic blue eyes that pretty much said, *I hope you win, Katie.*

That was it. She was going to puke. Something she hadn't done in school since third grade when Greg Harms had eaten his own booger in class.

Then she realized she was holding her breath, and blew it out. The judges had moved on to the last table, Lisa Banks and her misbehaving mice. They spent a few frowns and a couple of pen scribbles there and that was it.

Oh, Lord, please let me win. Just this once, let me win something. I promise I won't call Penny the b-word ever again and I'll stop watching Peter wash his dad's car with his shirt off. Please, oh please.

The judges spent about a minute or an hour conferring on the stage; she wasn't sure which, as time perception was not high on her abilities right now. Finally, Mrs. Wells stepped to the microphone. Then stepped back to confer with a judge on something, putting her hand on the mic.

Oh, geez, just do it. *Either let me win or shoot me, now.* Duffy, the janitor, could clean up the mess. He had a mop.

The room grew silent, save for the buzzing and hissing of a few projects. Someone's parrot said "pretty boy" and everyone laughed. Except Katie.

Mrs. Wells spoke. "Students and faculty, thank you so much for all your hard work putting together another successful Nitrovex Scholarship Fair."

There was polite applause.

"This year's entrants were exceptional, making it very difficult to choose a winner."

Lisa yelled *ouch!* as one of her mice bit her.

Say it, say it, say it, Katie willed.

"But first, the runners-up," Mrs. Wells said regally.

Oh, geez, Louise.

"For the third-place prize, a plaque, a five-hundred-dollar scholarship, and a gift certificate to Copperfield's Book Store..." A pause. "Katie—"

No!

"—Ferguson."

Yes! Katie clutched her chest. *I think I'm having a heart attack. That had to be a heart attack.* Could you have a heart attack at seventeen and a half?

"For our second-place prize. A plaque and a one-thousand-dollar scholarship, the winner is...Peter Clark."

The crowd applauded, a few of the boys whooped. Katie felt a twinge of guilt as Peter made his way to the stage, grinning. *Good job, Peter.*

"And finally, for our first-prize winner."

Oh, here we go. Katie folded her arms on her chest and squeezed, hoping she could stay vertical for the next thirty seconds. The room was still, silent, like runners waiting for the gun to go off.

"A plaque and a *five*-thousand-dollar-a-year scholarship go to..."

Pleeeeeeeeeeease...

"Katie Brady, and her beautiful mobile!"

I won. I won? I won!

Fireworks exploded in her head. Someone smacked her on the back, the crowd was applauding, some cheering. She stumbled forward, grin frozen on her face, up to the stage, students clapping, socking her arm as she went by.

It was like floating on a cloud. She'd won! All the hours, the work, the flat-out validation of it all. Finally, something good was happening. To her.

Mrs. Wells was waiting, smiling, holding out her hand. Katie shook it, accepted the plaque, and some piece of paper, the stage lights hot and blinding. The gym was large and wide, full of people cheering. For her. She looked to her right. Peter was there, on stage, clapping, grinning, his face full of joy, actual joy, for her. Her chest pounded. It was magical.

The stage lights dimmed, the gym lights went up and the applause died out as students began picking up their projects. Katie accepted thanks from all the judges, each shaking her hand. At the end of the line was Peter.

He hugged her. He smelled clean and bright, like sunshine. His arms were the safest, warmest place she'd ever been. She rested her head on his shoulder, and she didn't care who saw it.

She'd won.

* * *

The Present

Carol bumped in from the kitchen, breaking her daydream. "Here's the tea," she said, carrying two steaming mugs.

Kate took hers with both hands. "Thanks."

"So, what time is your appointment tomorrow?"

Appointment? *Oh, yeah... your job, remember?* "Um, nine a.m., sharp." And she still had some notes she wanted to go over before then. *And* she still wanted to get out to that plant yet tonight. "Which reminds me. Could I borrow your car?"

Carol's face went blank for a few seconds.

"I have a flat tire, remember?" Kate said sweetly. After the "coincidence" of running into Peter, she had some suspicions about her flat.

Carol was shaking her head. "Oh dear. I had planned to get groceries tonight. Forgot to yesterday, you know."

"I see." Something evil was churning in that gray head of hers.

"Yes, I need milk and bread and, um, sweet gherkins and…groceries."

Kate nodded. "Let me guess. You'll be gone all night?"

She smiled sweetly. "I forgot eggs. And cauliflower. I'd better make a list."

Kate put the back of her hand on her forehead and feigned a swoon. "Oh, whatever am I to do? I have a flat tire and Daddy never taught me how to fix one. Who can save me from these dire straits?"

Carol studied her fingernails, then cleared her throat. "Maybe Peter could fix your flat tire."

And there it was. "Do you ever give up?" she asked her friend.

"I just thought since he's handy with cars and he's right next door, and if he is just a friend, as you say, what harm can it do?"

What harm? Where do I start?

Kate looked to the ceiling. But what else was she supposed to do? She needed to get a lay of the land before her meeting tomorrow, but she didn't want to drive all over the county on a spare. And she sure didn't have the equipment to repair a flat. And it might save her an early morning service call at a garage. "Well, he's probably busy. You know, getting gherkins and groceries and such."

"Oh, I know for a fact he's not busy," Carol said eagerly.

"How's that?"

Carol pointed out the kitchen window. "He's out there washing his car."

Kate looked through the lace curtains. Sure enough, there was Peter, wearing running shorts and a white t-shirt, wrestling a red hose around to the side of a glistening vintage cherry-red Mustang convertible parked in his back driveway. Oh, geez.

He grabbed a sponge from the bucket and bent over to wash the wheels.

"Buns," said Carol.

Kate whirled. "Excuse me?"

"I need to get buns, too. And bananas."

Kate's eyes narrowed.

Carol stood, then moved to the counter. "So, I'm sure Peter would be happy to help you with your tire. He's very handy." She began writing out her grocery list, humming slightly.

Kate bit her lip. Did she want to ask him? The forced meetup at the diner hadn't been particularly comfortable. But that was probably because it was out in public where everyone could see them. And she knew all too well how gossip flew in small towns.

She stared out the window where Peter was now wiping down the car. It was nice. The car. Was nice.

"Katie? Kate?"

Kate turned to Carol, eyebrows arched. "Hmm?"

"How do you spell 'rutabaga'?"

"Try r-something-something-b-a-g-a."

Carol seemed satisfied with that answer, scribbled on her pad, then looked up, sweet smile returning. "Don't let me keep you," she said. She moved past Kate, pushing open the kitchen door, humming more. "Bye now. Gotta run."

Kate flashed her own smile, although not as sweetly, at her friend's back as she left. She waited a moment, then got up, walking to the back door. She put her hand on the knob, and paused, peering out the window. Peter was coiling up the hose, done with his work.

What if he said no? What if he said yes? Her heart was thunking. It was just a flat tire. Why did this feel like one of the biggest decisions of her life?

She took a deep breath, turned the knob, and pulled open the door.

Chapter Six

"Hi, neighbor."

Peter turned. She wasn't sure if that was a look of surprise or pleasure on his face.

He quickly wiped his hands on a towel and tossed it on a nearby chair. "Hey. Kate. Good to see you again."

Good, he's smiling. That part's over. Kate walked around the gleaming Mustang, still dripping from its wash. "Well, I figured I'd be a bad neighbor if I never stopped over once while I was here. This is your car?" She ran her hand down the gleaming chrome on the side panel. "Wow." She wasn't an old-car geek, but this one was nice. Sleek and powerful-looking.

"Thanks." He came over to her, rested his hand on the rear fender.

"Wait...didn't your dad used to have a beat-up car like this?" She asked, peering inside the passenger window.

"Yup. Same one."

"Oh." It hit her. His dad, yes. *Stupid, Kate.* She looked down, then up. "Peter, I'm so sorry about your dad. I knew he had...gone." She looked back at her old house. "Carol told me the rest. With you and your mom and all. That must have been really hard."

He nodded. "Thanks."

"I'm sorry you had to go through that." What else could she say? "Losing a parent...I can't imagine." As distant as hers seemed at times, picturing one of them gone, especially so soon...

And Peter's dad had always been great, teasing her. He always called her Special K, his little joke.

"Yeah. He really started to deteriorate when I was in grad school. And Mom, she could only do so much caregiving."

Kate nodded, not sure what else to say. He stood, blue eyes fixed on her, then folded his arms, shoulders wide and back. It was a strong stance, not sad or defeated. As if the process of grief had steeled him.

"How is your mom?" she asked.

"Good. Great, actually. Out in New Mexico, if you can believe it. Her sister lives out there as well. Mom does pastel painting for a hobby and works as a librarian. Lots of friends."

"That's good. I'm glad." There was a moment, then, a softening silence. She wanted to touch his arm, something to say she was sorry, to comfort him. She touched the gleaming chrome side mirror instead. "So, you did all this?" She shaded her eyes and peered in the back window.

He nodded. "With a little help from Lucius, a ton of weekends, and a lot of favors from Matt at JC's Body Shop." He ran a hand through his hair. "I promised his kid an A in Intro to Chemistry."

She looked up, trying to gauge his face.

His face reddened slightly. "That was a joke, by the way, in case you're thinking of telling the principal."

Kate forced a smile. *Does he even remember why I lost that fair?* "Well, I'm impressed," she said. His eyes smiled again. *Okay, remember why you're here.* She touched her palms together, fingers spread. "Yes, the reason I came over was I was wondering if you could help me with my flat."

"Your flat what?"

"Oh—flat tire." She turned and pointed to the street where the yellow Bug sat, sagging on the front left side, courtesy of Carol's sabotage. "I wanted to drive out to see the Nitrovex plant."

"Oh, I can take you."

Her head cocked. What? "Take me? In your car?"

Peter ran a hand through his hair again, and her pulse fluttered. "Yeah, sure," he said. "It'll be dark pretty soon, and after that, you won't be able to see much of the plant. I'll fix the flat when we get back."

"Really? You sure?" *Because I'm not.*

He shook his head. "No problem. I've got a work light and a compressor. Probably just a slow leak."

Her brain was flip-flopping. Take a ride with him? Together?

"Okay, sure, thanks," she found herself saying. "I just thought it would be good to look around before my meeting." There. She'd let him know it was just about business.

"Sounds practical. They've grown quite a bit the last ten years."

He headed toward the passenger door, but before he could reach it, she settled down in the black bucket seat. The car smelled of polished leather mixed with stale oily dust and a faint tinge of gas. She found herself oddly enamored.

Peter climbed into the driver's side and inserted the key, then turned it. The V8 engine thrummed to life, then settled into a throaty idle.

Peter revved the engine a few times, smiling.

She hadn't pegged him for a gear head, but she had to admit. This car was cool.

"You ready?" he asked.

"Sure." The top was down, and the late afternoon sun was pushing through the trees. She pulled her Armani sunglasses down from her head, smiling. This might actually be fun.

The vintage car rolled to the end of the driveway until it reached the street. After looking both ways, Peter gunned the engine. The car shot from the curb with a small squeal, the engine churning. In a few seconds, they were off Brick Street and cruising down Main street towards the center of town.

Kate was watching the shops move by the car window, recognizing most of them. "Hey, Bailey's Five and Ten is still there!"

"Yeah, it's Bailey's Variety now. They mostly sell cards and knick-knacks."

It was the shop where she used to get toys, and where she got her first My Little Pony that had started her collection.

It was as if Peter read her mind. "You still have your pony collection thing?"

She pursed her lips. "Maybe. You still have your comic book collection thing?"

"Mmm. Maybe. You still... chew your fingernails when you're nervous?"

She slid her left hand under her leg. "Maybe. You still shoot Pepsi out of your nose when you laugh?"

He shot a look at her and then turned his head back toward the road. "I only did that once, and that was, like, what? Third grade?"

She laughed at his embarrassment. "It was fifth grade, and you turned as red as this car."

Peter was silent, making a right turn onto Franklin Street, which led to the highway out of town. She wondered if she'd joked too much.

"So, everything look the same?" he said.

She surveyed the passing businesses. King Drugs, Copperfield's Books. She'd spent a lot of Saturday afternoons there in the Young Adult Fantasy section, buried in the latest Harry Potter book. "Pretty much, surprisingly. A little more touristy." Her eye caught what looked like an art gallery on the corner of Franklin and Elm. That was new.

"I guess not much ever changes in a small town, huh?" Peter said, slowing for a stop sign.

"Mmm. Some do, some don't, I suppose."

The car was picking up speed as they headed out onto the main highway out of town, the engine settling into a vibrating hum.

"Hey, Roger's Roost is closed? I almost forgot about that place." She pointed to a small stand by the side of the road with a large gold star encrusted with light bulbs on top of a white, rusting pole. "Remember when we rode our bikes out here that one time just to get a chocolate cone, but we forgot we didn't have any money, and the lady gave it to us, anyway?"

She heard him chuckle as he shifted the car down a gear, slowing to make a turn onto a side road. "Nothing like free ice cream." The Mustang regained speed as it headed south down Eagle Bluff Road, which led towards the Nitrovex plant.

At the faster speed, the wind was blowing Kate's hair in ruffled bursts. It felt good. She could see Peter looking over at her, smiling. The rush of the cool air seemed to blow out the cobwebs, the seasoned scent of fallen leaves and sweet grass reminding her of being a kid again. She had to decide whether that was good or bad, and it sobered her.

She could see white tank towers peeking over the trees.

"I suppose you come out here a lot?" she asked.

He shrugged, wheeling the car onto an access road. "Every so often. Two or three times a year for field trips. Got one coming up in a few weeks, I think."

The Mustang slowed as it reached the entrance to Nitrovex. The old stone-and-brick sign was still there, but the plant now stretched down the road. They drove past warehouses and a row of metal factory buildings with sequential numbers painted on the sides, all the way up to six.

"Wow. I think when I left there were only two plants," she said as Peter pulled into the large front lot. She'd visited her parents here, but that was just to their offices in a building which wasn't even here anymore. Nothing looked familiar.

"Yeah, it's definitely grown. Went international about six years ago and from what I understand, it's doing well. Some plants in Europe, one in Asia." The car had stopped and was idling. "Guess that's why you're here, huh?"

"Guess so." The weight of this project was hitting her again. Not only was this place a lot bigger than she remembered, but the piles of pill-shaped holding tanks and a maze of tangled pipes reminded her of how out of her depth she was with all this science stuff. She had read all their materials and almost memorized the Nitrovex website, but seeing it now…it seemed impossible.

Peter must have seen her staring. "I know, impressive, right?" He turned off the engine and opened his door.

Kate did the same, struggling slightly to push up out of the low-slung car. She pointed. "That building is new, right?"

"Yup. That's the new reception and office building."

A clean, bright two-story building of aluminum and brick stood out from the dirtier work-oriented buildings around it.

Peter touched her arm and began to walk. "C'mon. The offices are closed, but you can at least look around."

She glanced back at the car. "Shouldn't you lock it?"

He looked back, chuckling. "In Golden Grove? You *have* been gone a while."

* * *

They spent the half hour or so walking the grounds around the office building before heading back to the car. Then they slowly drove down the row of giant steel-sided factory buildings while Peter explained the purpose of each one. Anti-foaming agents, corn oil, chemical synthesis. All things she had read about and was still trying to grasp. It seemed like a first language to Peter though.

She was enjoying watching him ramble on about polymer-something-or-other and reaction chemistry. He was oblivious that she had absolutely no clue what he was talking about. He seemed as excited about chemistry as he had been about getting some new Star Wars toy when they were kids. His eyes were flashing, his crooked smile frequent.

"Well, what do you think?" Peter asked as they walked back to the car.

"I think I'm in over my head."

"Oh, you'll be fine. You don't need to know all of the science stuff, anyway, right?"

She frowned. "I suppose not. I mostly need to get the feel of what direction the company is going. Then I'll have to come up with some preliminary designs and strategies, present them to my group back home for approval before we make the proposal to Nitrovex."

Which she had only done before for small businesses. Never for a company this large.

Peter reached the Mustang first and held the passenger door for her this time. "Want to take the scenic way home? You're probably a little curious how the rest of the town has changed."

Was she? But he didn't wait for an answer. A minute later, the car roared back to life, and he was pulling out of the Nitrovex lot.

They took a turn on a new road, which led towards the west edge of town. The car slowed and made another turn. It looked familiar…

She peered out the windshield. "Is this…Palisades?"

"It is." Peter maneuvered the Mustang down a smooth blacktop road, and a brown wooden sign confirmed Palisades Park, in yellow letters. "The playground is gone, but the rest is pretty much the same."

"I loved that playground. It had that one long slide with the tunnel in it." She remembered going down headfirst, getting a friction burn on her elbow.

They breezed slowly between stands of trees, early evening sunlight mottling the shiny red hood of the car. It was picture perfect. They slowed and then stopped at a pullout. Down a short hill and through a few trees sparkled a wide lake.

She shaded her eyes with her hand. "I'm trying to remember…this is the place with the little beach, right?"

"Sure. Didn't you go there with the senior class after prom?"

A stiffer breeze blew in off the lake. She shivered once and folded her arms to warm herself. "I didn't go to prom."

"Oh…I thought you went with Adam?"

She shook her head. "By then I had one foot out the door. I couldn't wait to graduate." She glanced at him and then back at the lake. *And I didn't go to the Homecoming Dance either.*

Peter shifted in his seat and cleared his throat. "I always forget how cold it gets here. I should probably put the top up." He flipped a switch on the lower left dashboard.

A motor whined as the black top of the convertible unfolded, then snapped into place around them. The car seemed smaller, almost claustrophobic.

He shifted the Mustang into gear. "I guess we'd better head back."

As they traveled out of the park, Kate could think of nothing to say. It all felt so…weird. The shops, the plant, the park. What was it they said? *You can never go home again?*

They moved east through the outskirts of town, then back onto Eagle Bluff Road, the one high up next to the Mississippi. These were some of the older houses, almost Cape Cod-like, with green shutters and slate dormers, perched up on the craggy limestone bluffs overlooking the river. One of the more picturesque parts of Golden Grove.

Peter turned left onto Park Road, and now some of the houses were looking familiar. That white house was where she had her first sleepover with…she couldn't remember her name. The brick house—Neil something-or-other's—where she got stung by a wasp on his tire swing and his mom put baking-soda paste on her leg. Mostly memories from grade school. High school memories, on the other hand, were scarcer.

And then, as if on cue, the familiar brown and red brick of the high school building flowed past them on the right. It looked smaller, for some reason. It still said GOLDEN GROVE HIGH SCHOOL etched in stone over the wooden front doors, but a newer, brown and white sign on posts near the front said Community Center.

Maybe it was because she had just been thinking about wasps, but it felt like something had stung her inside. Not hot and sharp, but cold and deep. She looked forward through the car windshield as it rolled on.

Peter was as wordless as she was during the few blocks it took to travel from there to their houses. She felt bad, but she could think of absolutely nothing to say.

"Here we are." He turned the car into the concrete slabs of his driveway, rolled to the back, and stopped. The engine shut off and the small-town quiet took over again.

"Thanks for the ride." She tried to unbuckle to get out, but the latch wouldn't budge. She looked at Peter. "It doesn't seem to want to—"

"Sorry. It does that sometimes." He reached over, grabbed both sides of the chrome latch, gave a tug. She could feel the heat from his hands. "Try it now," he said.

She did, and it clicked open. "Thanks."

"Sure thing. Anytime."

She opened her door and pushed up from her seat. He was coming around the rear of the car, a new breeze ruffling his hair. It wasn't fair, his hair. She pictured herself running her fingers through it…

She glanced down at the buzzing Fitbit on her arm, relieved to have the excuse of the message scrawled across it. Time to go. "It's work. Checking in on me, probably." She looked up. "I'd better get back to the house and see what my boss wants. It might be about the meeting tomorrow."

"Sure." He looked down at his shoes, then up. "So, will I get a chance to say goodbye before you leave?"

She smiled weakly. "Sure. I'll be around tomorrow at least. Maybe Tuesday. Then it's back to Chicago."

Peter nodded. "Okay, then. So, see you later?"

"See you." She turned without another word and walked the familiar path across the grass back to her house. *Carol's* house. She didn't live here anymore.

She took a breath, then scowled. What was she thinking, tooling around the town with Peter like that? Seeing the plant was one thing, but the park, and the old school? She should have been back here prepping for her meeting tomorrow. There were preliminary design ideas and a lot of questions to write out if she was going to make at least a half-decent showing of herself.

She was in Golden Grove on business. Nothing more. She had work to do.

Chapter Seven

Peter lugged the air compressor back into his garage, dropping the coiled hose next to it. Kate's tire only seemed flat. He'd filled it, heard no air, couldn't see any nails. But it was dark, and he couldn't see much, anyway. If it was a slow leak, then she'd find out tomorrow when it went low again. And then maybe she'd need help again…

Okay, enough. *You've got work to do at school, remember? Your job? Grading papers?*

He pulled the Mustang's keys from his pocket, zipped his leather coat, climbed in and started it.

Stupid, stupid, stupid. What had he been thinking, taking Kate to the lake like that? He had seen how she had shivered. He figured it hadn't been a big deal, but he wasn't thinking like her.

The car almost drove itself to the school on the route he'd taken, what? Thousands of times by now? And how many thousands more would there be?

Out of town, west. His left hand gripped the wheel as he shifted into fourth, ignoring the speed limit. If Denny was out patrolling tonight, he might get away with a warning and a raised eyebrow. He hoped.

He gunned the Mustang a little too fast around a curve. Loose gravel from the shoulder scrabbled under the tires as they grabbed at the road. As fun as it was to drive the car, he had forgotten how touchy rear wheel drive was. Stupid. He slowed down.

What it must be like coming back to a town you thought you'd left behind forever.

And he was at least partly to blame…

***

Twelve Years Ago
Golden Grove High

Peter was hugging Katie. It was something he had wanted to do for a long time, holding her, his hands cradling the small of her back. He'd dreamed about that, and more, this summer while he'd watched her work on her project for the Scholarship Fair.

He was so proud of her for winning. She'd worked hard, yes, but she'd also persevered. He knew how much the scholarship meant to her, not only for college but for herself. For her art.

He stepped back, finally, hands still around her back. "Great job, Katie."

Her face was shining, a bright light. "Thanks."

He released her, reluctantly, then gestured with his head towards the gym floor. "Guess we better go start packing up."

She nodded. "Guess so." They began walking towards the stage stairs.

"I wouldn't be surprised if Mrs. Wells will want your piece for her personal art gallery," Peter said, trying to be encouraging.

Katie's eyebrows raised. "You think so?"

They'd reached their tables. Peter walked over to her mobile, still spinning slowly, delicately. He nodded. "Absolutely. Who knows? Some wealthy industrialist might see it, offer you a thousand dollars."

"Only a thousand?" she joked.

"Sorry, one *hundred* thousand. And a tour of Europe."

"That's more like it," she said, approaching his table with the rocket that had earned him second prize.

Having her here, so close, beaming at him, felt like a much bigger prize. She looked like a field of yellow flowers. He could feel her warmth as she stood a foot from him, smelling like heaven. *Lucky You.*

You got that right. It was all very unscientific and unnerving and fantastic.

She was waiting, smiling, glowing in her victory. *Do it now*, he thought. What better possible time could there be?

"So, um…" he began, then swallowed. Her face was the picture of expectancy, eyebrows up slightly, brown eyes sparkling. "I was wondering, if you weren't already going… with someone else… if you wanted to go to homecoming? With me?"

Her face beamed brighter, if that were possible. She nodded. "Yes—" she started to say.

There was a commotion behind them. He looked past Katie's shoulder.

Penny Fitch was talking with two of the judges at Katie's table. They were bent towards her, faces intent, nodding as they listened.

He heard the words "Peter Clark" and "rules" and possibly "disqualified." Something danced and dropped in his stomach. Katie must have seen his face because her own lost its smile.

"Miss Brady? Mr. Clark? Could you come here, please?" One of the judges, Mr. Riley, the football coach, was motioning them over.

Peter looked at Katie, then walked over, feeling as if he were being asked into the principal's office. Which had never happened. Katie followed beside him, face puzzled.

Mr. Riley gestured at Penny, who was standing next to him and to another judge, Mrs. Wells. Penny was looking everywhere except at Peter and Katie.

"We have to ask you a few questions, Peter. You too, Katie."

"Okay," Peter said, sweat breaking out on his palms.

Mr. Riley rubbed the back of his neck and focused on Peter. "Miss Fitch has informed us that you may have, willingly or unwillingly, broken one of the rules of the fair."

Katie's eyes widened. "What rule?" she asked, her body tensing.

Mr. Riley looked at Mrs. Wells, who only smiled weakly and wrung her hands in front of her.

"The rule about having utilized outside help," Mr. Riley said.

Katie lifted her chin. "Peter wouldn't do anything wrong with his project."

"Mr. Clark's project isn't the problem. You're the one who's been accused of receiving outside help. From him."

Peter felt a burning creep up his neck. It was the same feeling he'd gotten when his dad had caught him in the back of the garage smoking a cigar he'd stolen out of his tackle box. He shot a look at Penny, who was busy studying her shoes.

"That's not true!" Katie said, her hands balling into fists. "I'm an artist. He's a science geek. Why would I need help from him?"

"I'm sorry, but we need to check it out," said Mrs. Wells softly. "To be fair to the other students. You understand."

"We have a reliable source," Mr. Riley said. "We just need to verify a few things to see if they're true or not."

"Who? What reliable source?" Katie demanded, her jaw set.

Mr. Riley turned to Peter, rubbing his neck again, obviously uncomfortable at being put in this position. "Mr. Clark, do you have something to say about this?"

Katie turned to him. He didn't dare look at her face, but he didn't need to. He could feel the fire.

"I'm not sure," Peter said finally. What was going on here? What had Penny told them? And why?

"Let me ask you outright, then. Did you help Miss Brady with her project?"

Help her? Did Mr. Riley mean this summer? Was hanging out in her basement breaking the rules. His brain was scrambling. What could he say? He couldn't get Katie in trouble. But he couldn't flat-out lie, either.

"Not really," he said. "We're friends. We just talked."

"Not really? Are you sure? Miss Fitch says that you told her that you helped Miss Brady with her project all summer."

The fire from Katie had turned to a hard, cold freeze. Peter rubbed his own neck. How had things gone from great to horrible so quickly?

"Mr. Clark? Did you or did you not help Miss Brady with her project? Yes, or no?"

He looked around the room as if maybe someone could come whisk him away. His eyes ended on Katie. She was staring at him, eyes round, pleading, desperate.

"Maybe." Don't make me say it, he thought. Don't make me hurt her.

"Maybe?"

"Well, I answered a few of her questions." The words spilled out of his mouth. "Technically, I suppose, yes, they were about her mobile, but it wasn't—"

Mr. Riley didn't let him finish, cutting him off with a raised hand. "Then I'm afraid we have no choice but to disqualify Miss Brady from the competition. I'm sorry, Miss Brady, but rules are rules." He turned to Peter again. "Mr. Clark, you are now the first-place winner. Congratulations. And I'm sorry it had to be under these circumstances."

Peter's legs buzzed as if he'd been shocked. Congratulations? For what? Ruining Katie's life?

He took a step back, confused. Mrs. Wells was shaking her head. She offered a pale smile to Katie who still stood, unseeing, as frozen as a block of granite.

Penny had disappeared. The judges evaporated into the background. Students milled about, tearing down their projects, oblivious that something horribly, terribly wrong had happened.

"Why, Peter?"

He turned. Katie's face was a mask of pain. Except for her eyes. They burned and sparked.

"Why did you tell them that?"

"I...I couldn't lie, Katie." It was all he had.

She cocked her head. Normally it was cute, but now it was an ugly gesture of bitterness. "No, you just threw me under the bus. Was it Penny's idea of yours? Heaven forbid an artist would win the big prize."

"What? No, that's not it at all. I don't care about the prize."

She nodded furiously. "Right. Why would you? You don't need this scholarship. You can get a dozen scholarships for science. Every school offers them. They practically hand them out to anyone." She stopped, standing, fuming.

"That's not fair, Katie."

She put her hands on her hips and took a step towards him. "Not fair? That's funny, Peter, really funny. I'll tell you what's not fair. It's not fair you guys with the stupid rockets and tadpoles get the scholarship every year, just because stupid Nitrovex is a stupid chemical company." She took another step towards him, finger pointing at his chest. "For once, just once, I had a chance, and you blew it for me."

Peter stepped back, surprised at the fury in Katie's eyes, his hands reaching for a table, trying to steady himself. Instead, his heel landed on something hard. His foot rolled forwards and he fell backward. He'd stepped on the stupid metal pipe he'd knocked off earlier.

Arms flailing, he grabbed for the edge of his table and twirled clumsily into his experiment. Pieces crashed together. He swung an arm in a last attempt at balance, glancing off a red lever. Pipes hissed and hoses snaked as the largest tube fell forward and pressure released.

It was slow-motion in his brain but over in a horrible instant. A heavy white pipe hissed and shot from the table, wobbling directly towards Katie's sculpture.

Peter fell backward onto the floor, face down, but the sound of the destruction was worse than actually seeing it. Clashing and tinkling glass, metal dropping, objects clattering to the floor.

And above it all, Katie's high-pitched wail of disbelief. "My mobile! You destroy my life and now my art too!"

* * *

Present Day

The Mustang's tires squealed as he took a turn too tightly onto Park Road which led to the high school. The new high school. Not the old one where everything had gone so wrong with Katie.

No, Kate. That was twelve years ago. And things seemed to have worked out well for her. It looked like she loved her job, and she must be good at if they were giving her a shot at this Nitrovex deal. His online snooping of her company a year or so ago had shown a pretty big organization.

Yes, he nodded to himself. Kate Brady was fine. More than fine, now. Doing well in Chicago, nice clothes, nice watch, Armani sunglasses. He wouldn't have pegged her for that, but, whatever.

None the worse for wear. Better, even, successful. She looked good, she sounded good. *She looked good.* He pushed some hair out of his face. He could still smell some of her perfume on his hand. Must be from the handle when he opened her door.

He couldn't help feeling a little wistful for what might have been. Well, we all got older. We all moved on, didn't we?

He gave a short sniff. Except for him, he supposed. Still here in Golden Grove. He almost thought "stuck." But he made a habit of not using that word anymore.

He pulled into the school lot, then guided the car to the teacher's parking spaces. Not too much longer and he wouldn't be able to drive the Mustang to work. Once the snow hit, he'd be back to the Camry.

He parked next to a familiar blue Taurus. Good old Lucius. Been working here for as a teacher for forty-odd years and he still came in on Sunday nights. He put the Mustang in park and got out.

Time to get back to the real world.

The empty halls of the high school always seemed strange on the weekends, as they were usually full of banging lockers and a mass of teenagers. Some laughing and shoving, some silently moving on to their next class, lost in the background of popularity. For some reason, those were the ones Peter noticed the most. Maybe because he once felt like one of them. Or maybe because he had an over-inflated sense of justice. "Every kid deserves the same shot," and all that.

He unlocked the door of his small but well-equipped office and tossed his keys on the desk. For all the hassles sometimes he did love his job. He hadn't thought he would.

The first year was rough. He hadn't done much teaching in grad school, so the students rolled over him pretty well, and there was talk of him not being cut out for teaching. If it weren't for Lucius, he wouldn't have survived.

Once he settled down and finally found his groove, it all kind of seemed to come naturally. From there, it just got better every semester. Now there was this "Science Teacher of the Year" thing. He had to admit, he was flattered, but he'd trade it in a second for one more student who could name just ten elements in the periodic table.

He was about to start going over some lab papers when he heard a knock on his door frame. Lucius's familiar mustached face leaned in.

"Well, well. If isn't the merry matchmaker," Peter said, nodding.

The older man's eyes twinkled. "I suppose I should apologize."

"Yeah, I suppose you should."

"Would it help to say that it was all Carol's idea?"

"It might if I believed that."

"Well, then, give me some more time to come up with a better excuse."

"I doubt that's possible. What were you thinking, Lucius?"

"You're not mad, are you?"

"Yes, actually, I think I am. How embarrassing do you think that was for Kate? She's trying to keep a low profile, and you and Carol drag her all over town."

Lucius came in and sat on the edge of Peter's desk. "I suppose I didn't think of it that way. Did you at least have a good time? I heard you went for a drive."

Thank to neighbor Carol, no doubt. Peter bit his upper lip. Lucius wasn't going to drop this, was he? "That depends on what you mean by good. 'Good' as in she didn't kill me and leave me in a ditch somewhere, or 'good' as in she gave me such a frosty send-off I'm surprised my eyebrows didn't freeze off."

"So, there's still hope?"

Peter snorted. "Hope? Hope for what, exactly?"

"Oh, c'mon. It couldn't have been that bad."

"Lucius, the woman hasn't been back in this town for more than twelve years. She's not going to just breeze in carrying a truckload of memories, forget everything and waltz around like everything's fine. Especially concerning me. You should have known that."

Lucius nodded. "I suppose not. But I'm sure you'll have other chances."

Peter laughed and stood. "Chances? Chances for what? You think just because you orchestrate some lame attempt at getting us together bluebirds are going to pop up and start circling around our heads the moment we see each other? Besides, Kate's different now. She's successful, driven—"

"Pretty."

"Of course, she's pretty. She's always been pretty."

Lucius's eyebrows raised, but he said nothing.

Peter continued. "Her home is in Chicago, now. She's not interested in what goes on in Podunk, Iowa anymore. She's just here to do her job and then go. Which I'm more than happy to let her do."

"She's interested enough to be here."

Peter waved his hand. "That's just for work. When she's done, she's back in Chicago with her job, and her suit-wearing co-workers and her downtown apartment."

"Oh, c'mon, Peter. I've known both of you since high school. Well, you, mostly. And I could see how you looked at her in the diner."

"I looked at her with…interest. Like someone I hadn't seen in twelve years after someone I thought was my friend practically shoved her into me."

"With interest? We're talking about a woman, not a bank."

Peter's eyes squinted. "And what do you mean 'in' the diner? You weren't 'in' the diner."

More throat clearing. "Well, I just happened to look in. When I passed by."

"Mm-hmm. And how long were you 'passing by'?"

Lucius shifted his weight on the desk. "Did I mention it was Carol's idea?"

Peter pushed his chair under his desk and gathered some papers to leave. "Yes, you did, and this conversation is over."

"Okay, okay." Lucius splayed his hands out. "I'm sorry."

"Fine. Now can we—"

"So, do you know when you're going to see her again?"

Peter dropped the papers and sighed. "Let me explain this to you in a way that might penetrate your obviously over-curious brain. Kate is the north pole of the magnet; I'm the south pole. Kate is vinegar; I'm baking soda. Kate is water, and I'm hydrophobic." He cocked his head. "Any of this getting through?"

Lucius, smiling rose from the desk and put his hands in his pockets. "You always have to get so scientific about everything."

"Well, I am a chemist." Peter began stacking some papers. "Sometimes it's the only way to make sense of things. You should know that."

"So you don't have any feelings for Kate whatsoever?"

Feelings? How could he? They'd barely spoken ten words all of senior year, beyond the first, feeble attempts on his part to apologize. But that had fallen flat quickly. From there it was just eye contact and a few "hi's" until graduation separated them forever. Until now.

Feelings? "No. I want her to succeed in life. I want her to be happy. I want her to do well in her job. Which she seems to do very well, by the way."

"Mmm-hmm."

"You're obviously not convinced."

Lucius pulled at the corner of his mustache. "No, no, I'm sure that explains all those questions you've asked Carol over the years. About Kate."

Peter looked up. "What?"

"Yes, like, 'How's Katie been doing?' or 'Heard anything from Katie lately?' or—"

Peter's face grew stony. "She told you?"

"Now, don't get angry. You live in a small town, remember? Everything gets around."

"Apparently." Peter grabbed his stapler and began forcefully stapling papers together. "Well, you can tell Carol Harding and the rest of the town gossip club that my questions about Kate are just out of friendliness. I have lots of other people from class I keep up with as well." None of whom just caused him to staple the wrong papers together.

"Sounds like you have it all under control."

"I believe I do." He began rummaging in the top drawer of his desk for the staple remover.

"Just keep it scientific."

"Yes."

"Feelings just get us into trouble."

"They can tend to do that, yes."

"Just like that scene from *Star Wars* with the Ewoks."

Peter sighed, not looking up from his desk. "Lucius, don't start with the Ewoks."

Lucius took off his glasses and began cleaning them with a hanky he pulled from his pocket. "I'm sure that now—as a full-grown, well-adjusted man—you're never affected by crude emotions, which, as we all know, are just chemical reactions in the brain."

Peter refused to look up, sorting test papers. "Whatever you say."

"Emotions such as the death of a poor innocent, really, really, cute furry forest creature—"

"C'mon, Lucius. I was only, like, six or something. Cut me some slack."

"—lying on the field of battle, his best friend weeping over his lifeless, battered body, rocking it slowly, limp dead hand flopping back and forth." Lucius flopped his hand in front of Peter's face.

"Knock it off."

"Poor, poor, fuzzy little Ewok, cut down in the prime of life."

"I will never forgive my parents for telling you that story." Peter sniffed once.

Lucius looked up in mock concern. "Oh. I'm sorry—forgot about your allergies." He stuck out his hand. "Here—here's a hanky."

"Keep it." He gathered the now-stacked pile of papers. "I've enjoyed our little talk. I'm sure you've got some work to do. I know I do. And please, next time you think about doing some matchmaking, consider dropping a lit Bunsen burner down your pants."

Lucius rose from the edge of the desk, smiling. "Noted, my friend. I will see you later." He returned through the open door, stopping to look back once. Peter could hear his footsteps receding down the empty hallway.

He dropped the stack of papers on the desk and leaned on it with both hands.

Feelings. Chemical reactions in the brain. Usually caused more trouble than good, in his experience. That and trying to help someone and then getting reamed for telling the truth. He rubbed his hand through his hair. There was that scent of Kate again. *Lucky You*? Yeah, right.

He went to wash his hands.

* * *

Kate rummaged through her purse. "Carol, you have anything for a headache?" Her temples were pounding so hard it felt like her brain was going to bump out of her skull.

Tommy the cat appeared and swirled around her leg, looking for attention. "You're not helping," she told him. He gave up and eased toward the kitchen.

Carol breezed in past him, a concerned look on her face. "Your head hurts?"

"Just a bit. Not sure if it was the cold air or what." Kate slumped in the easy chair and propped her feet up on the black ottoman in front of it.

Carol nodded. "Yes, cold air can do that sometimes." She bustled back to the kitchen.

Kate followed her, eyes narrowed. Seemed like every other thing Carol said had some hidden meaning. Or was she just being paranoid?

She leaned back, hand on her forehead. Carol returned with some pills and a glass of water.

"Here you go, dear." She sat on the edge of the couch near Kate. "So, how was your drive?"

"Fine." Kate popped the two pills and chased them with the water.

"Just fine?" Carol was smiling but seemed worried by that answer.

"Just fine, yes. Fine is sometimes just…fine." She rubbed her throbbing temples.

"I suppose a lot of the town seems different?"

"Some." Actually, most of it seemed pretty much the same. She had gotten used to the fast changes of life around Chicago. Boutiques and restaurants popping up and disappearing like dandelions. Small towns seemed a little more loyal to existing businesses. Maybe because nothing much ever changed.

"It was a nice day for a drive. I'm sure Peter enjoyed seeing you again."

Had he? She wasn't so sure. She wasn't so sure she had. Her temples thumped. "I suppose."

"Did he take you past the Community Center?"

She had to think. "The old school? Yes."

"Oh, good. I mean, I wanted you to see it sometime while you were here."

Kate cocked an eye at her friend. There seemed to be something on her mind. Carol sat with her hands folded on her lap, just staring at her as if she had something she wanted to blurt out but was afraid to. She was as transparent as thin air.

"Well, I was there, and we saw it. You can check it off the list."

"It's where they're having the Homecoming Dance in a few weeks."

There it was. "Really?"

"Yes, the theme is 'Making it Rad in the Eighties,' and they're decorating it to look just like it did in the eighties. You know anything about the eighties?"

"Yes, I believe I read something about them in a history book once. It was some sort of decade, right?"

Carol never got her sarcasm. "Yes, well, they're having eighties music, and everyone is supposed to wear eighties clothes and have eighties hair. It's all going to be very…"

"Eighties?"

"Yes." Carol still sat with her hands on her lap, smiling, watching her.

Kate sighed. It looked like she was going to have to play this out or Carol would stay that way until February.

"Teachers are invited, you know. To the dance."

"Really?"

"Yes. They're allowed to bring dates, too."

"How nice."

"I don't believe Peter has a date yet, though."

"That's so very sad. But I'm sure some hometown girl will snatch him up soon enough." She thought of Penny Fitch. Her temples pulsed harder.

"I think someone sounds a little jealous."

"Don't be ridiculous. But someone *is* getting a little miffed at her nosy but lovable old friend who keeps dropping hints about her neighbor like slippery sledgehammers. I'm not interested. I have work to do. And I won't be around, anyway. I'll be in Chicago." Her brow furrowed. Unless she had to come back to do more follow-up for this proposal…

"All I'm saying is that you're here and Peter's there…" She pointed at Kate and then out the window. "And as long as you're here and he's there…"

"As long as I'm here and he's there, we're going to stay right here and there. Where we were. Or *are*. Or…" Kate threw her hands in the air. "You've been doing this to me all day. You get me all worked up, and then I do something stupid like asking him for a ride." She stopped. "Well, I'm not a dopey little high school girl anymore, and I can take care of my own life, thank you."

"He's fixing your tire."

She'd forgotten about that. "He is?" She cranked her neck to see out the front window. All she could see was the porch and the back of her car.

"Yes. I saw him go by the house with his tire-fixing thingy a few minutes ago."

Kate jutted out her bottom lip, thinking. Maybe she should go out. Say thanks.

"Maybe you should go out and thank him," Carol said.

Aggh! Mind-reader! *Get out of my head.*

Then stubbornness straightened her up. "No. We already said our goodbyes. It would be awkward."

Carol was silent, then put her fingertips on the table and stood, pushing her chair back. "Maybe you're right. I'm meddling. You're a big girl now."

She still had her smile, so Kate knew she wasn't angry. "Yes I am, thank you."

"I'll start getting some supper ready. Do you like meatloaf?"

Not really. But her only other choice was going out. Which meant maybe Ray's or a frozen burrito from the Stop-n-Pop. Worse, she'd have to walk past her wavy-haired neighbor with his tire-fixing thingy. "Yes. Meatloaf sounds great. Thanks."

Carol moved into the kitchen, leaving behind a swirling cloud of thoughts in Kate's head.

It was this place. The town. The buildings, the school, Nitrovex, the people. She sighed. Mostly the people. The ones with the bright-blue eyes.

No. Don't go there. Don't think it. Remember what happened? Broken dreams. Broken glass. Broken…everything.

* * *

Twelve Years Ago
Golden Grove High

Katie saw the shards of her mobile skittering across the floor under the cold glare of the gym lights.

It was a nightmare. It had to be. It couldn't be happening for real. Not after all her work, her time. She didn't deserve this. She had won.

But it was gone. The delicate pieces she had spent hours fitting together all summer and after school were scattered across the gym floor like an evaporating dream. Everyone had stopped and turned to look at her, every face petrified at the destruction.

Except for Peter, who was clumsily trying to get up from the floor. Peter, whose stupid science project had blasted hers to smithereens. It was gone, and heart screamed in a thousand different directions as she dropped to her knees.

But it was still nothing—not even close—to the sting of betrayal that pierced her soul. Nice Peter, loyal Peter—the one time she needed him to come through for—the *one* time, and he chose himself. Chose *Penny*. Over her.

She was too shocked, too angry to even cry. She hopelessly started to pick up a few pieces of glass from the floor, but it was over, it was gone. No one would be giving her a scholarship to anything unless it was to a trade school to learn how to sweep up garbage.

A hand touched her arm. "Katie, I'm so sorry. It was an accident. I'm so sorry."

Katie wrenched her arm away. "Don't even…just don't," was all she could say.

Peter kneeled down and began to help her pick up pieces. "At least let me help."

She whirled on him. "Haven't you done enough already? And what do you care? You've got your prize. You won. You and that..." She almost said it out loud. *Witch!* "Just...go back to your pipes and tubes and blow something else up."

Peter stood, looking back at his own project, now a pile of steaming tubes and dripping pipes. "Well, mine's kind of a mess, now, too."

"Oh, really? Well, you deserve it." She lowered her voice. "I thought you were my friend, Peter. I even thought you were..." She stopped. "I thought if anyone was going to stand up for me, anyone in this stupid school, it would have been you."

His voice was small, tiny, almost like a little boy. "I'm sorry."

"Yes, sorry, oh, that helps now." She almost laughed. "You ruined my life, Peter." The tears were unstoppable now, the pain wrenching them out of her heart in sobs. "You ruined my life."

He just stood there. His mouth opened as if he were going to say something, then he turned and went back to his table.

That was it. It was over. Not only was her project ruined, but Peter was gone. Even if she wanted him, she'd never have him. Not his stupid smile or his blue eyes or—or *anything*. Phase three, homecoming, all of it. It had all come crashing down with her mobile.

Her eyes stung from the tears. She knew everyone was watching her but trying not to, embarrassed by the scene.

The rocket, now a lifeless chunk of metal, steamed on the ground, dead and oblivious. It was everything Peter was, everything that was wrong with this town, all rolled into one flashing, destructive, mindless instant. Nitrovex, science, stupidity. One big, unmistakable explosive metaphor, a life scattered apart as surely as the bent wire and broken glass that littered the gym floor. Worthless, irreparable, and who would want to bother fixing it, anyway?

It was over, all of it—the scholarship, art school, the dance, Peter. All her hopes gone. She'd do her time, say hi in the hallways, be a good little girl, do her homework and get through school, and then she was gone. College, a commune, the moon, wherever, it didn't matter.

Kicking a piece of glass with her foot, she walked quickly to the back of the gym, bumping through students who were trying not to make eye contact. The tears flowed easily now, heartbreak giving way to anger and indignation, and she let them run. She didn't care. Let someone else clean up this mess. She pushed through the metal doors at the back of the gym.

She was as good as gone. Years of Golden Grove frustration and manipulating parents and Peter and worthless, meaningless art—all behind her. Once spring was here, once that diploma was in her hand she was leaving Golden Grove. Forever.

Chapter Eight

Present Day

Kate turned off the engine to her yellow Bug which she'd parked in a visitor space next to the main entrance at Nitrovex Chemical Corporation. This was it. Fresh start, Monday morning, time to get to down business. No distractions. Game time.

The flat tire was still full that morning. Carol called it a miracle. Kate called it Carol looking up online how to deflate a car tire so she'd have to take a ride with the handsome man next door.

She had to admit, though, she'd slept better than she had in months, which surprised her. She'd expected after all the ups and downs and her drive with Peter that her mind wouldn't be able to shut off. But it only took a minute or two of staring at the angled ceiling of her old room for her half-open eyes to close and her mind to drift off into a solid, long sleep.

She got out of her car and retrieved her briefcase. *Deep breath. You've done your homework. Put the past few days—and the past—behind you. This is what you really came here for, remember?*

She straightened a crease in her gray business skirt, then checked her reflection in the window of the car. Hair up, all in place, and proper makeup. Not too strong, very professional. She nodded, pleased with herself, remembering what had gotten her here. She was good at what she did, wasn't she?

The entrance to the Nitrovex main office was bright and airy and could just as easily be in a Chicago-suburb office park. Tall, thin windows were flanked by birch trim. It almost reminded her of her downtown office.

"Miss Brady?" A slim older woman in a trim business outfit approached her, hand outstretched.

"Yes," Kate returned, surprised that she was recognized.

The woman smiled. "I'm Sandy. Mr. Wells is almost ready to see you."

"I know I'm early."

"That's quite alright. You can have a seat here in the reception area. There's coffee there in the alcove." She was pointing to a neatly trimmed waiting area with similar light woodwork and aluminum-framed chairs.

She hadn't waited more than a few minutes when a booming voice caromed down the hallway. "That'll be fine, Jim. Just tell them to up it by ten percent."

A man in his late sixties strolled toward her wearing a seed-corn hat and jeans. A paunchy stomach hung over a big-buckled belt. Mr. Wells was just as she remembered, although a lot grayer and a little paunchier.

She almost smiled. He still looked more like one of the guys she used to see as a little girl hanging out on the park benches on the square, jawing about how bad the Cubs were that year. Not the head of a multi-million-dollar international corporation.

"You must be Kate," he said in the same booming voice as he approached, hand out.

"I must be," she said, shaking it. "Kate Brady, from the Garman Group."

He was studying her, eyes slightly squinted. "Your company said you used to live in Golden Grove?"

Terrific. She briefly thought about lying. "Well, yes. A long time ago. My parents are—"

He snapped his fingers and pointed at her. "Joe and Emily Brady. That's right." He grinned. "Always liked those two."

She returned the smile weakly. "Mr. Wells, I think the Garman Group can help you make Nitrovex even more visible in your industry." That's it. Get right down to business.

John nodded. "I'm sure you can, I'm sure you can." He spread his arms wide. "Well, why don't we start by having our VP of Operations show you around? Get the lay of the land? Then we can chat some more." He peered past Kate's shoulder into the waiting area. "Looks like she's just arriving."

VP of Ops? *Uh-oh*, and *oh no*. She'd done her research on the company and knew exactly who that was.

"Sorry I'm late, John," a bright and disturbingly familiar voice said.

Kate turned and squinted into the morning sunlight that glanced through the tall windows of the open lobby, hitting her teenage nemesis at just the wrong angle. Same long black hair and perfectly white smile. Just add twelve years, some crow's feet (yes! Even she gets old!), and a navy-blue business dress, and it was her, the Wispy Witch herself. Penny Fitch.

Penny was busy putting her sunglasses in her pocket and hadn't really taken notice of her yet. Kate cleared her throat and waited. She'd expected to meet her sooner or later but had hoped it would be later. Much later. As in, never.

But they were all adults now, right?

"Penny Fitch, this is—"

"—Kate Brady," Penny enthused, her hand extended. "So good to see you again!"

Was it? Was it really?

"Hi," Kate said, shaking Penny's claw. *You're a professional, remember?*

"You two know each other?" said John.

"Sure," Penny said. "Katie and I went to high school together."

Kate had the odd thought of what Penny's head would like if it just spontaneously exploded right now. Kind of messy, she guessed. But somewhat satisfying.

"Well, then, you two probably have a lot to talk about," John said. "Kate, I'll leave you in Penny's hands for a while."

That thought caused her skin to creep sideways. "Okay," she said, watching John saunter away down the hallway.

She turned back to Penny. The blaring sun behind her made it look like she had horns growing out of her head. Kate tried to smile but just grimaced.

Penny gave her a quick once over and a grin. "You look great, Kate. I almost didn't recognize you."

I kind of wished you hadn't.

"Thanks, you too." She wished she could have lied, could have said, *Wow, did you gain weight, or are you just pregnant?* But, no. Penny looked trim, light, and aggravatingly perfect. "John said something about a tour?"

Penny nodded. "Of course. Let me show you around the plant." She gestured with her arm towards a side hallway that led to some white metal double doors.

* * *

Two hours, a stuffy filtration mask, and a hard hat later, Kate had seen about as many vats of nameless brown liquid and endless white pipes as she could handle. She hadn't visited her parents at the plant a lot when they'd worked here as chemists, but she hadn't forgotten the acrid stink. Her dad had shown her around like this on some "take your kid to work day", and she'd thought she was going to permanently damage her sense of smell.

Penny had led her back to the main office area, the thrum and bang of the plant floor disappearing as the door closed.

"You can keep the hat." Penny was pointing to the white hard hat with the Nitrovex logo on it perched on Kate's head.

"Thanks." She might need it at her next meeting in Chicago if she blew this deal.

"I'll let John know we're done. Hope to see you around again, Kate." She stuck her hand out.

Kate shook it. Penny paused, then turned and left down a carpeted hallway.

Kate wiped her hand on her skirt. She realized she'd had her stomach muscles clenched for the last thirty minutes and exhaled. That was it, then? No apologies? No, 'sorry I was such a petty skank and ruined your life?' Just act like nothing ever happened, everything was just all hunky-dory, huh? Okay, she could play it that way.

But the tour actually hadn't been that bad. She'd half expected Penny to be one of those overly-extroverted sales reps she'd had run-ins with before, but she'd been…normal. Even professional. *Maybe we do all grow up sometime.*

John Wells was approaching briskly. "Well, then, what do you think of our little operation?" he asked, face beaming.

All she could remember were pipes and banging and guys in white hazmat coveralls, all with the urgent look of someone waiting for a vat of deadly chemicals to explode and flood the town.

"It was amazing. Just like I remembered it."

He laughed. "You mean you liked all those tanks and smelly mixing stations?"

"I've always been interested in science." She tried to sound convincing. It wasn't a flat-out lie. There was her friendship with Peter after all. *Yeah, right.*

He began walking back down the hallway. "Let's be real, Miss Brady. Most people don't get much out of seeing our little operation here. But I think what we do here is important. Not just chemicals for sewage plants or farms. You know we also make resins in paints used by artists?"

"I saw something about that, yes."

He nodded. "Among other things. You may not see it right up front, but you'd sure notice it if we weren't there. What I'm trying to say is that you may feel like you have your work cut out for you, but Nitrovex isn't just chemicals."

"We'll certainly do our best for you, Mr. Wells. And I hope you find we're the right company for this project." That was no lie. The significance of this project to her career continued to hover around her like a nervous cloud.

He smiled. "You can call me John if I can call you Kate."

She smiled. She liked him. "It's a deal."

He gestured down the hall, and she followed. "Now, let me show you our history room if I may. Did you know we were the first company in the US to produce epichlorohydrin derivatives?"

Chapter Nine

A week later, Kate was back in Golden Grove, hoping to be inspired before her second meeting at Nitrovex. She put down the heavy book on Carol's dining room table and rubbed her temple. *Nitrovex: Fifty Years of Innovation.*

More like fifty years of grinding monotony. She'd thumbed through the science tome, which was masquerading as a company PR piece, at least a dozen times in her office in Chicago. If she had to look at one more photo of a smiling, goggled technician pointing at a rat's nest of tubes she'd go crazy.

The table was loaded with all the materials Penny Fitch had shoved at her after her tour of the plant. They might as well have been written in Martian. Membrane technology. Hexavalent chromium reduction. Flocculant polymers.

It was all just a bunch of vague words next to pictures of dirty churning machines run by guys hidden in white hazmat gear. And this one: "sludge bulking." Sounded like some exercise Penny did to keep her stomach flat.

The wispy witch might pretend the pile of materials was intended to help, but Kate wasn't fooled. Penny was probably trying another round of sabotage.

She called out to Carol in the kitchen. "I'll give you twenty bucks if you can tell me what"—she squinted at a brochure—"'filamentous bulking bacteria' is."

Carol was at the sink washing dishes left from a Thread Heads meeting earlier in the day. "Sounds like the bug I got after my trip to Acapulco a few years ago. Maybe you should take a break. You've been at it all afternoon and now past dinner."

"I don't need to take a break. I need to get one." Kate sighed. "Clothing companies, web startups, those I can at least somewhat relate to." She flipped through a stack of Nitrovex brochures. "But phosphorus reduction and sludge dewatering? I'd have to be a…a…"

"Chemist?" Carol suggested.

Kate leaned back to look at her, shaking her head slowly. "Oh, nice try."

Carol continued to dry her dishes, back turned. "What do mean? I'm just trying to provide you with the best answer to your dilemma."

"Have you ever thought of being a politician?"

"All I'm trying to do is suggest the best ways for you to do well with your job. That is what you want, isn't it?"

Kate opened her mouth, then closed it. It was manipulative, it was sneaky, but she had to admit Carol might be right. Peter was probably the best person to help her get a handle on this project. She'd gone through every piece of material Penny had given her, watched every online video of swirling tanks of cow poop she could handle, and she was still left with a blank. And Garman was expecting an update on her progress on Wednesday.

She just needed a kernel of a concept, a base for everything she would use to promote the company. Coke was fun, fizzy water. Corvette was fast, loud cars. But unpronounceable chemicals? What did you do with that, come up with a mascot of a singing test tube?

Hmm. *Singing test tube.* She wrote it down. Then crossed it out.

She tapped the pen on her teeth, thinking, then writing.

Nitrovex: The Future of Hexavalent Chromium Reduction. *Today.*

Nitrovex: We Make Stuff That Cleans Your Poop So You Don't Have To.

Hi, I'm Peter the Pipe! Sludge need bulking? Polymers need flocculating? Need some deadly, brain-damaging chemicals to do vague, chemical-ly things? I'm your guy!

Nitrovex: Help Kate keep her job by liking this slogan.

Crap. This was impossible.

She sat back. Maybe she should break down and call her parents. Yeah, that would be rich. Kate calling her parents for advice on Nitrovex, the place where they'd worked that she'd always ridiculed as a kid. The place that almost got her into art school but always gave their scholarship to some science geek.

Since then, she'd made a point of making her own way and leaving her parents out of career advice. Well, she was paying for that now.

She bit her lip, then sighed. *I can't believe I'm saying this.* "Do you think Peter's home?" She half-wished he wasn't, that he was at school or somewhere, anywhere. That he didn't exist, and she was back in Chicago, in her nice, safe office, with someone else handling this hopeless account.

Carol entered the room, drying her hands on a dish towel. "Oh, I know he is. Can't you hear the hammering?"

Kate noticed it for the first time. Random hammering and occasional thunks on wood coming from next door.

"He's working in the back yard," Carol said, returning to the kitchen. "I'm sure he'd be happy to help you."

Kate just looked at her.

"What could it hurt?"

What could it hurt? How much time did Carol have?

But for all Carol's obvious machinations, maybe she was right. Let's look at this objectively, Katie thought. Peter knew chemistry, which meant he was already miles ahead of her in understanding what could hit Nitrovex's sweet spot. He'd lived here all his life and knew the company, especially the last few years.

She just needed that first step, that edge. Then she could take it from there. All she had to show for the last few hours was a doodle of gap-toothed, labcoat-wearing cow that looked suspiciously like Penny Fitch.

She only had a couple days before she had to report on her progress, and they'd made it abundantly clear that this was no small account. Lose this and she'd be designing flyers for baby showers and cleaning out Danni's coffee machine.

She put her head in her hands. "Carol, if you need me, I'll be over at Peter's."

* * *

Peter set the heavy wooden toolbox down next the huge oak tree in his back yard and looked up. His old tree house had been there for almost a couple of decades now, and the tree was beginning to grow around it. Slowly and unthinkingly, it was bending the boards and swallowing it up. Some things don't stop for time.

He picked out a hammer. He'd been meaning to get to this for months, and now was as good a time as any. Some things needed to be done, right? It had nothing to do with the yellow VW he'd spotted in Carol's driveway.

He shook his head at himself. It was a schoolboy move, and he knew it. It was just an excuse to be in the backyard, hoping maybe he would see Kate next door. Maybe he could talk to her. Finally apologize. Before she left again.

He climbed the ladder he had rested against the tree and began working on pulling off some of the loose boards at the base of the tree house. He tried not to think about all the fun he had had here. Building it with his dad, who almost fell from the tree and made him promise not to tell his mom. That brought a bittersweet smile. Then there were the sleepovers with his buddies on cool and humid June nights, staying up late, eating junk food and playing Grand Theft Auto on their PS2s.

And that night with Kate after the movie.

He began wedging out a stubborn nail. Shook his head at himself again. Why did he always get so sentimental about things? He was a scientist, for crying out loud.

A screen door banged, and he immediately glanced over. He swallowed, once. It was Kate, coming this way, holding a bottle of her Fiji water. She moved slowly around the short privet hedge that separated their two yards, arms folded casually, bottle dangling.

Try to act nonchalant. Be cool. "So, how'd it go at Nitrovex last week?" he asked, descending the ladder.

"Lousy. Penny Fitch was assigned as my tour guide."

Oops. He had hoped she wouldn't bump into Penny so soon. If at all. "You saw Penny?"

"Yes, I saw her. All five-foot-nothing of her and her perfect smile. She gave me a pile of materials on the company," Kate said with a sniff.

Mayday. Change the subject. Think of something. "Oh."

"But she can't sabotage me if I don't let her. I still have a chance to win this proposal."

"She wasn't that bad, was she?"

"Well, truth is…" She stopped.

"What?"

She put the bottle on a nearby chair and her hands in her pockets. "Truth is she actually seemed to know what she was doing."

"I think she does." He saw Kate's eyes narrow. "From what I've heard."

She nodded. "Maybe."

"So, aside from Penny, did it go well? You're back for another meeting?"

She blew a wisp of red-gold hair from her forehead. "More research. I'm fine with the general scope of the business, but the chemical stuff is tougher. The tour didn't help much, to be honest." She walked to a white metal lawn chair next to the corner flower bed and sat. "I thought I'd be able to bluff my way through the science part, but it's just a bunch of sludge bulk to me."

Peter cocked his head in her direction. "Oh, so you already learned about filamentous bacteria?"

That won a musical laugh. The laugh he remembered hearing here in this treehouse, on her family's porch swing, walks home from school…

"I wish," she said. "I'm still trying to figure out what a flocculant polymer is. Sounds like something illegal Randy Palmer used to snort behind the high school."

Peter laughed. "That's actually kind of funny."

"Thanks."

"No, I mean, Randy Palmer's a sheriff now, over in Jasper County."

"Really? Wow. I guess you never know about some people." She looked away, then stood and approached him, hands in pockets. "I have an idea. You think maybe we could switch places and you meet with John Wells tomorrow? You two seem to speak the same language."

"No chance."

"C'mon—you shave that face stubble, put on a nice, navy-blue business dress. You could probably borrow one of Penny's."

He shook his head for emphasis. "Definitely don't have the legs for it."

She gave him the once-over, then pursed her lips. "Oh, I don't know. I've seen you in shorts."

He put the hammer back in the toolbox. "Nope. I don't shave my legs for anyone."

"Well, then, can you at least tell me why I should at all need to know what a flocculate is?"

"Sure. Sludge needs a high-molecular-weight, high-charge structured cationic flocculate in order to be separated or dewatered."

She batted her eyes. "Oh, Peter, stop. You had me at sludge."

Peter nodded, wiping his hands on his jeans. "Good one."

She cocked her head up at the tree as if seeing it for the first time. "What are you working on?"

Peter wagged his thumb towards the huge gnarled oak tree. "Taking down the old treehouse."

Her shoulders slumped. "Oh, no. Why?"

"Well, the tree's growing around the boards now, and if I don't remove them, it'll probably kill the tree."

"Really?" She frowned. "I always liked that old tree house. I used to play dolls there with my friends when you weren't around."

Peter smiled. "I know."

"What, really? You were spying on me?" Her eyebrows arched.

"I wouldn't call it spying. I would call it paying very close attention from a distance. Besides, I kept finding little Polly Pocket shoes in the cracks of the floor. Pretty big clue."

She smiled, looking down at the grass. "Well, I guess all good things come to an end."

It was a statement that seemed to carry more weight than it should have. He watched as she turned, touching the rough gray bark of the old tree, looking up at the jumble of scrap boards joined together in a crude box in the center of the tree. The limbs of the giant oak seemed to cradle it in its arms. "Do you really need to tear it down?"

Peter joined her. "Well, how about a last look around? Most of it's still there. The ladder should work." He tugged on the first couple of boards nailed at intervals up the side of the tree. Kate grabbed the first and started to climb, Peter holding her side for safety, hoping his palms weren't too sweaty. *Lucky You* fogged his brain a little. "Make sure they aren't loose."

He watched her reach the top of the climb and disappear over the side.

Her head popped out a small side window. "Come on up." She disappeared inside again.

Peter followed, testing each board as he climbed, and soon joined her in the cramped space. It smelled like damp, old pine. A few boards were loose, and some were even rotting, but most of the roof was still there, and the floor seemed safe. He hadn't been up here in years. No reason to until now, he supposed.

"Smaller than I remember," he said, scooting to a place opposite Kate, who ducked her head under a branch poking through the roof.

"Pretty cozy." She pointed at a board. "Look—there's the drawing I made of the two of us."

She was pointing at a sketch of two kids done in magic marker, one rail-thin with oversized round glasses and the other in a dress. "Hmm," he said. "I'd say I look about the same. You look as good as always."

She shot him a glance as if she wasn't sure if he was making a joke. "Thanks."

He peered out the larger window on the opposite side, looking down towards the back fence. "Man, the snowball fights we used to have." He pointed to a black burn mark near the window. "Shot a rocket from here one night when my parents weren't home."

He wasn't sure, but he thought he saw her flinch at the word rocket. *Stupid, Peter.*

"Look, Kate…" He stopped. *Go on, get it over with.*

She was looking at him, her brown eyes liquid, her hair falling in a flowing river over her shoulder.

He swallowed. "I want to apologize. For the whole Scholarship Fair thing in high school."

She shook her head. "No, it's not necessary."

He shook back. "No, please. I know it hurt you. A lot. Not getting that scholarship, and my experiment destroying your mobile. You'd worked so hard on it. I can't imagine how you must have felt."

Kate looked down, but she had a small smile. The evening sun arced through a crack in the treehouse, lighting her hair with even more gold. *Not fair.*

"It's not a big deal," she said. "Besides, you did me a favor."

"How's that?"

She gestured with her hands. "Well, if I had gotten that scholarship I would have gone to some place like Mason and gotten a degree in art, instead of graphic design. I'd probably be sitting at some abandoned gas station trying to sell velvet Elvis paintings right now."

"That's probably a little extreme."

She held up her hands, fingers out. "Trust me, one of my friends has an art degree, and he's still living with his parents. Makes wind chimes out of those tiny liquor bottles you get on the airplane. He spends his weekends trying to sell them to bored housewives at flea markets. A graphic design degree has gotten me a far better job, thank you."

"Hmm," was all he could think of to say. "Sounds like a very practical approach."

"I'd like to think so." She wasn't looking at him anymore. The sun had dropped further, and she was in shadow again.

It struck him then. She'd moved on. She'd said as much. Living in Chicago, climbing the corporate ladder. Fiji water and Armani. She wasn't a Golden Grove kid anymore. Like him.

Kate pulled her knees up and brushed some dust from her jeans. "Didn't we used to come up here to do homework?"

"Mmm-hmm." He glanced at her. "It's also where..." He stopped. *Don't do it.* "Never mind."

"What?" When he hesitated, she reached over to swat him. "C'mon, what?"

Now that he brought it up, he knew she'd never let him off the hook.

"You know. The night a bunch of us went to see *Toy Story 2*? In seventh grade? After the movie, I was up here looking at stars with my telescope. You came up and brought me some Oreos."

"Yeah?" Kate pushed some hair back from her face nonchalantly.

Peter's shoulders dropped. She was going to make him say it. "Okay, the kiss, remember? Our first kiss?"

She nodded as if she just remembered where she'd left her car keys. "Oh, that. Yeah, sure I remember. I think."

"You think? You don't remember your first kiss?"

"Well, yeah." She cleared her throat. "Sure I do."

"Wait..." Peter's eyes squinted. "You mean...?"

She laced her fingers together around her knees and shrugged, looking out the window. "Well, it wasn't exactly my *first* kiss."

"It wasn't?" he said, irritated at how his voice sounded so small.

He must have looked a little too disappointed. "Well, it's not really that important, is it Peter? I mean, that was a long time ago."

His eyes narrowed. "Who was it? Robert Bowman?"

"No, it wasn't Robert Bowman."

"Tim Polowski?"

"No, of course not. You know, I really don't even think I—"

"Kent Wilkins?" He looked at the ceiling, thinking. "Uh, that Steve guy with the freckles? Martin what's-his-name in your art class? Dennis—"

"It was Brian McDermott and we were at a birthday party in his basement and my friends dared me to kiss him so I did and that was all there was to it," she blurted.

"Brian McDermott? 'Fissure Chin'?" Peter gave a short laugh.

Kate folded her arms. "Well, you just had to know, so there."

"Brian McDermott." He nodded. "Did you know he's a plastic surgeon in Texas?"

Kate's eyes widened. "Really?"

"Yup. You could have been the wife of the only plastic surgeon in the country who needed more work done than his patients."

Kate flashed a sarcastic smile but said nothing.

Peter looked out the window. "Well, it was *my* first kiss."

"Oh, come on."

"You were wearing a purple dress and had those yellow flower clip things in your hair that you always wore, one on each side. And you smelled like strawberries from your Strawberry Shortcake perfume."

Kate stared at him. "I did?" she said softly.

"And you were wearing orange sandals, and all I could think of was 'Please, God, don't let our braces get stuck together.'"

"They didn't, as I recall."

Peter turned to face her, smiling. "So you *do* remember."

Now it was Kate's turn to stare out the window. "Sure. Everyone remembers their third kiss." She untangled her legs, crawled to the ladder and turned to climb down.

"Mmm-hmm. Wait—third kiss?"

Kate's head disappeared down the ladder with a sly smile.

Chapter Ten

Kate left Peter struggling to get down from the treehouse and stepped through the fresh-cut grass, smiling. The vacant look on his boyish face when she left was priceless. Boyish but also rugged now with its two-day stubble.

She made her way to a pair of chipped white metal garden chairs set next to a vine-covered gazebo in the corner of Peter's yard. The chilly metal felt good through her jeans. She stretched her legs, kicking off her shoes. The grass was cool, almost cold, but it felt good between her toes. Couldn't do that on the concrete outside her high-rise apartment in the Chicago Loop. She could only afford a low floor, so she couldn't even see Lake Michigan. Her view was of rows of anonymous windows in the next building and sky-crane-dotted construction down the alley where there would be more anonymous windows soon.

Not that she was there all that much. Mostly just to sleep and eat when she wasn't working. She'd only been back to Golden Grove a couple of times and it was already starting to seem like a completely different life.

She watched Peter make his way down from the treehouse quickly but carefully, making sure his feet hit the rickety boards that served as the ladder.

He spotted Kate. "I thought you'd disappeared."

She gave him a wave. "Right here. Want to join me?"

"In a minute. Let me clean this us first." He began collecting the hammer and other tools he'd left on the ground and dumping them in a long wooden tool box.

She noticed the cut muscles of his legs under the cargo shorts, and his carved arms. Still lean, but now… She almost thought the word sexy and pushed it to the side.

She crossed her legs at the ankles, looking around. She remembered this part of his yard from when she was a girl. Although it had seemed bigger then. Everything had seemed bigger then, she guessed. It was strange sitting here, like she was inside some time capsule. Or, more accurately was on the outside looking in. A place she had been once but had left behind. It was a surprisingly lonely feeling, as if she didn't belong anywhere anymore.

"Getting dark earlier," Peter said. He had joined her, taking the chair opposite her, putting his arms on the rests on each side. He'd put on a navy-blue jacket. His form was an orange outline in the last rays of the sun behind him, his glasses were mirrors hiding his eyes.

"It's not past your bedtime yet, is it?" she teased.

She assumed he was smiling when he spoke. "Not yet. And you're the one that always had to be home by eight-thirty, remember?"

She shook her head. "That was just because my parents wanted me to study so I could be as good in school as Peter Clark."

"Mmm. Is that why you stopped coming around as much in high school?"

"We had different crowds. You were science and cross-country. I was in the art crowd, if there even was such a thing here." That stung more than it should have. "It was a long time ago, right?" she added, as if that somehow explained everything.

"Seems like it." He leaned forward, elbows on his knees, face closer. "Sometimes, though, it seems like just yesterday."

She nodded, not just to appear to agree with him, but because he was right. Sitting here, their houses on either side. It felt like they could be ten again. She wasn't sure why it felt that way, but it did.

They talked. Talked until after dark, sitting on the metal chairs by the gazebo. She had forgotten how quiet it was here. No car horns or sirens echoing down concrete canyons. Just a few crickets chirping and the occasional dog barking somewhere in the distance. A car crunching down a road a street or two over.

Just the two of them, the night slowly hiding their features until all that were left were silhouettes against a clear sky dotted with stars. The sun had long set, leaving them the light from the distant street lamps and a dim glow from the half-moon that was just rising above the trees behind Peter's house. She wasn't sure what time it was anymore, and she didn't care to check her watch. Certainly past 8:30, but her parents would never know.

Peter was describing an incident with his chemistry club last year in such an excited voice she couldn't help but smile. He seemed like the boy she remembered, under the manly stubble. No pretensions. What you saw was what you got.

It struck her that of all the dates she'd had with men back in Chicago, she'd never talked as much with them as she had with Peter tonight. In the city, there was lots of small talk, business talk, sports. Her dates were good-looking guys, nice, but kind of flat. Like a painting, not a sculpture, to use an art analogy.

Not that she'd made much time for relationships. She didn't have much to spare if she was going to make any headway at Garman.

But with Peter conversation was easy. Maybe it was just what happened with old friends. All the shared history.

Old friends. That's what they were, right? Just old friends.

Peter was finishing his story. "They couldn't get the burn marks off the ceiling. I had to promise to come in over the summer and paint it. Guess that's the last time I let them mix red phosphorus with potassium chlorate."

Kate laughed.

"What?" Peter leaned forward toward her chair, head cocked.

"I don't know, nothing, I guess." She leaned forward as well. "It's just, like… you've really found your niche here. Teaching I mean. I don't know a molecule from a mangstrom and even I can see that."

"Angstrom," he corrected.

"See?"

He sat back. "I suppose. I mean, I do enjoy it. There's just something about when a kid gets it, you know? When something in the intangible world becomes real because of an experiment or a new way of explaining it. It's almost like you can see a light go on in their eyes."

"It must be really rewarding, Peter."

"It is. I mean, I never thought I'd like it this much, but…" He gestured at the yard, the house where he'd grown up. "Here I am, right where I started."

She wasn't sure if that was sadness in his voice or not. She folded her arms around her. It was getting cooler. "Carol mentioned you might be leaving. I mean, not leaving teaching, but maybe getting another job. Somewhere at a larger school."

He paused, his body angled toward her. It felt like he was studying her, but she couldn't quite tell because of the dark. "That's just Lucius talking. He has a friend at a private school where he taught once. They have an opening for a science teacher. A place in Chicago, actually. The Dixon School."

She leaned forward impressed. "Really? The head of my company has two kids that go there. Pretty prestigious. Are you going to take it?"

"I don't think so. I'm pretty happy here."

"But aren't you going to even interview?"

"If I know I'm not interested, why should I waste their time?"

"Well, to see if maybe you'll like it. You'll never know until you try."

Even in the dark she could see him stiffen. "It's not like I have a lot of time to interview everywhere. I've got a lot of responsibilities here. I know it's just a small-town school, but there are a lot of kids here who depend on us. For some of them, it's a make-or-break time for them. If I left, I'd feel like I was letting them down."

She could tell she'd struck a nerve, but pushed on. "But what about you? You've put your time in. Everyone knows how you took care of your dad and mom, and that's great, that's huge. But you need to think about your own life, too. Maybe there are other students in Chicago who need you just as much. Maybe more."

He shrugged. "Maybe."

"The pay's probably better, too, you know," she said.

"Oh, I'm sure."

Was that sarcasm?

He continued. "But there's more to life than money, right?"

Kate knew success wasn't only about money. It was about your hard work being appreciated, about climbing the next rung on the ladder. "Why not just do an interview, explore the opportunity—"

"Look, Kate, I don't want to be a jerk about this, but can we change the subject?"

Had she hacked him off? This ground was beginning to seem all-too-familiar. Geez, she sounded almost like her parents. His career was none of her business.

She checked her watch. "Oh, look, a message from my office. I'd better check it. I'm sure you've got work to do, too. Papers to grade or something…"

As she stood, so did he.

He stepped closer. "Oh, hey, so…you seemed like you wanted to ask me some stuff earlier. About your proposal?"

She waved her hand. "Oh, no worries, it's fine." She'd been so busy chatting she'd tabled her chemistry questions for the time being.

He put his hand on her arm. She shivered, but it wasn't from the cold night air. "Okay, well, if you do need any help just let me know, okay?"

They were only a few inches apart now. When did that happen?

She instantly felt like a girl on her first date, standing on her porch, waiting to see what the guy was going to do. She could feel the pulse pounding in her ears, the heat from his hand.

What should she do? What did she want him to do? Her voice was almost a whisper. "Thanks. I will."

His hand lingered on her arm for what seemed like an hour. She could barely see his face in the glancing light of the street lamps. Just the outline of his tousled hair, his glasses. She realized she hadn't kissed anyone with glasses since…

"Okay, then, I guess I'll see you?"

Her thoughts broke, the buzzing in her ears stopped. It was just her and Peter and the crickets again.

"Sure," she said, as his hand left her arm. She took a breath. This wasn't why she was here. This was just a distraction. She took a step back.

Peter had begun walking back towards his house, then turned, looking back over his shoulder. "Good night, Kate." His shadow continued towards his house.

She watched him go, wondering why she was still just standing there, feeling as if some huge, important moment had just floated by and disappeared.

Chapter Eleven

"Well, you're up early, Katie." Carol entered the dining room. She was still in her flannel pajamas, pink with tiny roses.

"Just trying to stay on top of things." Kate heaved a sigh, happy to take a break from her computer screen. At the end of another frustrating week in her office, she had decided she might as well be frustrated close to her project. She'd called Carol late on Friday and asked if she'd mind having her as a guest again. Three weekends in a row.

Carol disappeared into the kitchen and returned in a few seconds carrying two cups of steaming coffee. Kate accepted hers gratefully and took a long sip of the much-needed caffeine. She didn't want to confess how badly she had slept after her drive. Then some dumb cardinal began singing its head off in the spruce tree outside her window at five thirty. She was too restless to sleep after that.

It had nothing to do with Peter, well, aside from the fact that she'd lost the nerve to ask for his help last time. She needed something to present to Danni and her team at Garman this week, and so far she was still stuck with Penny the cartoon cow who looked like she'd been sniffing too many flocculates, whatever they were.

Carol sat down across the table. "My sewing group is coming this morning. I hope that won't interfere with your work?"

"Don't be silly. I'm the guest here. This is your house. I can always find a spot at the library. What kind of sewing project are you working on? A quilt?"

"The Thread Heads are taking a break from sewing today. We're finalizing some details for the carnival at the Community Center next week."

Kate looked up from the list of Nitrovex products she was studying for inspiration. Maybe lightning would strike. Who knew? "The Community Center sounds like it means a lot to you."

Carol shrugged. "It means a lot to the community."

Kate didn't understand the attachment to Golden Grove. "Why not travel, see the world? Take a cruise, or go to Europe?"

"Oh, Katie, that's not me. Besides, all my friends are right here—always have been. Why would I want to go anywhere else?"

Why would anyone *not* want to be anywhere else? Sure, Golden Grove had charm up the wazoo, but even charm gets boring after a while. Right? No Starbucks, no theater, no museums, no skipping work to watch the Cubs playing a day game at Wrigley. Only about five restaurants, if you didn't count the Stop-n-Pop and its microwave burritos. Which she never, ever would. There was Ray's, of course, and his one-of-a-kind shakes. Forgotten how awesome those were. And Copperfield's Bookstore, where they used to order a out-of-print art books for her even though it probably didn't make them much money. And parking free instead of paying thirty bucks for a morning.

Okay, so maybe not *everything* about Golden Grove was bad.

Carol took a sip of coffee "So, are you planning to drop-in on Peter again tonight? It seemed like a success last weekend. I didn't even hear you come in."

Here we go, right on schedule.

"I was home by eight-thirty," she lied.

"Oh? Did he help you with your project?"

"We never quite got around to chemistry, actually."

Carol did more coffee stirring. "Oh?" There seemed to be a lot implied in that one syllable.

"We kind of got sidetracked. He's tearing down his old tree house."

"Yes, I noticed that this week." Carol continued to study her.

"We just…talked."

"Well, I'm glad you too are becoming reacquainted. You know, sometimes old friends are the best."

"I'm sure Peter already has lots of friends." Kate tapped a few computer keys. Better check her email.

"You might be surprised. It's just not good going through life feeling like you've missed out on something good, believe me." Carol was staring at her coffee cup, stroking the rim. There was something beyond that motherly gibe.

Kate couldn't help but feel curious. "Did you miss out on something in particular?"

Carol didn't speak for a moment. "Oh, nothing. I should leave you to your work."

"No, really. What is it?" She could tell something was on Carol's mind. She'd been getting these wistful hints on her last two visits, too.

She finally spilled. "Oh, it was a long time ago, and we were both in high school. Like you and Peter were. But it's fine."

"You and Percy?"

"No, this was before Percy and I ever met."

Oh. Normally, she might have teased her friend, but this seemed different. She closed her laptop lid. "C'mon, you can tell me."

"No, I've already said too much. Besides, we were a lot younger then. We both got happily married to other people, and we're too old for that sort of thing now."

"Wait…he's here in Golden Grove isn't he?"

"No, no…my goodness, we're happy to be just friends now. This isn't about me, it's about you, remember?"

Kate leaned forward. "You and Lucius Potter? Oh my gosh, that's so adorable." She put her hand on her mouth. "What was he like?"

Carol pointed a finger at her. "Now, Kate, if you tell a soul about this—"

"Oh, don't worry, I won't. Was he cute?"

"Was he cute? Is that all you girls think about these days?"

"Oh, come on. Some things never change, right?"

Carol said nothing but slowly turned beet red.

Kate slapped the table with both hands, smiling. "He was cute! That's so sweet. You and your high school sweetheart. Did Percy know?"

"Oh, Katie, now stop. It was a long time ago. We were just kids, way before I ever met your Percy."

"Did Mister Potter—Lucius, I mean—have a mustache back then?"

"No, he did not have a mustache. My point was supposed to be—"

"What was he like? I bet he held the door for you and carried your books home from school." She almost squealed. "Did you go to the sock hop together?"

Carol snorted. "The sock hop? How old do you think I am?"

Kate shrugged. "I don't know. Sock hop, mosh pit, love-in—what did you guys do back then?"

"I think we're getting a little off track."

"Are you kidding? This is the juiciest conversation I've had in the last month. Maybe the last year. So, did his mustache tickle?"

"His mustache does not tickle—I mean—he didn't have—"

Kate's eyes grew wide. "*Does* not? You didn't just say that." She squeezed her friend's arm. "Carol, you mover, you."

Carol stood up, face still red. "Oh, you're getting me all flustered. Now shush." She turned and went into the kitchen.

Kate waved her hands. "Okay, okay, I'm sorry, I'm sorry." She got up and followed.

"Well, I should hope so." Carol rummaged for something in the refrigerator.

Kate realized she had taken the teasing a little too far. "Look, here, just come back and sit down. Tell me what you were going to say."

Carol sighed and plopped down at the kitchen table. Kate took a seat opposite her. "What I was trying to say was if you don't take some chances you might just miss out on something better than you thought, that's all."

"What happened with you and Lucius?" Kate said softly.

Carol hesitated. "Well, we were good friends in school. Just like you and Peter. He lived down on the south side of town, down where the bowling alley is? It was all farmland then."

"Did he ever take you out on a date?"

She smiled, gazing at the table, flicking a crumb from the tablecloth. "We used to go roller skating in Compton. They had a rink on the edge of town, Rhonda's Roll-a-Rama."

Kate almost laughed, but the pensive look on Carol's face stopped her. "So you too were a pair, huh?"

"Oh, no, not really. I think we both liked each other, you know, but our parents didn't quite see eye to eye. He was four years older than me, you know. He was so dashing. Tall and thin, with horn-rimmed glasses. A lot like Peter, actually." She seemed to remember something, staring into space. "He had these long sideburns, and he smoked clove cigarettes."

"Wait, Lucius smoked?"

She chuckled, putting her finger to her mouth. "Got caught once outside of shop class. I don't think his parents ever found out. If they had, they probably would have sent him to military school. They were pretty strict. Did you know his dad worked at Nitrovex?"

Kate put her chin in her hand. "I didn't."

"It was a lot smaller back then, just starting out. They didn't think much of their son wanting to go to college, for some reason. Maybe they thought working a factory floor was more secure than getting a degree at some college. I think he smoked just to try to act rebellious."

Kate had a sudden picture of a young Lucius, with mutton-chop sideburns and a walrus mustache, long brown hair blowing in the breeze. Decked out in a rainbow-colored headband, sitting on a rumbling purple chopper, revving the engine. And Carol on the back of it, wearing a Nehru jacket with beads and fringe, arms around his waist, wearing mirrored granny glasses. Flashing a peace sign.

"So what happened?"

Carol sighed. "Well, as I said, my parents didn't think too much of it, me being about sixteen and all and him almost four years older."

"So that was it? You never got together?"

"We tried, but remember, he was older. He went off to college when I was just starting high school. Oh, he snuck back a few times early on or we'd meet down the road in Millersburg or some place. I told my parents I was going bowling with my friends. I'd never lied to them before."

Kate's mouth curved in a small smile. She was trying to imagine her kind little as a rebellious teenager.

"And, of course, we wrote each other. Nice long letters about what we were doing, and school and such. Not so much what we were feeling though. First, it was a couple of times a week. Then it was once a week, then every month, and then we just...stopped."

Kate felt the silence hanging in the air, the only sound the ticking of the old schoolhouse clock hanging on the wall. She put her hand on Carol's.

"And then you met Percy?"

Carol nodded, smiling. "In college, yes. Swept me off my feet, you might say." She took off her glasses and peered through them, then laid them on the table. "Lucius managed to avoid the draft—flat feet, I believe, but don't tell him I know that. Met his wife a few years after college. We never really saw each other until he came back here to teach."

"Wasn't that kind of awkward?"

"Oh, not so much. We were practical. You got on with life. You can't always dwell in the past, you know." She paused, looking down. "Still, it is a part of who you are. My dad used to say 'Who we are in the present includes who we were in the past.'"

Something, a feeling, a notion, tugged at Kate's thoughts, but it never materialized. She felt…not really sad, but wistful? Was that the word? And the uneasy part was she wasn't sure if it was for her friend or her. She rubbed her temples with her hand. Man. Being back here was really messing with her emotions.

"Well," Carol stood suddenly. "Enough of that. I have to get ready for the ladies." She hustled into the kitchen. In a few moments, Kate could hear pots banging and water coming from the faucet. And…was that sniffing? She couldn't be sure.

* * *

The doorbell rang, and a clatter of happy female voices echoed from the front hall. Tommy, Carol's cat, shot past her and into hiding under an upholstered chair.

Kate understood exactly how the cat felt. She hadn't planned on being at the house when the Thread Heads showed up, but she was on a roll with her work. At least, she thought she was. Talking to Peter had given her an idea about how she might pursue the Nitrovex project. Scientists weren't all lab-coat-wearing dweebs.

She pushed her laptop into its case and quickly gathered her things while Tommy eyed her and the invading Thread Heads suspiciously from under the chair.

She intended to hop over to the city library and work from there. It was probably the best place in town to hide out and find good Wi-Fi. Then she had a conference call with her bosses this afternoon. And Monday, back to Chicago with her spectacular, scintillating and hopefully impressive proposal for re-branding Nitrovex.

Almost as if on cue, her phone rang. It was Danni's ringtone. It wasn't unusual for her boss to call on the weekend. She punched the answer icon on the phone, covering her left ear to block out the increasing chatter from the living room as more ladies arrived.

"Hi, Danni."

"Hello, Kate. How's everything?"

"Going great. Just working on the proposal now." She brushed some crumpled doodles of dancing test tubes into a nearby wastebasket.

"Good, the board will be glad to hear it." A pause. Pauses were never good. "So, I just wanted to give you a heads-up. Frank Madsen will be sitting in on your meeting this week."

Kate's pulse quickened. "Mr. Madsen will be there?"

"Yes," Danni said. "I'm sure it's just one of his routine visits to keep tabs on us."

Routine? There was nothing routine about the highly invested owner of the company checking up on a project. On her project. She sat down in a chair.

"Kate?" Danni was saying. "You there?"

"Sure—yes. I'm fine. We'll be fine."

Danni must have heard the worry in her voice. "So, how's the proposal going?"

Kate stared at the blank sheets of paper among the scattered Nitrovex materials on the table. "Great, great. I'm actually in Golden Grove working through some ideas." She rubbed her face with her palm.

"Okay, good. Looking forward to the presentation this week." Danni said. "Don't let me down."

The line went dead, and she set her phone down, staring at the table. *Don't worry, don't worry, don't worry* buzzed through her brain.

She sat up. *Don't worry. Remember, you're good. You know what you're doing, right?* There were still days to create a good, tight concept to present.

A sketch of a grinning ear of corn in a hazmat suit peeked out from under her laptop. She crumpled it and tossed it into the wastebasket with the rest.

"Katie? Could you come here a moment?"

Kate's head popped up. It was Carol leaning in at the door of the dining room. "Hmm?"

"All the ladies want to say hi."

Now? Kate stood, then finished piling her papers together. "Okay, I can for a minute. Then I really need to get back to work."

"Is everything okay?" Carol was looking at her the way her mom used to look at her when she thought she'd forgotten to study for a test.

Kate waved her fingers. "Absolutely." She brought her things and followed Carol into the living room where groups of two or three older ladies were chatting happily.

"Is that little Katie?" a large woman said as she came at her with arms outstretched. She just had time to set her laptop and folders on an end table before enduring a crushing hug from the large woman who smelled overwhelmingly of lilacs.

"It's me," she returned weakly.

The woman was holding her at arms' length as if waiting for Kate to say her name. "Oh, come now. Don't say you don't remember your old second-grade teacher?"

Kate's mind scrambled. Second grade, second grade, old room, smelled like crayons and Comet cleanser, and…lilacs. "Mrs. Rooney?"

That got another crushing hug. "You do remember."

"Sure, of course," Kate said with what little breath she had left.

Her old teacher released her. "Look at you, all grown and beautiful. My little artist." She turned to her smiling friends. "Katie was the best artist. Always drawing in class, leaving me little notes and pictures."

The other women cooed and smiled.

"I remember it like it was yesterday," Mrs. Rooney continued. She looked up, head tilted, eyes closed, pointing with her finger. "You had a chair in the second row by the window. Half the time I'd call on you you'd be staring out the window at Mrs. Malcom's flower garden or a bird or some such." The other ladies tittered politely.

Okay, this was getting embarrassing. "Yes, that was me, I guess." Mrs. Rooney remembered more about her school days than she did.

"Yes, and when you weren't staring out the window you were staring at your little friend Peter in the row next to you."

Kate could feel her face warm. Yup, this was undeniably, officially embarrassing.

"Little Peter, little Peter," her teacher continued with a sigh. "You two were inseparable. Always at recess together." She whispered: "I once caught them holding hands by the monkey bars." The other ladies tittered again.

This was getting out of hand. "Yes, well, that was a long time ago."

"Little Peter, little Peter," Mrs. Rooney said again, smiling and shaking her head. "Although not so little anymore, now, is he?" She gave a nudge to one of her friends, then returned her gaze to Kate. "And still an eligible bachelor, if I'm not mistaken."

Kate just smiled. *You're not, and someone get me out of here now.*

Mrs. Rooney plowed on. "Eligible and handsome, if I might say."

"And so polite," a shorter woman contributed. "And a very good teacher, from what I understand. My grandson would have failed his class without his help. Came to his house to help tutor him."

The other ladies nodded in approval. "I've heard the same from my granddaughter, Stacy. She loves his class, and she never liked science at all."

Yes, terrific, we all agree that Peter is a great guy and a fantastic catch. Let's all start a Peter club. You can be President. Now, how do I get out of here?

Kate looked to Carol for help, but only got an approving smile and nod.

"Have you been able to see Peter while you're here?" Mrs. Rooney continued. "He's just next door, you know."

No kidding. "Oh, yes, I've seen him once or twice."

She caught Mrs. Rooney staring at her ring finger for a moment. "You, know, I imagine someone will be snapping him up soon. He can't stay single forever."

"I'm sure someone will," Kate said, hoping her agreement would end the topic.

No such luck.

"I've seen him with that Penny Fitch a few times," one of the ladies said.

What? Peter hadn't said anything about that. Or Carol…

Mrs. Rooney nodded. "Oh, yes. And her being divorced and all, I'm sure she's on the prowl."

Divorced? On the prowl? An image of Penny with wild black hair and fingers like claws popped into her head.

"Oh, now, Rose, don't start any rumors," Carol said.

"Well, you never know. None of us are getting any younger." More titters and nods. "And, as I said, he's the town's most eligible bachelor."

Carol came forward. "Well, ladies, I suppose we should get to it."

"Yes, it was nice to see you all again," Kate said, backing away.

The bevy of ladies began moving into the dining room, their chatting picking up where it had left off.

Kate quickly picked up her things and headed for the front door. She hadn't run a gauntlet like that in a while. The weird thing was, aside from the embarrassing prodding about Peter, it was nice to see everyone. At least Carol had a group of friends to hang out with. All she had were Saturday night Netflix binges and the occasional after-work pizza with a few co-workers.

She'd have to have a talk with Carol later about all this. Penny Fitch? What was that all about? Just a bunch of ladies trying to start a rumor?

Well, she had more important things to do than worry about Peter's social life. And the Thread Heads confirmed it. He was doing well here. Not only well, but he was actually helping kids. Just like he'd said last night.

She glanced at her watch as she shouldered her way out the front door and down the steps. That conference call with her bosses was in a few hours, and she had a ton of work left to do if she was going to convince them she was not only on the job, but killing it.

She couldn't help glancing at the house next door where the town's most eligible bachelor lived. The treehouse still stood, for now, quietly being swallowed by the tree. And the boy who had built it? He seemed stuck here, too, slowly being engulfed by Golden Grove.

Chapter Twelve

The Screamin' Bean was Golden Grove's main coffee shop, next to Ray's Diner, of course. It was usually empty late on Saturday afternoon, save for a scattering of college students hunkered down with earphones on, studying. And Sam Price in a corner booth, hunched over a manuscript. Sam was one of Golden Grove's authors, currently the ghost writer behind the "Lottie Long" cozy mystery series, although he didn't publicize the fact.

"Hey, Sam," Peter called over. "Who you killing off today?"

Sam looked up. "Hey, Peter. Not sure yet. Either the one-eyed priest or the librarian with the limp. Have any suggestions?"

"How about a school district budget committee member with an evil laugh and red pen that never runs out of ink?"

"I'll see what I can do," Sam said, eyes twinkling as he went back to work.

Lucius and Peter chose a table with two chairs by one of the two plate-glass windows that overlooked the town square.

A light rain rolled down the wide diner windows, clouding the view outside. It was getting cooler almost daily. There'd be the first frost soon, then the long slow descent into winter would start.

Peter nursed his coffee. He and Lucius had been talking the usual. School business, how the cross-country team was doing, the art teacher who was pregnant and quitting after this year. But he was more interested in talking about another topic. The one that hadn't left his mind the last few weeks. The one with the red-gold hair and the perfect dash of freckles around her nose.

"Heard you dropped a beaker on Friday in lab," Lucius was saying.

Peter shrugged. "It was slippery. Nothing was in it."

"Always gives the kids a laugh, I bet."

"Hey, if it gets their attention I'll drop a brick on my head."

"Wouldn't be because you were distracted by anything, would it?"

He said nothing.

"Heard our visitor is back in town. You should invite her over to help with the treehouse again."

Peter heaved a sigh. "I see Carol has you on speed dial."

Lucius smiled. "Just looking out for our friends."

Friends. He wasn't sure what that word meant anymore. Were you friends with someone if you daydreamed about how the sunset made her hair flame gold when you were trying to grade lab quizzes? He must have been lonelier than he'd thought.

"Anyway, it's raining," Peter pointed out.

"So ask her inside. Kind of nice seeing her all grown up," Lucius said.

No, they were not talking about this.

Lucius continued. "It's interesting. I've been teaching so long I see a lot of students come back. I recognize their faces or their walk or voice. Some change a lot, and I can't recognize them. Some look pretty much the same."

"I can't tell with Kate. It's like she's in there somewhere," Peter said. "The real Kate. The 'Katie.' Behind the designer watches and alkaline bottled water, underneath the gray business skirts."

Lucius cocked his eyebrows. "Underneath the skirts?"

"You know what I mean."

Lucius nodded, seeming to consider something. "I do know what you mean. You want her to be who you think she really is."

Peter shrugged. "She can be who she wants."

"I just wondered if maybe you want her to be someone you once knew."

"And who is that?"

"The girl next door. The one you grew up with." His voice grew softer. "The one who got away." He cleared his throat. "So to speak."

Peter's eyes narrowed. "We're talking about Kate, right?"

He shifted in his seat. "Of course. What I'm saying is you remember Kate the way she was, and now you're seeing her as who she is. And you're trying to decide which one is which."

"Which one is the real Kate? I think I can tell you pretty easily." He ticked off his fingers. "Successful, talented, fashionable, driven, confident." Beautiful. Brown eyes. Out of your league. And, once she'd done with her Nitrovex proposal, out of your life. "I told her myself last weekend. Everyone grows up. She's chosen a nice life for herself." He took a sip of his own coffee. "She's moved on. This is just a brief stop in her old life, and then she's back to the big city."

Lucius nodded. "Hmm. You seem a little bitter about that."

"No, this isn't about me. I'm happy for her. She's done well. She's where she belongs now."

Lucius nodded. "Maybe. Can't help think that for all her success, she's still alone."

Peter shrugged. "Well, you keep telling me how great I am, and I'm still alone."

Lucius nodded. "True. I'm just wondering if maybe sometimes people should try being alone together." He pushed his coffee cup forward and began sliding out of the booth. "Now, if I'm going to be half as successful as either of you two, I'd better get over to the school. Have to order some new beakers for the lab." He smiled.

Peter watched him leave the coffee shop. The front door dinged, and he was gone.

Alone together. Sounded like the title of a bad pop song. But it seemed to describe his feelings about Kate. Maybe, at one time, they'd had a bit of a chance. But that was a long time ago, when they were kids. A lifetime ago. No, *two* lifetimes ago. One flying high in Chicago and the other stuck in the mud of Golden Grove.

His jaw set. They were just friends. Old friends, enjoying a little time together.

He drained his cup, set it back in his saucer. Outside, his hometown bustled along. Cars going to work, to shop, people moving along the sidewalk, talking, laughing, couples holding hands under umbrellas.

He pushed himself up from the chair. He had work of his own to do. That's about all there seemed to be to do anymore, about all he had left here. No family, no life, no future. He sighed, pushing open the door and stepping into the cold drizzle.

Maybe he'd stop and grab an early dinner to take with him to the school. He could grade some papers. There was usually some school activity most Saturday nights. Better than eating alone. Again.

* * *

The double-thick chocolate-chip pecan pie shake had done nothing to lift Kate's mood. She sat in a back-corner booth, the only customer in Ray's. She stirred the shake with her long spoon, staring at it, hoping maybe Ray had dumped some kind of instant answer juice into it that would make everything become clear.

Her next meeting at Nitrovex was going to a complete disaster if she didn't come up with an idea. John Wells had to be running out of patience. He'd already arranged an on-line update via Skype earlier this week, where Kate had stumbled through her presentation like she was a high school girl giving a book report she'd just written the night before.

Which wasn't too far off. She'd been up until one a.m., trying to find a decent angle on Nitrovex. Something, anything that would at least get Garman to the next round of companies under consideration until she could find that one killer concept she knew was out there.

John Wells had been mostly silent. If it hadn't been for his inborn Iowa politeness he probably would have laughed in her face. Good thing this wasn't a Chicago client or the meeting might have ended with a phone call to her boss and her flying from a twenty-second-story window followed by her laptop and the glossy pages of her proposal.

Penny was there during the conference call too, occasionally offering suggestions. Some of them were helpful actually, but Kate had the sense that when she left they were going to both have a huge laugh over the dopey chick who thought she could leave her hometown and make it big in the city.

And she hadn't come up with much more today.

Something was missing, and she couldn't put her finger on it. What was worse was she knew there were other companies presenting *their* proposals, and they probably weren't using a dancing cow in a lab coat.

Kate felt doomed. She'd then had to bluff her way through a meeting with her team at Garman, her subsequent report to Danni filled with enough platitudes and buzzwords to (hopefully) buy her a little more time. But she needed something much more concrete to bring back to her team in Chicago on Monday.

She rested her chin in her hand, looking out the rain-spattered front window of the diner, past the curling pages of pancake-breakfast notices and missing-cat posters. Out to the city park, where the old cannon stood in a flower bed of orange and yellow mums. Somewhere out there was a great solution in someone's brain, but it sure wasn't hers.

She returned to her shake, took a hard sip from the straw, then stood. She had never had a problem coming up with the artistic ideas, but how anything to do with chemicals could be anything but a vat of swirling brown sludge was eluding her.

She thought about calling Danni, telling her they were wrong. That she was wrong for the job. They should bring in someone else before she completely blew this account.

Maybe she could come up with something to at least keep this lame train rolling. That elusive angle, that basic foundation to build on, the core of what made Nitrovex unique. Okay, stop and think. Picture the essence of the product and let the ideas flow.

She closed her eyes. Her brain could only picture a tangle of endless white pipes nested amongst a sea of meaningless tanks, all backed by the deafening soundtrack of the crushing hum of machinery.

The essence? Let's see, boredom? Dullness? The futility of man's struggle against the inevitable clutching fingers of death?

She shook her head. What she needed was the perspective of someone who loved this stuff. Someone who appreciated caustic potash and hexafluoro-whatevers. She sighed. Someone with a crooked smile and understanding, stupidly blue eyes.

Someone who had just walked through the front door of Ray's.

* * *

"Kate, hi," Peter said, ambling over.

Hi, yourself. She gave a little wave, he hesitated at her table.

"Okay if I sit?"

"Sure," she nodded, her mouth dry. She took a sip of her shake, realizing it probably looked huge to him, the metal container and glass both loaded up. "I was, uh, going to save some for Carol. For later," she lied.

He slid into the booth, crooked smile and all, and she lost her appetite. Okay, tough girl, here's your chance. Ask him.

"What brings you in?" she said. *Wrong question*, her brain barked at her.

He scanned the room, then glanced at his watch. "I was supposed to meet Lucius here at three for coffee. He called and said he had something to go over with me." His eyes returned to hers. "I'm beginning to wonder if he's going to show."

She smiled the same smile she used for selfies. Fake. She cleared her throat. "Oh, well, then since you're here and all, I was kind of wondering if maybe you might be able to help me out with something." Smooth segue, genius.

He leaned forward, smile still working its magic. "Sure thing. What can I do?"

There's a loaded question. "It's this Nitrovex project. All of the chemistry terms, the flocculants and stuff." She fluttered her fingers. "I think I got a C plus in chemistry in high school, if that." She normally didn't do the damsel in distress routine, but she was desperate for a breakthrough. She tried batting her eyelashes as helplessly as possible.

"Something in your eye?" he asked.

Eyelash bat fail. She rubbed her eye. "Just an eyelash. So, do you think you can help me out?"

He nodded, eyes studying her. For a second she thought he was going to say no, and her heart jumped.

"Sure," he said finally. "I think I can give you a refresher on the basics."

"That would be so helpful, thanks."

"No problem. I've got to grade a few papers tonight, so I could meet you at the school. There's basketball practice so the doors should be open. Meet you at the front doors at six-thirty?"

She nodded. "Sounds great, thanks."

He began sliding out of the booth. "I better give Lucius a call, see what's up."

"Okay. I'll see you tonight at six-thirty then?"

The smile flashed again. "It's a date," he said, and left.

She watched him go. Allrighty, then, it's a date. A chemistry date. Yay. She wiped her sweating palms on her pants, breathed in some air, and pushed her shake away. *Yay.*

* * *

Kate set her purse down on Peter's desk at the front of the chemistry classroom. She looked around at the rows of black Formica tables, each with their own sink and chrome gas nozzles. She sniffed. The air smelled acrid, like sulfur and things long since burned. She wrinkled her nose. She preferred the thick waxy smell of paints and paper in the art room down the hall.

"So this is where you spend most of your time?"

Peter was at a bookshelf near the window putting away some books. "Most of it. I've got an office down the hall, but I'd rather hang out here. Easier for students to find me."

Kate walked around his desk, touching the various knick-knacks on it. Models of molecules, small homemade trophies with cryptic sayings on them. Probably inside jokes from students. She joined him at the shelf, scanning the titles. *Organic Chemistry Study Guide*. *Quantum Chemistry and Molecular Interactions*. Wow. Real pager-turners.

"Thanks again for be willing to help," she said.

He pulled out a folder and walked around the desk to his chair. "No problem. Beats grading papers." He moved back to his desk and opened a drawer. "Sorry I couldn't help more the other night."

She looked up, remembering that night. "No, that's okay." She spied an official-looking paper on the corner of his desk under a folder and two books. Spirograph swirls around the border of parchment paper. She pulled it out from under the books and read it: *Board of Education of Iowa confers on Peter Hargrave Clark Science Teacher of the Year.*

She cocked her head at him. "This is your award?"

He looked up, then down again. "Yup."

"Why don't you have it in a frame. It'll get all wrinkled here."

"I'll get to it sometime."

She opened her mouth to say more, then stopped. Instead, she put the paper down neatly on his desk and returned to scanning his bookshelf. A weathered spine of a book with a photo of a hand holding a beaker of pink liquid caught her eye.

She pulled it out. "Isn't this our old chem book?"

Peter looked up from his desk, then back down. "It is. Bring back memories?"

Kate hefted the book. "Yes. Of back pain." Science books were always so heavy. She didn't remember much about chemistry, but she sure remembered how her back ached every day she had to haul this thing home in her backpack.

She opened it. On the inside cover was scrawled "Peter Clark" and under it "SuperChemGuy" with stars drawn around it. She smiled. "So, Super Chem Guy, do you ever get out? I mean, away from town? Surely there must be some incredibly exciting chemistry conventions you get to go to or something."

Peter looked up, then chuckled. "Oh, yeah. Pretty much every other weekend there's a wild convention for high school chemistry teachers in Vegas. Champagne in beakers, dancing girls, the whole deal. And SuperChemGuy was just my old AOL account name."

She bit her lip, thinking. "I think mine was ArtGurlForever or something dumb like that."

"ArtGurlsRule."

She raised an eyebrow, but said nothing. She reached to put the book back on the shelf. A few loose notes dropped from under its back cover onto the floor.

Kate picked them up, scanning them. "Ooo! Love notes!"

"What?" He got up and came around the desk. "Those are probably just old chem quizzes." He tried to take them from her, but she turned before he could, keeping them out of reach as she unfolded one, scribbled pen on notebook paper.

"*Dear Marvel*," she read, "*I must protest the use of ammonia as a re-agent in the latest issue of Spider-Man, Number 167. Also, the common reaction of the burning of butane would be to produce a blue flame, not a pink one as is shown in panel five on page twelve.*" She laughed. "Oh my gosh…I'm sorry, Peter, but you were such a geek."

"Yeah, well, says the girl who painted a My Little Pony mural on her wall and then talked to it every night."

"I did not talk to it. It was just…pretending. And you said you'd never tell."

"Just give me the rest of those." He reached over her shoulder and grabbed the papers from her hand then stuffed them in between two books on the shelf.

She almost wished she could see if there was a note from Penny Fitch. It was ancient history, but she couldn't help it.

Peter snorted. "Why don't we just leave behind memory lane, okay?" He pulled her by the elbow to a chair near his desk, then returned to his own.

Kate saluted as she sat. "Aye, aye, Super Chem Guy."

"You said you needed some advice on your proposal?"

She was enjoying seeing him flustered, brushing his unruly hair back from his eyes. His face was clean-shaven today, and he smelled like fresh laundry and spice. But he was right. It was time to get down to business.

"Okay, so you know I'm supposed to be coming up with this brilliant new makeover for Nitrovex."

"Okay."

"But I just can't seem to get a handle on it. I mean, most of the companies we work with are creative companies or in the service industry. We look at what makes them tick, what's at their core, their foundation, then come up with a slogan. Like 'Moving into the Future' or 'Technology at the Speed of the Mind.' Stuff like that."

"Catchy."

"Thanks. You can use them in your next letter to Marvel Comics."

"So, what has Nitrovex thought of what you've come up with so far?"

She remembered the long silence from John Wells. "What's a word that means hate but only worse?"

"Loathe?" He rubbed his chin once with his palm. "Um, despise? Shrink back in horror? Vomit profusely?"

"Let's just stick with hate. He hated it."

"Oh, c'mon, it couldn't be that bad." He moved his chair closer to her, his arm touching hers. "Show me what you got."

"Okay, but just remember, I'm not responsible for any loathing or shrinking back in horror it may cause." She punched a couple of keys on her laptop. A graphics program popped up, then an image of a smiling cow holding a test tube filled the screen.

Peter burst out laughing, then stopped, clearing his throat.

Kate's eyes narrowed. "That was just a preliminary sketch. You weren't supposed to see it."

"No, Kate, I'm sorry. It's good. If Nitrovex were an ice-cream truck." This time, he covered his face as he laughed, wincing in anticipation of the swat she did give him.

"Hilarious. Artistic advice from a guy who couldn't even finish a paint-by-number picture of a puppy."

"Hey, you're the artist, not me."

"Exactly, which is why I need the help of your simple, unemotional little scientific brain. What am I missing?"

"Besides a dancing test tube? Not sure."

She winced. "I tried that."

"Really?" He rubbed his chin again. "Maybe if you gave him a little hat…"

"C'mon, Peter, I'm serious."

His laughter had subsided. "Okay, okay. I'm sorry." He wiped his eyes. "Look, you're dealing with engineers and scientists here. Neither the people at Nitrovex or the companies they're dealing with are going to care about whether the logo has a cow or a pig or a corn stalk in it. They're not that literal."

"So how do I come up with a tagline for a company whose main product seems to be something that keeps raw sewage from getting foamy?"

"Well, how about 'Technology at the Speed of Poop'?"

Kate shook her head. "I knew this was a bad idea."

Peter's shoulders were shaking. He held up his hand. "Wait, wait, I got it. 'Nitrovex: Bowel Moving Into The Future.'"

Kate stood up. "Thanks a lot for your help."

Peter grabbed her by the hand. "No, Kate, wait. I'm sorry." He pulled her back into her seat.

She sat, crossing her arms.

"Look," he said, "John Wells is the guy you have to convince, right? So maybe if you just concentrate on what he likes you'll find something to land on. Look at his background, where he came from, why he started the company."

"Maybe. But he seems more cowhand than chemist to me."

"He may look that way, but he's a sharp guy. Graduated third in his class at Iowa State."

"Well then, we're back to how do I relate to chemicals again."

Peter stood. "I think part of the problem is you need to get reacquainted with the wonderful world of science. Come with me into the lab." He stood.

Kate, getting up with a sigh, followed him to a long black table. "Okay, but you're asking a lot from an art geek."

"Don't worry. I'm Science Teacher of the Year, remember? Okay, let's start with the basics."

* * *

An hour later and Kate felt like her brain was going to melt.

"Well, that's close," Peter was saying, "but remember, a mole is a unit quantity. A molecule is a group of atoms."

Kate threw her hands up in frustration. "Okay, I'm done. I don't suppose you've got anything in here that can change whatever's in this glass into wine." She pointed to a beaker of liquid next to the sink.

"Oh, c'mon—you shouldn't give up so easily."

"You shouldn't underestimate the value of wine."

Peter shook his head. "Remember the old chemistry joke: Alcohol is not the problem…it's the solution."

"Okay, first—really? Chemistry has jokes? And second—I totally don't get it."

Peter frowned. "Strange…that one always knocks 'em dead at our incredibly exciting chemistry conventions."

Kate made a face.

"The joke is, ethanol is a pure substance, but the alcohol we drink is always a mixture of things—like grapes or water and alcohol—so technically it's a solution."

"Wow. That's so…not funny."

Peter nodded, left side of his mouth curling up. "Yeah, you kinda have to be a chemistry geek, I guess."

Kate put both hands on the table. "If you can tell by my face and its utter lack of expression, I'm not laughing. And I don't think this is getting me any closer to a solution—and if you make another solution joke, I will hit you with whatever this bottle is called."

"What I'm trying to show you is that there is an art, even a beauty to chemistry. It's what makes up the world. Like, when you paint a painting, you use different colors, right?"

"Sure."

"Well, everything we are, our bodies, this chair, is made up of molecules, of chemicals, each combining in different ways to make something greater."

She cocked her head. "Wow, Peter. That was actually…poetic."

"Yeah, I kind of surprised myself there, too."

Kate rubbed her eyes and stifled a yawn. She felt exhausted, and it wasn't even late.

"Say," Peter said. "I don't have any bottles of Chardonnay stashed in the classroom, but how about some dinner sometime?"

Kate stood. She'd enjoyed her time with Peter, but all this science stuff had drained the life out of her. And she knew the clock was ticking on this project. "Thanks, but I'd better get back to work. I've got a proposal to present back in Chicago next week."

She wasn't sure if his shoulders had drooped. "Sure, right. I suppose we won't be seeing you around much anymore?"

She wasn't sure herself. What if this meeting this week went poorly? What if they yanked her from the project and put someone else in? She felt a twinge shoot through her stomach. "I think I should be back, if all goes well with my ideas."

He nodded. "Good. I mean, it's been good seeing you again."

She gathered her things. "You too," she said, mustering a smile. "and thanks for your help."

He looked at the clock on the wall. "I guess I should get to grading those papers. I think I'll take them home, though. I just need to grab them from my office."

She nodded. "Sure. I'll meet you at the front door?"

"Sure. I'll drive you home. Well, not home. Not to Chicago. To Carol's."

She was noticing their partings were becoming more awkward, neither certain whether to just say "bye" and leave, or something more. As if they were some kind of couple and needed to…what? Shake hands? Slap each other on the back and butt heads? Kiss?

She guessed it was more about whether or when they would see each other again. Just because she was staying at the house next door didn't mean she could assume she would see him again before she left.

The twinge jumped in her stomach again. She didn't know if she'd even be back in Golden Grove.

Okay, deep breath. Stupid thoughts.

She hoisted her purse on her back, turned a corner in the hallway, only to bump into someone.

Freckles, braces. It was like looking in a mirror and seeing herself in high school.

Chapter Thirteen

A couple of books and an art board clapped to the floor. Kate bent to pick them up, apologizing at the same time. "I'm so sorry, I didn't see you there."

"No, it was me," the girl said, her face flushed. "I wasn't watching where I was going, I guess."

Kate picked up the books, noticing the covers. Milton's *History of Art and Drawing the Human Body*. She hadn't heard of the second but the first was the same book she'd used when she was in high school. She handed the books to the girl, who tucked them into her purple backpack.

She flipped over the art boards in order to pass them to the girl. The one on top was a sketch of a rearing horse, no rider. She slid that one to the side to see the one under it, which was an acrylic painting of a tulip, up close and in detail. Both were excellent.

"Did you do these?" she asked the girl, who was shifting her weight from one foot to the other.

"Yes. In art class."

Kate noticed the girl hadn't once looked her in the eye. "They're very good."

There was the hint of a smile on the girl's face that quickly vanished. "Thanks."

Kate handed over the boards. The girl took them then sidled to a nearby table where she dumped her backpack. Kate followed, curious. Work could wait for a few minutes.

"You're here awfully late."

The girl never turned. "I got permission from Mr. Clark to work on my experiment tonight. I was gone yesterday. And I'm going to help with Homecoming decorations later."

"Oh, yes. 'Keeping It Rad In The Eighties', I believe." She paused. "So. Are you in Peter's—Mr. Clark's chemistry class?"

"Chemistry 201." The teenager began busily arranging equipment on the table.

"201? You must like chemistry."

"I guess."

Kate moved closer, putting her things on the table next to the girl's backpack. She stuck out her hand.

"I'm Kate. I'm a friend of Mr. Clark. He's been helping me with chemistry, too."

The brief smile returned, and she shook Kate's hand gingerly. "I'm Stacy." She went back to work, pulling a thick, heavy-looking textbook from the depths of her backpack.

"Hi, Stacy." Stacy…the girl one of the Thread Heads had mentioned the other morning?

She tried to ignore how much the girl reminded her of herself at this age. Shy, pretty but probably afraid to think it. Her brief smile had shown a glint of metal. Braces. Kate had forgotten how much she'd hated to smile when she had braces. Two whole years of high school photos with just a tight-lipped, grim Mona Lisa smile, not to mention junior high. Courtesy of some orthodontic condition she could pronounce. One thing she hadn't forgotten how much high school could suck.

"So, do you take any art classes?" Kate pointed to the drawings next to the backpack.

"There aren't many to take, but I've done some extra-credit painting."

"What year in school are you?"

"I'm a senior."

"Oh, almost ready for college?"

"I guess."

"And you like chemistry, too?"

There was a lot longer pause as if Stacy was deciding something. She didn't look up, just said, "Not really," in a small voice.

Kate's eyebrows arched slightly. "But you're taking the second chemistry class? I'm guessing that's what the two-oh-one stands for, right?"

"Yeah." Another pause. "My parents think I need to get as much science as possible. For college. So I can get a good job."

Now where have she heard that before? "Let me guess. One or both of your parents work at Nitrovex?"

That got a direct look in the face. "How did you know?"

Kate chuckled. "Lucky guess. I bet half the town works there."

"I guess."

Kate noticed Stacy's unopened chemistry binder on the table. It was covered in intricate doodles. Animals, shapes, filigree, all intertwined. She opened the binder and saw more doodles in the margins as well as whole pages of drawings. Cats, lions, a girl with hair streaming in the wind as she stared from a cliff out at the ocean, hands clasped behind her back.

"Stacy, these are really good."

Stacy's head popped up. Her face grew pink when she saw Kate looking through her binder. "Oh. Those are just things I do. In my notes when I'm bored."

"Well, they're good."

Brief smile. "I like art the best, but my dad wants me to do something in science, like be a doctor or something."

Kate felt a burning in her neck. Sheesh. Some things never change. "Well, I suppose that's practical...but have you considered getting an art major? Or something in graphic design?"

Stacy's shoulders shrugged. "I might take some classes in college if I have time. But I'm not sure if my dad would go for it."

"Well...I'd be happy to talk to him. If you like." Okay, where did that come from? She didn't even know this family.

Stacy paused what she was doing and looked up. "You would?"

"Sure. I like art, too. Do you remember—have you heard of My Little Pony?"

Stacy cocked her head. "The toy?"

"Yup." She waved her hand through the air. "I painted a full mural on my wall. When I was a kid. All eight ponies, with a rainbow, grass, a bridge over a creek." She rubbed her chin with her finger. "I think I even had Queen Chrysalis up there somewhere."

Stacy smiled fully for the first time, dimples forming on her freckled cheeks. "Wow."

Kate laughed. "Yeah. Pretty geeky, huh?"

Stacy returned to her work. "I don't know. Sounds kind of cool."

Kate leaned on the table with her elbows. "Well, I thought it was. At least then. I switched to business and graphic design for college. Got to be practical, right?"

"I guess."

The girl seemed disappointed. It reminded her of the tone her parents had used when she said she was going to art school instead of college. Except this was in reverse. "I did do a lot of art in high school, though. Even entered the Scholarship Fair."

There was a new brightness in Stacy's voice as she turned. "Really? Did you win?"

Kate almost winced but kept her smile. "Not really. But things turned out fine." Hadn't they?

"My art teacher is making me enter the fair. She says my project is really good."

Kate nodded. "Judging from what I saw, I bet it is."

"It's a really big painting I did of my farm. I painted it on barn wood."

Wood. Good. That should be rocket-proof. "I hope you win," Kate said.

Stacy just nodded.

Kate's eyes wandered to the yellow-papered bulletin board in the hall, filled mostly with class notices. They rested on a collage of photos pasted on green poster board: Peter and his class outside somewhere, laughing, playing, making faces. She smiled. "Where was that taken?"

Stacy turned to see what she was looking at. "Oh, that. That was our field trip at the beginning of the year. Mr. Clark took us out to Palisades Park to shoot off some rockets we had made in class."

"You made rockets?" Her stomach flipped once. Again with the rockets.

"Yeah—Mr. Clark said it was an experiment on combustion and propulsion. We did it with the physics class. It was fun. He's really cool."

"He's certainly something." Kate remembered the scorched marks on the floor of the treehouse.

"Yeah. The school didn't have any money for it, but he paid for it all himself, anyway. Then he took us all out for ice cream."

Kate scanned the rest of the photos. She found one with Stacy, small smile, away from the more boisterous part of the crowd, but still hanging with a few friends. It was an all-too-familiar reminder. "So, are those your friends?"

Stacy looked up and then down again. "Yeah."

Kate squinted at the photo again. "What's that on your jeans?" She thought she saw a pattern. "Is that needlepoint?"

"No. It's yellow paint."

"Paint? Did you have an accident in art class?"

"No. It was nothing. Just some guys."

Kate's eyes narrowed. "What guys?"

Stacy shrugged. "Just…guys." She moved a glass slide over by a gray microscope. "It's no big deal. A couple of guys were messing around and flicked me with yellow paint in art class. It's just high school, my dad says."

A litany of similar memories flashed through Kate's mind. Laughing and pointing in the hallway. Braces jokes. Snickers and glances. Not being picked for teams at PE. Small things that piled up into big things. If you let them.

"Well, you're right about one thing. It is no big deal. You know you're not all the things people say about you, right?"

Stacy nodded but kept working. "I know," she said softly.

"And it shouldn't be 'just high school' either." She could feel her ears warming.

"I know," Stacy repeated, then glanced at Kate before returning to her test tubes. "I bet you probably didn't have…I mean, you're so pretty…" She trailed off.

"I didn't have problems in high school?" Kate finished for her. She almost snorted. "Sorry. Stacy, the stories I could tell."

Stacy now turned, head up, eyes wide. "Really?"

Kate pulled out a stool at the bench and sat down. "I had braces until I was sixteen. My name's Katie Brady, so, of course, I was Katie Braces for most of high school. Then there were the boys who would bark or moo when I walked by. And the girls weren't much better. One of them saw me reading a Harry Potter book. Started calling me 'Hairy Pitter' in PE." She paused, remembering. "Even the friends who you thought were your friends could turn on you."

"I thought you would have…I mean, you're not…"

Kate touched the younger girl's shoulder. "Hey, Stacy? Listen to me. Just because you can't fit into a size six doesn't mean you're worthless. And just because you were born with your teeth at the wrong angles doesn't mean you aren't beautiful. At all. Right?" She gave Stacy's shoulder a squeeze for emphasis.

Stacy nodded yes. "I wish I was as pretty as you."

"Hmph. Remember when your mom used to tell you to eat your vegetables? Moms still do that, right?"

"Yeah?"

"I took mine real seriously. That's about all I ate for a while after college. It was kind of a mission for me at the time. I thought that if I made myself look beautiful on the outside, it would make me beautiful on the inside, too. But after a while, I realized that was pretty much a lie."

"Well, you are beautiful." Stacy smiled shyly.

Kate touched her new friend's shoulder. "I was always beautiful, Stacy. And so are you. I mean true beauty, not the stuff people see on the outside. That doesn't always mean it's true. Believe me, once people get to see the real beauty you have—the beauty it takes time to see—it means a lot more. And lasts a lot…longer." She found her eyes staring at the photo of Peter the class had pasted on the bulletin board, his blue eyes dancing over his joyful smile as the class clowned around him. She sighed.

"So, Kate…so…you like Mr. Clark, right?"

Kate was jolted out of her thoughts. "Hmm? What?"

Stacy was staring at her. It was obvious Kate had been gazing at the photo for a few seconds. "Mr. Clark. He says you went to school together."

"He does? Yes, we did. A long time ago."

Stacy turned back to the table and began organizing her notes. "What was he like? Back then, I mean?"

Kate laced her fingers together, thinking. "Well, let's see. He was tall and skinny and wore glasses. Some of the boys called him 'Peter Clarker'—you know, like Spiderman?"

Stacy giggled.

"And, umm…oh yeah—he was into rockets back then, too."

"Really?"

Kate nodded, then whispered. "Almost burned down his treehouse once."

That got a wide-eyed, open-mouthed smile. Stacy seemed to remember something. "Oh, yeah—once Mr. Clark was showing us inert gasses and he lit a bag on fire because he thought it was helium, but it was really hydrogen."

Kate nodded. "Okay, I have no idea what that means, but I'll assume something blew up."

"Yeah. There was this big ball of fire." She pointed to a dark spot on the ceiling tiles over one of the tables. "You can still see the smudge on the hanging light."

Kate pursed her lips. "Hmm. I'd only heard about the one where he mixed two things together. Red-something and phosphor-something?"

"Oh, yeah. That wasn't my class, but I heard about it. The school made him paint the ceiling."

Kate leaned forward, warming to these bits of Peter gossip. "Okay, what else you got?"

"Oh, this one time, he was mixing something in a beaker and it slipped and dropped and spilled on the table and sprayed on him." She covered her mouth with her hand. "He looked like he had wet his pants for the rest of the class."

Kate laughed. "Okay, that one I'm definitely remembering."

"Yeah." Stacy folded her hands in her lap. "He's the best teacher in school. I wish he was an art teacher."

Kate nodded. Stacy continued before she could speak.

"I was just wondering if you thought that maybe he—well, not him, of course…" She looked down. "But someone like him could be…" She pushed some hair back from her eyes. "Could like someone? Like me?"

Kate drew in a deep breath and exhaled. "Oh, Stacy." She touched her shoulder again. "Of course someone could and someone will."

Stacy smiled broadly. "Okay." She seemed to have a thought because she sat a little straighter. "You should go to the Homecoming Dance with him. Mr. Clark goes every year." More giggles. "He's a good dancer."

Peter? "Really? It'd almost be worth seeing that." Then she remembered. "But I doubt if I'll be here. I live in Chicago."

"Oh. I thought you lived here." And with that, the girl turned on her stool and flopped open her chemistry binder.

Kate observed her for a moment, then hopped off her own stool. "Okay, enough girl talk. I should get on the road. But remember, if you want to chat, let me know, okay? Here—" Kate took Stacy's cell phone that was on the table and punched in her number. "I'll put it under 'Hairy Pitter' so you know who it is."

Stacy gave a couple of laughs. "Okay."

"Don't stay too late. It's Saturday night, remember?"

A small but genuine smile. "I won't."

Kate gathered her things again, her eye catching the poster board, automatically finding Peter's familiar smiling face. Seeing him now less the gawky, cute boy she had known and more the complex man she was discovering. But maybe too late.

She glanced at Stacy as she left the room. She was busy with her chemistry experiment. Although now with a slight smile on her face. And she was humming.

Kate hadn't been just giving her a pep talk. She really was beautiful. Sometimes you just needed to have someone say it, someone who wasn't your parents or their friend or your teacher.

She left, her footsteps echoed down the empty hall. How many other Stacy's needed to hear that here? Maybe that was what had kept Peter her all these years. Not just what he could teach in the classroom, but outside of it. So many Stacy's…

She saw her reflection in the trophy case at the entry of the school and stopped. Basketball, football, track. She squinted. A plaque with the Scholarship Fair winners of the past years rested on its back near the corner of the case. One row over, eight brass nameplates down. Peter Clark.

Her reflection stared back from the glass.

Stacy seemed to believe her little pep talk. But did she?

Her eye caught another set of reflections in the glass. Down the hall, an open door, Peter and…Penny Fitch? What was she doing here?

She froze. Penny was laughing (of course), touching Peter's arm, tossing her perfect jet-black hair. Peter, smiling in return, hands in his pockets, doing his "aw-shucks" schoolboy pose. Another arm-grab by Penny and she disappeared back into the room, just as Stacy joined her. Homecoming decorations? That was why Penny was here?

And now Peter was coming her way. She suddenly found the 1969 First Runner-Up Girls Tennis trophy in front of her very interesting.

* * *

Peter saw Kate standing in the empty hallway, staring at the trophy case. "I see you met Stacy," he said, ambling over.

Kate turned, nodding. He couldn't make out her expression. "Yes, she's a very hardworking girl, staying here so late at night. Helping out with the Homecoming decorations."

His eyes narrowed. Had Stacy told her that? "So, Stacy give you all the dirt on mean old Mr. Clark, did she?"

Kate nodded. "Some, but probably not all. I heard you're pretty good at ceiling painting."

"Man, you blow up one bag of hydrogen and you get branded for life."

"Better than going around all day with wet pants."

When she moved towards the front entrance, he followed. Great. The wet pants story. "Well, anyone who said being a teacher is easy is lying."

"I doubt if anyone who's ever had to teach has ever said that."

"True."

They stopped by the front door. A pair of students came in from outside, looked at them, looked at each other smiling, and scampered on, tittering. Great. More rumors.

She pushed herself from the door post. "I should be getting back. I've got hours of work ahead of me."

He nodded. "Sure." *Ask her.*

She beat him to it. "Can I text you if I get struck on some science term?"

"Sure. Anytime."

She smiled. "Never know when I might need some more science pointers."

He nodded. "Good. I'll be here."

They stood silent for a moment. "Drive you to your car?" Peter said finally.

She gave a short curtsy. "Thank you, kind sir."

"Don't mention it." Peter edged around her to get the door.

The walked together through the front doors and out into the sunset. The rain had stopped, but fast-moving clouds scudded across the sky. A few leaves rustled at their feet.

"Just like the old days."

"What's that?" he said.

"When you used to walk me home from school."

"It was a lot closer then. Be about a five-mile run from here."

"True." They shuffled along silently. She held her purse in both hands in front of her, kicking leaves as she went.

He thought of something someone told him once, or maybe he had read it. You remembered the bad things about the past and forgot about a lot of the good. Right now, he was thinking about Kate the little girl, walking her home from school, her purple My Little Pony backpack bouncing on her shoulders. The Kate he had grown close to, not the one he had drifted apart from in high school. The one he was wondering if he had lost, or if maybe he'd been given another chance to find.

They shuffled on. He started kicking leaves with her, smiling.

Just like the old days.

Chapter Fourteen

Frank Madsen looked up from Kate's report on his laptop, peering at her over his reading glasses. "And this is the extent of the report so far?"

Kate fussed with the collar of her shirt. The conference room seemed awfully warm today. "Yes, so far. It's just the preliminary report. Nitrovex is turning out to have a more extensive reach than we—than I thought."

Madsen nodded slowly. The three other senior members of her group continued to shift through the thin stack of papers that made up her report. None of them were smiling.

That's it then, back to the business cards. She wondered if the KwikCopies on the corner had any job openings? She waited for someone else to speak, fingers laced together.

She'd spent the trip back to on Sunday with the radio off, a yellow-lined notepad and a pen on the passenger seat beside her. Thinking, driving, taking notes. More notes once she got to her apartment, Then a quickly made slide presentation when she'd hit the office this morning. She hated doing things so last minute, and she was annoyed with herself for feeling so out-of-her-depth.

The talk with Peter had helped. She'd pursued the Nitrovex problem from a different angle, a more personal angle, and had managed to cobble together some new ideas for her proposal. Enough, hopefully, to convince the group that she could finish the job. Which meant another trip back to Nitrovex and Golden Grove.

And Peter?

She couldn't decide how she felt about that. She'd even thought that blowing this deal might be a good thing. She'd never wanted to go to Golden Grove in the first place—dreaded it, in fact.

But there was her job to think about. Danni had made it clear what the expectations of the group were. A failure here would most likely be a career killer. And her career was something she'd worked on too hard and for too long to consider losing.

She straightened her spine. At least she could pretend that she knew what she was doing. Even if she was about to get fired.

Danni spoke up. "Although the report is rather…thin, I think we may have something to work with."

Good ol' Danni. Thank you, Danni.

"Although there's going to have to be a lot more work done regarding the basic premise of your proposal. For example, what are some of the core concepts you're working with? What about the international aspect of the company? How does that fit in with Nitrovex's Midwest origins?"

"Yes, the international aspect. Well, I feel that first, we must come up with the foundation—the core of what makes Nitrovex unique. The essence of the company may seem very basic, but the overarching theme of its products is much broader than we suspected. To that end, I feel we must do a deeper examination of all the different aspects of the company's very diversified holdings, especially in Europe, where they are making significant inroads in, um, flocculating solvents."

It was a stall, a non-answer. She felt like a politician, or a beauty contestant trying to answer her question about world peace without really saying anything.

"Flocculating solvents?" a group member said.

Kate nodded. "Yes." Just yes. She couldn't say much more about flocculating solvents, especially since she'd just made it up in order to save her job.

"I see that you've spoken almost exclusively with the owner, Mr. Wells?" Madsen was asking.

Kate nodded, shifting in her seat. "Yes, he's been very helpful in giving me the backdrop, the history of the company."

No one changed their expression, just stared at her, waiting.

"Yes, and I'm also consulting with another local expert. And I'm hoping to meet with the grandson of the owner next week. He's much more versed in their European operations, as well as the future of the company."

It was kind of a lie. Well, it was mostly a lie. Okay, it was a flat-out lie, and she wished she hadn't said it. But she did know that Corey Steele was supposed to be back in Golden Grove soon, and she was sure that John would be happy to set up a meeting with him.

Finally, one of the members nodded. "That should be very helpful. A better picture of the future of the company is what we'll need."

"Should" not *could*. For the first time since the meeting had started, she felt like she had a chance at not being booting form the account...

"However..." Madsen said.

Oh, geez, not a *however*.

"...we're going to have to have a much more extensive report at the next meeting if we're going to trust you to present the full proposal."

Kate nodded vigorously. "Yes, of course, much more complete, I promise you. Once I have a few more pieces of the puzzle in place, I'll be able to suggest a full package. Logos, slogans, and branding."

Logos, slogans, and branding, oh, my. She had none of those, yet. She said an internal thank you that she'd left Penny the Toothy Cow out of her logo suggestions at the last minute.

Madsen jutted out his chin as he nodded, thinking. "Well, at this point, this is probably still our best bet. We can't negate the edge we may still have with Ms. Brady having lived in the town of the client." He turned to her. "Is there any way you might be able to exploit that further? Maybe meet with more of the town folk? Connect with them, let Wells know you're still one of them, so to speak?"

Still one of them?

She swallowed. "Absolutely. I've already been quite successful in that regard." A flash of Peter's smiling blue eyes crossed her mind, and she blinked. "With Mr. Wells, the owner. We've developed a very good rapport." That part was true. The genial owner of Nitrovex seemed to have taken a fatherly shine to her.

"Very well," Madsen said. The other members began shuffling their papers together, closing laptops, indicating the meeting was almost over. "Get back to Nitrovex soon. Meet with the grandson, this Corey Steele, if you can. I don't have to remind you that there are other companies bidding on this job, most of them bigger than us."

"Yes, understood," she said, her neck sweating.

Madsen shut his own laptop and stood. "We'll expect a more complete report at the end of next week, this time with some logo and slogan examples."

It wasn't a question; it was a command.

"Absolutely," she said.

The members left. All but Danni, who came around the long oval table. "Looks like you got a second chance," she said.

Kate smiled weakly, stacking her papers. "Yes, thank you."

"Don't thank me. I was just about to blow the whistle on your little song and dance."

A cold fist gripped Kate's stomach. "Well, I, uh, know it wasn't the best proposal I've ever done."

Danni's expression was neutral. "We've all had to fluff up the edges of a concept at one time or another. But flocculating solvents? That's a new one."

"I'll do better next week. Full report, branding, everything."

Danni nodded. "You'd better, or I won't be able to run interference for you." She sat on the table edge. "You sure you're up for this, Kate? It's a big job, your first major account."

Kate's back stiffened as a little courage returned. "I am. I know I am. I've already got a few new ideas I didn't present today."

"Good. As long as they're better than your happy cow, there." She pointed at Kate's laptop screen, where half the face of her toothy cow logo was peeking out from under another window.

She felt her face burn. "Oh, they will be."

Danni stood. "I expect you to work on this through the weekend."

She left Kate alone with just the hum of the fluorescent lights overhead and her thumping heartbeat. She blew out some air slowly, sweating as if she'd just gotten done with a workout.

For the first time since working at Garman, she wondered if it was worth it. The missed vacations, the extra hours. But, all jobs had their boring parts, right? Like grading papers. That was just what work was.

She felt a twinge of envy for Peter. She bet he got to go home at night, see friends, have pie shakes with Lucius. A thought surfaced. Maybe she should set up shop on her own. Get back to design work, where she started.

She shook her head, needing to clear it. Well, right now, her job was here. And she knew that just being pals with John Wells or depending on his politeness wasn't going to win any contract. She was going to need to do a lot more work. A lot more, and without distractions this time.

*　*　*

Peter set the last dish in the dishwasher, closed the door, then leaned on the edge of the sink, breathing out a slow sigh. Through the kitchen window, the branches of the ancient elm in the backyard waved, each breeze setting free a new set of leaves.

It should have been easy, this thing with Kate. He shouldn't have been so distracted at work, forgetting student's names, forgetting a lab study session and arriving late. Looking out the north window of his house just in case a bright yellow Volkswagen was parked in the street. Wondering if she was even coming back again.

It was stupid, like he was a high school kid again, like the kids he saw in the hallways, drama feeding on drama. But he wasn't. He was grown, but he was acting like them, wasn't he?

He wiped his hands on a towel and dropped it on the counter. The family portrait hung in its spot, next to the back door, where it had been the past fifteen or so years. It was the one they took at Sears in Iowa City when he was in ninth grade when he'd insisted on wearing his V-neck shirt. Good thing he hadn't had any chest hair.

It was times like these, alone in the house, when he wished his dad was still here. He could call his mom, but he knew she'd probably tell him to "be himself." It wasn't bad advice, and she meant well, but sometimes he just wanted to know what Dad would say. But that wasn't going to happen, was it?

He moved to the living room, grabbing a book on the way. Good night for a fire in the fireplace. He hadn't had to turn the heat on yet, and he always hated to do so. Always meant summer was really gone, and winter would be setting in any day. As if he could ever stop something as inevitable as seasons changing.

That's what this felt like. Inevitable. Or was a better word impossible? As if he had no choice, as if he couldn't avoid having to decide about Kate, once and for all.

He gathered a few pieces of kindling from the rack next to the fireplace, placed them over the crumpled newspaper in a pyramid. In a few minutes, the blaze was crackling.

He hadn't moved, hypnotized by the orange flames wicking up the sides of the logs. He almost laughed, a thought popping in his head. He knew the principles of combustion, had taught it for years. It read in his mind like and internal textbook. "A chemical process which occurs when oxygen reacts with another substance producing sufficient heat and light to cause ignition."

But the simple dance of the flames was pure beauty, the flip side of the science, the mesmerizing one. So, was that him and Kate?

She might be proud of his artistic metaphor. If she were here.

He sat for a long time, the room dark, except for the flames of the slowly dying fire.

Chapter Fifteen

Geez, what was it with Golden Grove and its crazy conventions? First the bearded guys and now there was a barbershop quartet contest going on this weekend. The only available hotel room Kate could find was at the Super 6 on the edge of town.

Not the classiest of accommodations, but she decided it was her best option. Peter would be close by in case she needed more science help, but not so close as to be a distraction. She needed to hunker down and get to work. No pie shakes, no convertible trips to the park, and no hanging out with him in his backyard or at the high school.

Eat, sleep, and breathe Nitrovex. Her nose wrinkled. Well, not breathe.

She spread out her computer on the tiny desk in her hotel room and tried to get to it, Danni's words echoing. *You sure you're still up to this, Kate?*

Maybe not.

The barbershop quartets on either side of her thin-walled hotel room were in full swing. She counted twelve rounds of "You Must Have Been a Beautiful Baby," thirteen run-throughs of "Bye Bye Blackbird," and a too-many-too-care number of renditions of something called "Ma, She's Makin' Eyes At Me," which absolutely had to be the number one song played in hell.

By midnight, it was too much, and she headed for Carol's house, letting herself in using the key under the garden gnome that looked like Karl Marx with a hangover. Which also described her mood perfectly.

The next morning, wrinkled and still fully-clothed, Kate turned over on Carol's stiff couch, dreading to look at her watch. A furry tail twitched on her face, and she blew out a puff of air. Tommy flipped off the arm of the couch and dove under a chair.

Carol was a little surprised to see her too. Okay, she clutched her heart when she spotted Kate on the couch. But she quickly calmed down, excited that her prodigal girl was home again.

An hour and a decent cup of coffee later, Kate rubbed her temples.

"How's your head, now, dear?" Carol asked.

"Better." The Tylenol she'd downed with the tall glass of orange juice was starting to kick in. The two nails that obviously must be sticking out of her temples were slowly disappearing.

"Well, I'm sorry you didn't sleep well last night." She sighed. "You'd think the manager wouldn't let them practice so late like that."

Lida Rose, I'm home again, Rose...

Kate sat up, held the cool glass to her head. "I considered murder, but I would have had to dig four graves, and after the drive from Chicago, I was just too tired."

"Here, I'll get you an ice pack from the freezer," Carol said, heading for the kitchen.

The doorbell donged, and the nails returned. Ouch.

"Can you get that, Kate?" Carol called. "It's probably Rose dropping off my casserole dish."

Better not be *Lida* Rose. "Sure," Kate called back, heading for the front door. She could see a shadowy figure outlined behind the lace curtains. If that was Rose, she must play a lot of basketball.

She pulled open the door, her heart bumping. "Okay, hand over the casserole dish, mister, and no one gets hurt."

"Hi, Kate," Peter said, the crooked smile in danger of giving her heart palpitations. "No casserole dish, just a clock." He held up an apple-shaped red clock with little twigs for hands. "Carol dropped it off early this morning and asked me to fix it for her."

Kate nodded, eyes narrowed. How early? And when exactly had Carol noticed her on the couch? "Okay, then, what's the password?"

"Let me in, I have a clock?"

"Nope."

"Uh, should I come back later?"

She shook her head. "Not even close. Last chance."

"Kate is the most beautiful girl I've ever seen?" His liquid eyes danced with a smile, and now her elbows were buzzing.

Uh-oh, elbows now?

"Close enough," she said, stepping back as a breeze played with his hair. Why was this town always so breezy? "You may enter."

He did, brushing by her, all smooth and clean and zesty.

Carol entered the room, a huge smile blossoming on her face. "Oh, Peter, hi."

Peter held out the clock. "All fixed. Just needed some new batteries."

Carol took it from him, handling it as if it were a vital piece of equipment from the Space Shuttle instead of a cheap dime-store clock. "Oh, thank you so much. I don't know what I would do without you."

Kate watched, arms folded, nodding slightly at the performance. *Bravo, Carol.* She turned to Peter. "So, clock savior, how was your week?"

"Well. You look good. You must be making progress on the project?"

"Mmm-hmm." She gave a noncommittal nod. He was being gracious, and she liked it. Her hair was flopped the wrong way, and she wasn't wearing makeup. And now that she suddenly remembered that, she turned quickly. Oh, geez.

He made his way in but still stood. Polite.

Carol had returned from dropping off her precious two-dollar cargo. "Peter, will we see you at the carnival tonight?"

He nodded. "I'll be there. Have to man the balloon booth. Pop a balloon, win a prize."

Too bad there wasn't a kissing booth, Kate thought haphazardly, then squinted. Okay, easy. Must be the lack of sleep.

"Kate, why don't you come to the carnival tonight? You'll need a break, won't you?"

"Carnival?" she said in her best *who me?* tone.

"Yes, the Community Center Carnival. Remember, that's what the Thread Heads were meeting about last time you were here? It's a fundraiser we do every fall. This year it's for the wounded veteran's group. Peter will be there."

As if that was supposed to be the clincher. "Well, I suppose maybe I can take a break. For a few minutes."

Peter was just standing there looking like a big gorgeous puppy, arms folded.

"Actually, I could use some help with the face painting booth," Carol said.

"What time?" Kate asked. Well, she really would need a break later. Anyway, she could hunker down all day tomorrow.

"Starts at seven," Peter said.

Kate thought, then nodded. "Okay."

"It's a date," Carol said.

Kate glared at her.

"Good," Peter said, heading back to the door. "Sorry, I've got to go. I still need to pick up the helium tank for the balloons."

He wafted by, and Kate inhaled.

"Ladies," he said, and let himself out.

"Such a nice man," Carol said dreamily.

Kate sauntered over to her friend. "You know, he's single," she said suggestively. "Have you ever heard of May-December romances?"

That got her a swat. "Oh, stop. And thank you."

"For what?"

"For agreeing to help. Gives you a chance to see some of the community again."

She hadn't thought of that. Mixing with the denizens of Golden Grove again? She sighed. Well, it was for a good cause, and maybe it would give her some inspiration for her proposal. After all, that was at least part of why she'd decided to drive to Golden Grove and work here instead of Chicago this weekend, right?

"Are the men in Chicago as nice as him?" Carol asked.

"Excuse me?"

"Are the men in Chicago nice?"

"Yes, Carol, they're very nice. They open the door for you, sometimes they bathe, and they don't dip your pigtails in the inkwell."

"As nice as Peter? He's been such a nice neighbor to have. So helpful."

"Sure he's nice. He's nice to everyone. He's got a virulent, terminal case of nice. When God was handing out niceness he looked at Peter and just said…'nice!' He's the niceness king. If niceness were an Olympic event—"

"Katie. Kate?"

"What?"

"You're babbling."

Kate put her hand on her forehead. "I know. I need a nap." She sat on the couch. "But doesn't it make you a little crazy sometimes that he's so…you know…" She flopped her hands, searching for the word.

"Nice?" Carol offered.

Kate put her hands over her ears. "Yarggh, stop saying that word."

Carol burst out laughing.

"What?"

Carol waved her hand, still chuckling. "Look at you. Most women complain because men are too mean or stupid or lazy, and you're getting all bent out of shape because someone's too nice."

Kate scrunched her lips, then sighed. Carol might act like a matchmaking busybody at times, but she was a friend. More than that, almost a surrogate mom.

"I guess that's the point. He's just being nice to me like he's nice to everyone else." Like, Penny Fitch at the high school.

"Are you sure of that?" Carol approached, touched her arm. "Why don't you ask him if it's more than that?"

Ask him? Like, with words? Did Kate even really want to know? They'd had a rough enough time just getting back to square one as friends, hadn't they? And, yeah, maybe there was some flirting, but that was harmless, right?

Did she really want to risk complicating a friendship by having to wallow through some painful "Do you *like* like me?" conversation like a blushing, blubbering school girl?

Carol touched her arm again. "Kate, what is your heart telling you?"

What was this, a Disney movie? She smiled, gave her friend an arm squeeze back. "It's telling me I need to get to work."

Chapter Sixteen

Kate followed Carol up the concrete stairs. Even though the vinyl letters on the back door of the old gym announced Golden Grove Community Center, too many memories still made it high school to her. The same metal railings, same worn slatted maple floors. It was the smell that got her most, that scent of dust and wax and history. She swallowed.

She'd wondered on the walk here whether there would be some kind of big moment when she stepped inside the gym. Some heart-stabbing revelation, dropping her to her knees in a flood of anguished memories. This was the heart of it all, right? The Scholarship Fair, the betrayal.

She scanned the corners of the room, along the walls, half-expecting there to still be bits of broken glass hidden along the edges.

But, nothing. It was just a normal room full of milling people.

Carol, carrying a small box, led her across the floor. People milled all around her, some carrying more boxes, toting children. None she recognized. Yet, anyway.

The carnival was opening its doors in about fifteen minutes. The plan was to stick close to Carol, help at the art booth, not wander. Maybe say hi to Peter at the balloon dart booth, of course. Had to be neighborly.

Speaking of which…

Peter waved from the hallway. Hmm. Could a wave be sexy? She decided it could.

"Ladies, lovely as always," Peter said, blue eyes simmering.

Whoa, was Carol blushing? The schmoozer. Wait, was *she* blushing?

"Should be a big crowd tonight." Carol grinned, shoving the box at her. "Kate, can you take these paints to that table, please? I have to check in with Marcie."

"Here, I can take that." Peter reached for the box and led the way to the face-painting booth.

"Thanks," Kate said once they were at the streamer-decorated table.

He gave her a friendly thunk on the shoulder. "I'll be across the way. If you need me."

He ambled through the growing crowd, half a dozen people stopping him to say hi on the way.

Carol returned. "Okay, we set here?"

"Oh. Sorry." Kate began to sifting through the box. It was packed with brushes, sponges, and small jars of various colors. "I've never done this before," she told Carol, who was busy sorting bills in a metal cash drawer.

"Oh, nothing to it. I did it last year. Here." She pushed a laminated card across the table. "Here are the designs they can choose from."

Kate slid the paper towards her. Butterflies, teddy bears, flowers, hearts. Seemed simple enough.

The gym was becoming noisier as more people filtered in. She swallowed, smiled at a family wandering past. A little girl tugged at her mom's hand, pointing at Kate's table.

"Maybe later, sweetie," the mom said as they moved on.

Kate fumbled with the brushes, her heart thumping. She felt more nervous than if she'd been giving a presentation to the whole Garman board in a bikini. It was the people. She felt out of place. They all seemed to know each other, laughing, big sudden grins as a new friend approached, kids playing together. Yeah, one big happy small-town family.

She surveyed the room. Spin-art booth a few tables way. Cakewalk in the corner, in front of the stage. Plastic ducks in a blue wading pool across the way, a boy pulling one out to see if he'd won a prize.

She hadn't recognized anyone yet. Maybe she'd escape the night after all. I mean, she'd been gone for twelve years. But all it would take would be one Kate sighting, and the word would spread. Get the pitchforks and torches, Katie Brady is back.

Why had she agreed to…? Right. A good cause.

She sighed. Okay, relax. It was just for a few hours, right? It might even be…fun.

A girl, probably about four, was approaching, an older woman in tow. Probably her grandmother. Kate cocked her head. She looked familiar, but she couldn't place the face.

"Hi," the girl said shyly.

Kate leaned forward, hands on her knees, smiling. "Hi, there! Want to get your face painted?"

The girl looked at her grandmother for approval. "Go on, tell her what you want," the woman said.

Kate pushed the sheet with the sample designs closer. "How about a flower?"

The girl shook her head no.

"Um…here, a kitty?"

Head shake. No.

"Doggie?"

No.

C'mon, kid, you're killing me here. "Butterfly?"

That got an enthusiastic nod.

"Okay. Hop up in the chair here and we'll get you a nice butterfly."

"Purple," the girl said as she sat. Then, after a reprimanding stare from her grandmother, "Please."

"Purple it is," Kate said, unscrewing the cap from a bottle. She began outlining some butterfly wings in purple paint, the little girls holding still. Kate smiled. She had a spray of freckles on her cheek. "I like your freckles," she said as she got out a smaller brush and the black paint. *Need to outline this thing, otherwise, the balance will be off.*

"Thank you," the girl said.

"Excuse me," the grandmother said. "Is your name Katie?"

Kate froze drawing the curl of the proboscis. *Me?* She looked up. The woman's head was cocked, waiting, small smile on her face.

Kate forced a smile. "Yes, Kate, actually," she said, returning to the girl's cheek.

"I thought I recognized you. I'm Betty Locklear. Your old piano teacher?"

Kate closed her eyes. Yes, of course. Mrs. Locklear. Summer of what? Third grade? The weekly death marches to her house four blocks away to pound out butchered songs from that green piano book.

"Hi, Mrs. Locklear. Yeah, it's me." She shook her old teacher's hand.

"I thought so," Mrs. Locklear said. "Are you back in Golden Grove?"

Kate returned to her patient girl, choosing some green paint for wing polka dots. "Just visiting. Work, actually. I'll be gone soon." Yes, let her know this is not a permanent gig.

"Well, it's so good to see you. I always enjoyed teaching you, even if it was just for one summer."

Like Peter, she was being gracious. Kate had begged her parents to let her take lessons, promising to practice every day. Which she had. Then, when she'd found out she didn't have a little something called musical ability, she'd begged them again to quit.

"Thanks," Kate said. "Sorry I was such a lousy student." Was twenty years too late for an apology? Or was twelve...?

The woman waved her hand. "Oh, stop. At least you tried your best. That's all I ever asked."

Kate finished the final flourishes on her butterfly. She wasn't sure if butterflies had curling antenna with hearts on the ends, but, whatever. Artistic license.

She held up a hand mirror to the girl, who beamed, then looked at her grandmother for approval.

Mrs. Locklear nodded. "Very nice. Very, very nice, Katie," she said as the little girl hopped down from the stool. "Go show your mom."

"Thanks," Katie said as she began cleaning her brushes.

"Oh, I'm sorry," Mrs. Locklear said, touching her chest. "My granddaughter's name is Katie, too."

Oh. Oops.

"But you did do a very nice job, too," she said, passing over a five-dollar bill.

"Thanks," Kate said.

Mrs. Locklear leaned close, giving Kate a squeeze on the shoulder. "So nice to see you again, Kate."

"You too." In that moment, she felt like she'd known this woman all her life.

Carol bustled up. "I see you had your first customer."

Kate saw her namesake over by the duck pond, showing off her cheek to three of her little friends, pointing back at her.

"Yeah. Looks like I might get some referral business, too." She felt a small surge of pride.

About an hour, eight butterflies, three kitties, five flowers, and a customized zombie head (no blood, please) later, she needed a break.

"Carol? Mind if I take a look around?" She'd noticed a cotton candy booth over by the concessions area near Peter's balloon dart booth. It was her one weakness. The cotton candy.

Carol waved her off. "Go. Have some fun. Maybe play some of the games. I hear the balloon booth is paying out pretty well."

"I'm sure it is." She took her wallet out of her purse and extracted a couple of twenties, stuffing them in her pocket. "Can you watch my purse?"

"Certainly."

Kate set her purse on the floor under the table. She'd never do that in Chicago, but Golden Grove? Please. She could probably leave it open on the table with twenties hanging out of it and some Golden Grove good Samaritan would come along and hide it for her.

She moved off to her right, taking in the booths there that she hadn't seen yet. Guess the M&M's in the jar. Ping-pong-ball toss into the plastic cup. Photo booth with goofy props.

So far, she'd escaped recognition, except for Mrs. Locklear and another teacher, Mr. Harms, her eighth-grade science teacher. And Dale Schwartz, the Community Center director (high school). And Denny Anderson (grade school, middle school, high school), who was now a cop, which she could believe. And you could also count his wife Jenna, who sat in the desk in front of her in Mrs. Turlowski's fourth-grade class.

Okay, so her mission to remain stealthy wasn't going so well, but it hadn't been that bad. Almost fun, really, seeing people you hadn't seen for a while, knowing how they turned out, what they were doing. Some even had kids, which is how she'd met Megan Burns, a girl she was in art club with.

Okay, no need to get too sappy. At most, she'd probably only need to make a few more visits here. She needed to remember that.

A crew of high school students were topping off the water in a dunk tank. An idea teased her brain. "Who's getting in?" she asked the girl with the hose.

"Bunch of teachers, Sheriff Anderson, Mayor Watts."

Bunch of teachers? Interesting. "Mr. Clark getting in?"

The girl checked with her friends, then turned back. "Not that I know of."

"Oh. That's too bad. I heard he was going to," Kate said. What? It was for a good cause.

The girl's eyes grew round. "That would be awesome if he did."

Kate smiled. "Let me see what I can do."

The cotton candy booth was calling her name, and she obeyed, getting a large purple spool of it fresh from the drum. She hadn't had cotton candy in years.

"Cotton candy, your favorite," Peter said.

She turned, choking on a huge wad she'd just stuffed in her mouth. He was standing to her side, eyes glinting.

"Oh," she said in a muffled voice. "Want some?"

He shook his head. "No, thanks. More of a caramel apple guy, myself. One, please? No sprinkles?" he said to the high school girl behind the next table.

Kate nodded, swallowing a mouthful of spun sugar. *So, now that he thinks I'm a pig...* "How's the booth going?" she asked.

He took the apple from the girl, passing over two dollars. Kate couldn't help notice the lingering look she gave Peter. *Back off, girly*, she thought.

"Booth is going well. I'm taking a break to help set up the dunk tank."

Wait, dunk tank? This was going to be easy. "Oh. Are you, uh, the guest of honor?" she asked.

He pointed at his chest? "Me? No way. My students would destroy me."

"Yeah, but, it's for charity, remember?"

A boy, a student, bopped up. "Mr. C, someone said you were getting in?"

Peter narrowed his eyes at Kate. Now it was her turn to point at her chest. "It wasn't me," she said, laughing. "But I think it's a *great* idea, don't you?" She directed this to the boy, who grinned and nodded.

"C'mon, Mr. C. It's only a little water," he coaxed.

A new set of students showed up.

"Yeah, c'mon, Mr. C," Kate said. "Mis-ter C, Mis-ter C," she began chanting, making sure not to make eye contact with Peter.

The students picked up the chant. "Mis-ter C! Mis-ter C! Mis-ter C!"

Peter opened his mouth, then stepped back, bringing his hands up in surrender. "Okay, okay, you hooligans, I'll do it."

A cheer went up. There was that schoolboy look of his, and her heart did a little jig.

"Geez, it's not enough I have to make sure you don't blow up the lab, you want to drown me, too?"

The students laughed, then jostled around him, moving him towards the booth.

Kate followed. "Oh, Peter, I'm so proud of you," she said in her best fawning frontier woman voice.

"Save it, sister. And don't *you* get any ideas."

"Me?" she said.

"Yeah, you. You've got a mean streak."

"Well, now that you mention it, I *have* been working on my curve ball lately."

"You probably couldn't even get it to the target, much less hit it."

A taunt? Okay, buddy. She put her hand in her pocket, felt the wad of cash she'd put there, then grinned. "I've got a roll of twenties that says otherwise."

"Well, you can take your roll of twenties and—"

He couldn't finish, as he was being dragged towards the tank.

She had a last glimpse of him as he took off his button-down shirt and gave a crooked smile and—was that a wink?

Oh, she was absolutely, positively getting in on this action.

* * *

"You sure you can make it from there?" Peter taunted from the tank. "Maybe you should step a little closer."

"Maybe you should take a deep breath," Kate called back, then let loose with her first pitch.

The ball sailed wide and thunked harmlessly into the canvas backdrop.

The crowd gathered around the dunk tank groaned a collective *oh!*

"You throw like a girl!" Peter called through cupped hands. He was sitting on his perch in the tank, legs dangling.

"I am a girl, you idiot," Kate yelled, winging the second ball.

This one hit square on the protective plastic in front of Peter's face with an echoing *thwack*. He recoiled instinctively, grabbing the seat. Way off, but oh so satisfying.

"Sorry, did I scare you?" she called, batting her eyes.

He shook his head. "Not since you wore that Frida Kahlo costume in fourth grade." He made a slashing gesture across his forehead, mouthing the word *unibrow*.

Ooo. Below the belt, mister.

The crowd had grown, a mix of students and townspeople, some pointing and smiling. Okay, she thought, jaw set, but grinning. This was now officially serious business.

Two shots left. She hefted the next ball as she eyed Peter, who waved from the booth. "Any day, sweetheart," he called.

Sweetheart? She cocked back and threw. Her arm felt like it was flying out of its socket. The ball shot straight for the red and white circles of the target, then curved and dinged the edge, careening across the gym floor. The tank's arm whanged and wobbled but stayed, and Peter remained dry.

Another *oh!* from the crowd.

"Oh, so close!" Peter yelled, cupping his hands again. "C'mon, Kate. It's for charity, remember?"

She flipped the remaining ball up and down in her hand. *Last one.*

"Nail him, Kate," Lucius called from a booth across the floor. A few of the guy students began chanting, "Mr. C! Mr. C!"

"Ready to get wet?" she called to Peter.

He answered with a grin, folding his arms. "Take your best shot!"

She nodded. *Oh, I will, mister.* She bent forward, eyeing the target. Someone in the crowd whistled. An unusual competitiveness gripped her as her eyes narrowed.

She reared back, aimed, and threw.

The ball thunked harmlessly against the canvas backdrop.

Oooh came the groan from the crowd. Kate stood with her hands on her hips. Peter almost seemed more disappointed than her, and something tugged at her heart.

She walked up to the booth. "Gave it my best shot," she said.

He nodded from his perch, chin jutting out. "That's all you can do." He paused, then cocked his head. "Double or nothing?"

She stroked her chin, then glanced over her shoulder to the crowd, who began cheering her on. "Tell you what," she said loudly. "Why don't we just cut to the chase?"

The crowd cheered harder. She turned back to Peter, whose smile was slowly evaporating.

"Wait. Kate?"

She grinned, pulled out a twenty from her pocket, dropped it on the ground, and then shoved the target arm as hard as she could.

Peter plunged, and the look on his face was delicious.

The crowd went crazy.

"It's for charity, remember?" she said sweetly as he popped up, sputtering.

* * *

Twenty minutes later, he joined her at Carol's booth, hair wet, in a pair of sweats, a freshly-scrubbed look on his face.

"Enjoy your bath?" she said without looking up. She was busy painting a flower on a five-year-old's face.

"Surprisingly refreshing," he said, swiping a hand through his hair. "Thinking of getting one of those tanks for home."

She nodded, finishing a striped daisy petal. "I'd be happy to assist you with the dunking again."

"No, I think tonight's humiliation is enough for now."

Kate patted the girl's hand. "You're done, sweetie."

The girl admired her cheek in the hand mirror on the table, then scooted off to show her friends.

"Do you next?" Kate asked, standing. "I was thinking something aquatic." She faked surprise. "I know! How about I draw some gills on your neck?"

"Funny. How about you try the tank next? There's an opening at eight-thirty."

She shook her head. "No thanks. I prefer to do all my bathing in private. Besides, you'd probably cheat."

"I would not. And look who's talking?"

She could tell the minute he realized what he'd said. His expression froze, but oddly the old reminder didn't bother her.

She grinned at him. "I paid for that privilege fair and square. For charity, remember?"

He nodded, stepping closer and looking relieved. "How about lunch, then? Tomorrow?"

Her neck flashed. She'd been so worried about being in the gym, in being in Golden Grove again, but it all felt like such a long time ago.

Which was the problem. Her smile faltered. "Oh. I can't. I have to work on my proposal all day." Work seemed like another life, another world at the moment.

He nodded, understanding, but the spark had left his eyes. "That's okay. I understand."

She wasn't sure she did though. The carnival continued its happy swirl around them. Kids running from booth to booth, pockets of laughter breaking out around the room, circus music whirling from the PA. She must have unconsciously warmed to it. The easy conversations with the townspeople, as if they were already old friends. The honest acceptance into their little group here. It all felt so…safe.

She realized she hadn't said anything for a few seconds, rubbed her cheek with her palm. "Yes, sorry," she said, scanning the glowing room.

"How long are you staying this time?"

"Just until tomorrow." Her brain seemed to be in a slight fog.

"When will you be back?"

It was so direct, she swallowed. Not "if," *when*. "I won't know until after the next meeting with my boss."

"Oh, Okay."

She wanted to say something. Something to reassure him. He looked so lost. "Look, maybe—"

"Mr. C!" a student called behind him. "They need you at the balloon booth. They don't know how to run the helium tank."

"Be there in a second," he called over his shoulder, then turned back to Kate. "So, let me know when you're back in town, okay?"

"Okay."

He gave a quick squeeze of her arm and left.

And then the light seemed to go out of the room, and she felt like a stranger again. Someone who had just wandered into the place, sat down, and was pretending to be a part of the fun and familiarity.

"Kate? You have a customer."

Kate turned blankly. It was Carol, smiling, gesturing with her eyes to a girl standing patiently by the table, miniature smile on her face.

"Oh. Sure, hi." She sat down on the chair next to the paint kit, then leaned over. "What's your name, sweetie?"

"Eloise."

"Eloise, very pretty. What would you like me to paint?"

The girl pointed to the sheet of examples. "I want a heart," she said in her tiny voice.

Kate swallowed, forced a smile, picked up a brush. *Oh, sweetie. Don't we all. Don't we all.*

Chapter Seventeen

The shower always felt good after a run, Peter thought. The boy's locker room at the high school was clear Monday nights. Cross-country practice was early morning now. It was easier to just shower here than go home, especially since he still had more work to do.

Work. Great, yippee. Spend three weeks slicing and dicing his way through a budget proposal, trying to save the school some money yet still give his students a chance, and all he'd have to show for it was cuts.

He was in a bad mood, and a run usually helped. *Release endorphins, increase neuron growth, increase phenylacetic acid.* But biochemistry was failing him tonight, and he knew why.

It was more than a week since he'd last seen Kate at the carnival. For a few days, it was fine, no problem. He'd thought she'd probably be back by the weekend to continue working on her proposal at Nitrovex. Maybe he'd ask her out to dinner this time.

But she hadn't come back over the weekend. Her terse text said she wasn't sure when she'd be back in town.

The reality was, he hadn't wanted to face that fact. Surprising, right, for someone who was supposed to love the scientific method? Ask a question, do background research, construct a hypothesis, test with an experiment. Procedure working? No? Yes? He grunted.

The facts were: Kate lived in Chicago. She loved her job. He (still) lived in Golden Grove. And he loved *his* job?

He glanced down at the locker room bench where his budget-request sheet, covered in red strikethrough lines, jeered at him.

How was he supposed to love this job when he was being hamstrung by budget cuts? When he couldn't give his students what they needed to learn, to succeed?

That Science Teacher of the Year banquet he'd attended in Des Moines almost made it worse. Lots of smiles, clapping, smacks on the back. *Great job! You're a credit to your whatever*, and all the other platitudes that seemed to be worth about as much as the paper this budget sheet was printed on. Then it was back to reality.

One that now might no longer include visits from Kate.

He began unpacking his running bag, sifting through his street clothes.

"I thought I saw your car here."

Peter finished pulling on his shirt and saw Lucius, hands in pockets, leaning against a locker. He saluted him. "Yup. That's me. Conscientious Clark, here to the bitter end."

"Oh. I'm guessing you saw the budget report, then."

Peter tapped the paper. "Looks like they'll had to replace the red toner cartridge in the printer after this one."

"Actually, there's no red toner cartridge in a printer."

Peter scowled. "I know. But please let me have at least one sardonic comment? Or has that been cut from the budget, too?"

Lucius gave a small grin and sat.

"So, what're you doing here?" Peter asked.

"You weren't in your office. I was worried."

Peter stood, found his belt and began threading it through the loops on his jeans. He glanced at Lucius. "I don't need checking on, *Dad*."

"Uh-oh."

"Uh-oh, what?"

"I only see that look when something's wrong."

"I told you. Budget cuts."

Lucius stared at him, waiting.

"Nothing's wrong," Peter reaffirmed.

"Mm-hmm. You lose your lucky calculator again?"

"No." Peter sat down, pulled on his right shoe.

"Dent in the Mustang?"

Silence.

"Okay, that leaves, let's see, dead classroom turtle, Pluto not a planet anymore, or…anything to do with a *Star Wars* prequel."

"None of the above."

A pause. "No Kate, this past week, I heard."

Must have gotten that from the Carol hotline. "Nope."

"She coming back?"

"Not sure."

Lucius sat on the bench beside him. "Too bad. I owe her twenty bucks for promising to drop you in that dunk tank."

Peter stopped tying his shoe and sat up, eyes questioning.

Lucius smiled. "Just kidding."

Peter pointed. "Look at my face. Not laughing."

"Sorry. I like Kate."

"Well, so do I. And if you ask if I *like* like her, so help me…"

Lucius waved his fingers in surrender. "No, no." He paused. "Kind of hard to figure out, isn't it? How you feel about someone. What to do about it."

Peter pulled on his other shoe and began to lace it.

"Yes, people are complex," Lucius continued.

"I'm sorry, did I ask a question?"

"I'm just saying it's not easy to figure someone out completely. A lot goes into making who we are."

"Yeah, about a hundred-and-sixty dollars' worth of chemicals."

"I meant our past, our choices."

"Are you getting at something? Because I've got to go try to figure out how to teach the difference between acids and bases with a budget of"—he checked the paper next to him— "fourteen dollars and ninety-eight cents."

"Okay. My point is—"

"Sorry, stop. I'll save you the time of more song and dance. Getting closer to Kate would be a mistake. Being friends, fine. Resolving past issues, great. But we live in different worlds now."

"Oh, I don't know. She seemed pretty at home painting faces at the carnival."

Peter saw her in his mind, then, laughing, teasing the kids while she painted their faces. A natural with the students. He sobered. "Right, and then she left. She doesn't live here anymore, Lucius. Her life—the life she *chose*—is in Chicago, with her high-rise office and her Armani water or whatever. She's moved on. She's in the city. That's what she's chosen. She's not a small-town girl anymore."

"And you're still in high school. The same one you grew up in, in the same town."

Peter held his head. "Oh, geez, please don't psychoanalyze me."

"Sounds like you might be a little jealous."

He was done getting dressed and stood. "Well, you know what? Maybe I am. Maybe I'm tired of having to bleed every semester during budget season, trying to beg for enough materials so my students can have half a chance at learning something. Maybe I should interview for that job in Chicago. Maybe it's time for me to move on." *Maybe this will be my only chance.*

"That's a lot of maybes."

"Maybe."

Lucius stood as well and clapped him on the back. "Don't worry about the maybes. They're pretty much all that life is made up of."

"I prefer things be a little more concrete."

"You're a scientist. You like things to be neat, quantifiable, and reproducible. That's not how people work."

"Except for the reproducible part."

Lucius nodded, chuckling. "True. Well, I expect you're tired of my sage advice by now. I've got my own bleeding to stop back at my office." He turned to go, then paused. "See you tomorrow?"

Peter turned. "I'll be here."

"Oh, and Brenda asked if you squared away things with Nitrovex for that field trip?"

Peter dropped his head back, stared at the ceiling. He'd almost forgotten about that one. "Yes, if there's any money left to put gas in the bus."

"I'll help you car pool if it comes to that."

Lucius pushed open the locker room door and was gone.

Peter was alone. The locker room was big, boomy, and empty. The only sound was the steady drip from one of the faucets in the shower room. It plunked, rhythmically. Something told him it was all somehow symbolic, but he couldn't put his finger on it. Kate might be able to give him some metaphorical hints, but she was in Chicago.

He stood, grabbed his papers, slung his workout bag over his shoulder. The Dixon School brochure was still in his office, and it was time to take some action. There was an early out on Friday. Maybe he could get a substitute for the morning and set up an interview at Dixon that afternoon.

Maybe it was time for him to move on. As much as he loved this town, he wasn't going anywhere. Maybe this was the opportunity he needed. Maybe it was where he was supposed to be. In Chicago. Where Kate lived.

He pushed through the locker room door.

Yup, Lucius was right. That was a lot of maybes.

* * *

Great, Kate thought, examining the fresh gouge in her driver's side door as she closed it. *Another ding in my car.* No note, of course.

She hoisted her purse and made her way to the elevator of the downtown Chicago parking garage under Garman's offices, dodging a drooling slick of some nameless liquid someone had dumped out of their car door.

She went through her mental checklist. It was Wednesday, which meant a meeting with her whole group on project updates, policy changes, and blah blah blah. Then she had to sign off on the Hampstead deal that Milly had been working on while she was working on Nitrovex. Then another meeting, this one with human resources to go over a new sexual harassment policy she needed to make sure she followed—like that was an issue for her—but they had to tell her face to face by law or something.

She sighed as the elevator doors opened to Garman's offices. She'd done more design work in one day with her face painting at the carnival than she'd done here in months. But, like Danni said, that was the price of moving up. The joys of management.

Management. Such a limp, hopeless word. Implying that the highest thing you could achieve was to just to *manage,* to just get by.

Is that what she was doing here? Getting by?

She'd reached her office, nodding to another co-worker passing her down the hall as she pushed open the door. The neat, utilitarian space was the same as always, except today it was filled with the gloom of the softly raining morning. She flipped on the overhead lights, and they brightened the room, but harshly. Moving to her desk, she dropped her keys and her purse there. She had a sudden impulse to open the window, to let some of the fresh air in, no matter how rainy it was. But she knew that was impossible. Windows this high didn't open, of course. For her own safety.

Her eyes automatically drifted to her philodendron plant she'd moved to the windowsill. She'd forgotten how much she'd liked the green color, how refreshingly alive it was. It had turned brown now.

Her phone buzzed. She checked the screen. "Hey, Milly," she said. "I'll be right there."

Her first meeting was in three minutes, and Danni didn't like it when you were late.

Maybe, if she was lucky, this afternoon she'd get to sit behind her desk and do some actual work on the next Nitrovex presentation she'd be making to Danni and the board. Garman had made it through another round of cuts, but they didn't have the job yet.

And the handsome, blue-eyed elephant in the room? Well, she didn't have time to think about him, did she?

Chapter Eighteen

"Mr. Clark, good to see you. Thanks for coming." A tall man in a tan tweed coat directed Peter to a chair across from his desk. He sat.

Sun streamed in through the tall windows banked by maroon velvet curtains. Dixon's upper-grade students filed by the window outside, each in their navy-blue uniforms. It was all prim and proper and perfect.

The visit part of Peter's Dixon interview was over. The school had lived up to its brochure. Stately grounds, arcing old trees, attentive students marching on their way to class. Top-notch facilities, with separate labs for organic and inorganic chem. He had to share a room with the physics class back in Golden Grove. And the chess club.

"Your CV is impressive," the man, Stephen Volders, was saying. *Stephen*, not Steve, Peter had found out. He was the Director of Admissions and seemed as serious about his job as the wall of diplomas staring at Peter from behind his desk.

Volders was sifting through the folder Peter had brought along as a backup for his emailed references. He nodded, then glanced over his reading glasses. "Adam Butler. You worked with him?"

Peter nodded. "A summer internship in Colorado. Before my second year of grad school." When Dad was beginning to take his turn for the worse.

Volders nodded again. "Well, you certainly seem qualified, Mr. Clark." He put the folder on his desk and tapped the papers inside until they were square. "May I ask why you're considering teaching at Dixon?"

Peter had been wrestling with that very question on the four-hour drive here, and he still didn't have an adequate answer. He cleared his throat. "I feel it's time in my career to challenge myself with higher goals, to see if I can contribute to society in a more healthy and productive way."

It was either something Miss Iowa would say in the final round of a beauty pageant or a convict's appeal for early parole.

Volders nodded but said nothing.

Great. He doesn't believe me, either, Peter thought.

"And, what do you think of our facilities here?" Volders asked, gesturing towards the grounds.

Peter tried to sound enthusiastic. "Very nice. I'm more used to a view of a rusty dumpster outside my office window." He smiled, but Volders didn't. Okay, strike one.

"Yes, we pride ourselves on keeping tidy grounds. Of course, appearance isn't everything, but it is important for students to take pride in their surroundings. If a student has pride in his environment, he will have pride in himself. If he has pride in himself, he will be a better student. Do you see what I mean?"

No, but okay. "Of course," Peter said.

Volders stood, folding his hands behind his back as he paced to the window. "We have high standards of academic excellence at Dixon," he intoned, looking out the window. "Our parents expect it, and our students do as well. Three of our students have gone on to become Rhodes Scholars." He turned, obviously waiting for acknowledgment.

"Wow," was all Peter could think to say.

"Yes, indeed." Volders returned to the window, wiping a smudge from the wavy glass with his sleeve. "And with such a high degree of achievement, you can understand why we also expect to see that kind of dedication and decorum from our faculty."

So, I'm betting you've never been in a dunk tank. "Of course," Peter said again, shifting in his seat.

Volders turned. "I've asked two of our current faculty in for a brief interview if you don't mind?" Not waiting for a reply, he strode to the door and opened it. Two serious-looking teachers filed in, a woman in a high, tight bun and a shorter, older man with poofy gray sideburns.

Peter squelched his smile. If Lucius were here, he would have joked that they looked like Susan Calvin and Isaac Asimov. But he was pretty sure that these three wouldn't get his inside joke about classic science fiction.

The pair shook his hand in turn wordlessly and then sat. "Shall we begin?" Volders said with a wave of his hand.

* * *

Brief interview? The next hour was a crawl of questions. They were the usual:

How did you hear about the position? *Through my lovable but meddling friend, Lucius Potter.*

Why do you want this job? *Because I'm really into tweed.*

Tell me about a challenge or conflict you've faced at work, and how you dealt with it. *Well, last fall, Jake Showalter, our starting quarterback, got his middle finger stuck in a test tube on a bet, and we had to take him to the ER because he had a game that night.*

What's your dream job? *Pilot of the Millennium Falcon.*

He felt like a prisoner in a black and white war movie: *Vat is the chemical equation for photosynthesis? Ver are your troops? How many? Talk, pig!*

By three-thirty, Volders stood and it was finally, blessedly over. He wasn't sure if he had passed the grilling session, but by then he didn't care. He just wanted some fresh air.

All three of his interrogators stood. "Thank you so much for your time," Volders said as the other two filed out the way they had come. The door closed, and Peter stood as well.

"Mr. Clark, we appreciate you taking the time to answer our questions. I know it was a lengthy process, but you can understand our need to assure the highest quality of faculty here at Dixon."

"Of course." It was Peter's new answer to everything: You understand that tweed is essential to the ability of students to process new concepts? *Of course.* Sports are, of course, secondary to studies at Dixon. *Of course.* If you want this job, you will have to eat this houseplant on my windowsill without using your hands. *Of course.*

Volders stuck out his hand, and with that, the interview was over.

Peter wove his way through the campus towards the visitor's lot where his car was waiting. Students passed, some deep in conversation, most giving him a brief smile. It was a friendly enough place, certainly a gorgeous campus. And the average student GPA? He'd have to be nuts to turn down a job here. Wouldn't he?

He found his Camry. Dark blue, six years old, vaguely out of place among the sprinkle of Mercedes and BMWs.

He got in, closed the door, reviewing the interview.

For about three minutes. Then, as he had about six times on the trip here, he got out his phone and punched up the map.

The Garman Group was already listed with a gold star, south of his current location.

He put the phone down and sighed. He hadn't texted Kate he was going to be in Chicago for the interview. He didn't want her to think he was stalking her or something. Or that he was looking at this job just to be near her.

He didn't want *her* to think that, but he wasn't so sure himself.

No, this was about his career. Just like she was working on her career. If he didn't shake the branches, see what was out there, how would he ever know if there wasn't something better?

He chewed the side of his tongue, nodding, thinking. Yes. How would he know?

Kate had even encouraged him to interview for the job.

He started the car, put it in gear, then touched an icon on his phone, setting it face up on the console.

His map app chirped cheerily. "Twenty-six minutes to Garman Group."

* * *

Kate sipped her coffee absentmindedly as she walked down the hall back to her office, scanning notes in one hand. It was mid-Friday afternoon, but she still had a lot to do before she could head home. And not just the Nitrovex proposal. Milly had informed her that morning that one of her previous clients wanted additional branding for their website.

She pushed open her door with her foot, still studying the notes. By next Thursday? No way…

The harsh grind of an electric pencil sharpener jolted her gaze up. There, sitting at her desk, in her chair, was Peter.

"I used to have one of these," he said, examining the point of a newly sharpened pencil as if it were a diamond. "Then a student thought he'd stick a pen in it." He looked up, smiling.

She almost dropped her mug. "Oh, geez! What in the world are you doing here?"

He was wearing a crisp button-down white shirt that hugged his wide shoulders, and a thin striped purple tie. She moved to the desk, dropping her papers on the corner. Coffee could wait, and she didn't need the caffeine anymore, anyway. Her heart was beating overtime.

He stood, walked to the windows, putting his hands on the ledge. "Just came to see how the other half lives. Nice view. Are those real live pigeons?"

Her heart was still flip-flopping. Peter? Here? "What…did Milly let you in?"

He turned, his eyes dancing, and nodded. "Nice girl. Slipped her a five to let me sit in your chair. Very comfortable. I like that lumbar-support thing."

She joined him at the window, knees still a little wobbly. Peter, here. In her office. She looked around quickly. Was it a mess? No, not too bad. How was her hair? She should have worn her new Michael Kors dress…

"Sorry, I should have called," he said.

"Yes, I think so," she said, but not angrily.

He folded his arms. "But, I thought, I was in town anyway, so why not stop by?"

Yes, why not? But also, why?

He turned to his right and pulled something out of a small, white paper bag sitting on the window ledge. "I brought you a present." He held it out in the palm of his hand.

It was a snow globe.

The gold etching on the base said "Welcome to Golden Grove." Tiny brick houses in a row on a brick-lined street, miniature and picture perfect. And instead of snow, orange and yellow leaves swirled in the sunlight reflected through the window. He probably had picked it up at Bailey's; they had dozens there for tourists.

She shook it. The leaves spun like a miniature tornado. If she'd had time for metaphors, she would have called it her heart, but, oh, *please*.

"Thanks," she said, looking up.

He smiled, and it felt like sunlight. *Steady*.

"Just a little reminder," he said. "Someday, when it's gray and dark outside, or you're feeling down, maybe it will remind you of another place."

Sentiment? From Peter? That was almost as surprising as him standing here in her office.

She put the trinket on the window sill. "So, why are you here, really?"

He nodded, hands up. "Sorry, yes. I should have said earlier. I was up in Highland Park. At the Dixon School."

More heart thumping. *He did the interview?* "You did the interview?"

"More of an interrogation, really."

"So, how did it go?"

He shrugged. "Pretty well, I guess."

Pretty well in Peter-speak usually meant very well.

"So…are you still in the running for the job?"

"I suppose so. I'm sure there will be a lot of other applicants. It's a pretty prestigious school."

"You suppose so? We need to work on your self-promotion skills."

He shrugged, some of the light leaving the room.

Kate touched his arm. "Okay, I'm sorry. I guess…I'm not meaning to push you."

The smile returned. "No problem."

"Nice office," he said, nodding.

"Thanks. Not sure if I deserve it though."

"Really? Now who needs work on their self-promotion skills?" He crossed his arms. "Why do you say that?"

She shrugged. "No reason, really." Then she traced some dust from the windowsill. "I used to do more actual design work. When I started. Now it's like half my job is meetings." Why was she telling him this?

He nodded. "Meetings. Tell me about it. Had enough of those even today."

"I never liked doing interviews. All those awkward questions: What is your biggest weakness? Where do you see yourself in three years? If you could do anything and get paid, what would it be?" She shook her head.

"So, what would it be?" he asked.

"Hmm?" A halo of sun framed his head.

"If you could do anything, what would it be?"

She took in a breath. The question hung in the air, and she had no idea how to answer it. "Oh. Well, it would be something with graphic design. Logos, posters, brochure layouts. I did a book cover for a friend once—that was a blast."

He was just nodding, wordless.

"I suppose what I'd really like to do would be to have my own design studio." Where was this coming from? But the idea sparked something inside her.

"Why don't you do that," he asked, still in halo.

She shifted so she could see his face, and leaned against the edge of the window sill. "Oh, that would be way down the road. Besides, start my own company? Way too risky for me right now."

Peter was just nodding slowly, smiling.

She popped up, an idea in her head. "Look, how long are you in town?"

"Oh. I was planning on going back tonight."

She shook her head. "Not until you've had dinner."

He grinned. "What did you have in mind?"

Her head cocked. "What is your opinion on Marinetti's Deep-Dish Reuben Pizza with Zucchini Pickle Relish?"

The grin grew. "Sounds horrible. When do we eat?"

Chapter Nineteen

Peter's stomach had almost recovered from last night's Paisley Thai pizza at Marinetti's, although some residual growls still rumbled through his gut. Must have been the banana peppers Kate had insisted on. But it had been good. Fantastic, actually.

His Camry rolled through the theatre district to the address Kate had given him. He saw the stairs that led up to the Chicago el platform at State and Lake. She wasn't on the corner yet, but he was early.

He pulled back into traffic to circle around the block. She'd insisted on taking the train from her West Loop apartment so that he didn't have to drive all the way there and then back downtown.

They'd stayed at Marinetti's until closing last night, leaving only after an obvious glare from a surly hipster waitress stacking chairs on the table next to them. From there Kate had dropped him off at his hotel, a last-minute room at a plain but comfortable Radisson.

He'd agreed, and without too much arm-twisting, to stay overnight so they could catch some downtown sights before he had to head back to Golden Grove today. He wasn't sure if he could afford the time, especially after missing all of Friday. He had planned a quiz for Monday in Chemistry 102, and there was a lab test next Friday he needed to prep equipment for. But he was pretty sure he could get the work done with a few longer nights at the school.

Besides, he hadn't been to downtown Chicago in a long time, not since he was a kid. And there was Kate, too.

There was Kate, yes. She had been lively, bubbly last night at the restaurant. Laughing easily, touching his hand. Probably because she was on her home turf, so to speak.

But it had seemed like they could have been anywhere in the world and it wouldn't have mattered. It was just the two of them at a small table in the corner, each with a glass of Montoya Cabernet, doodling on the paper tablecloth using the crayons they left to keep kids busy. She was obviously better at it, sketching ponies, shading in hearts, even attempting a cartoonish drawing of his face. She'd insisted on tearing it out of the tablecloth and stuffing it in her purse. "My masterpiece," she jokingly called it.

He'd circled the block, and there she was, waving, wearing a cute, double-breasted black jacket, black leggings, and a smile. His heart danced as he pulled over.

"Need a lift, lady?" he said, in what he hoped was a taxi-driver voice.

"Don't usually go with strange men," she said, opening the door.

"Don't usually pick up such beautiful women," he said as she got in.

Her grin expanded. A car honked behind them. "Whoops," she said, closing the door. "Any ideas on where you want to go?" she asked.

He pulled into traffic. "I've always wanted to go to the Art Institute," he said.

He could sense her eyebrows raising. "You sure? It might put you to sleep. All that boring art stuff." She shivered for effect.

"I can take it."

"Okay, then. Let's see…turn right up at this light."

* * *

Peter had managed to score a parking space only two blocks from the museum on South Columbus, a feat which Kate pronounced miraculous. Chalk one up for the small-town guy, he thought.

By noon, they'd breezed through the Indian, African, and Asian art galleries, some of the ancient art, and had spent the last hour or so roving through the second level. Peter had to admit he'd been lost when it came to the pieces on the lower level, but now he made a show of pointing out a variety of paintings to her. In particular, a Gauguin and a Van Gogh in the Impressionism wing.

Now they moved into the Modern American Art section.

"So, over here," Kate was saying, pulling him by the hand, "this is Edward Hopper's famous—"

"'Nighthawks,'" Peter finished for her. "Yes, a particularly stark piece."

She stared at him as if a horn had just popped out of his head. "Right…" she said.

He turned, then nodded. "This is one of my favorites," he announced, pointing to a large painting of what looked like a disintegrated planet resting on a huge wire spool. "The Rock." He stroked his chin. "So blunt, yet so surreal."

Kate was wordless she followed him into a room across the way.

He rushed over to a square painting of an unremarkable seascape. "A particularly stunning example of a Whistler, don't you think?" he said, pointing. "Notice the broad, rough brush strokes."

He could feel her staring at him, and it was great. She reached out, socked him in the shoulder.

"Okay," she said. "You're going to tell me how you know all these paintings or I'm really going to smack you."

He turned, eyebrows up in mock surprise. "Hmm? Oh." He turned back to the Whistler, hand to his chin, studying it as if he were considering buying it. "I guess you could say I've always been a connoisseur of the arts," he said in his worst English accent.

Her arm raised, and he stepped back, his own hands up in defense. "Okay, okay," he said, laughing. "My parents had this game, Masterpiece?"

Her head cocked. *Go on?*

"It was an auction game. You each had these paintings with different values and you had to sell them. All the photos they used were from the Chicago Art Museum. I didn't know that until I saw about three of them here."

Her arm lowered, her head still cocked. But there was the slightest hint of a smile. "I knew something was up. How come we never played that game?"

He shrugged. "Don't know. My parents had to almost force me on game night. I preferred a good round of 'Hoth Ice Planet Adventure' myself."

She gave a burst of laughter, which echoed in the marble hall. "Come on," she said, looping her arm in his. "I saw a coffee shop a while back. Interested?"

He nodded. "Yes, the coffee shop. One of Edward Hopper's most famous paintings, it deduced the blending of interior and exterior lighting into a pastiche of red-golds reminiscent of Picasso's blue period, minus the blues, of course."

She fanned herself. "Ooh, I just love it when a man talks art."

"Edward Hopper. Post-impressionism. Still life. Uh, yellow. Paintings. Frames." He shrugged. "Sorry, that's all I've got."

She smiled softly. "That's okay. It's enough."

Their eyes locked for a smiling, golden moment. His watch beeped.

Peter pulled up his sleeve, turned it off. "Sorry. That's my reminder for my one o'clock lab. Forgot I still had it on."

She pouted. "You have to go?"

"Don't think anyone will be there on a Saturday." The reality of Golden Grove had intruded though. "But I'll be needing to head out in a couple of hours. Got two lesson plans to go over before Monday, and missing yesterday…"

"No, sure," she said, clasping her hands in front of her.

"But I still have a few hours. Show me more of the museum?"

"I think I've tortured you enough. I was thinking we should eat, and then the Museum of Science and Industry should be next," she said.

His eyebrows shot up, and he nodded. "You sure? It might put you to sleep. All that boring science stuff."

She shrugged. "I figured if you could stay awake here, so can I. Besides, I've always been curious to see that exhibit that shows the molecular structure of uranium-235 as typified by the constant remanagement of carbon atoms in relation to Einstein's theory of relativity."

"Well played."

"Thanks."

They walked on, arm in arm.

* * *

After an overly expensive but tasty lunch of ham and egg croissants, fruit, and a local designer coffee, Peter retrieved his Camry from their lucky parking spot, and they tooled south on Lake Shore Drive.

"Traffic always this bad?" he asked, risking a lane change in front of an oncoming black Hummer.

"Probably a festival in Millennium Park," Kate said, "or a convention at McCormick. Or maybe just normal Saturday traffic. Hard to tell."

They made it to the Museum of Science and Industry by two, although it took another half hour to find a parking space and buy tickets. Saturday's were busy here.

Once inside, they grabbed a map and wandered into the rotunda, which echoed with voices and the screeches of kids.

"Mmm. So, where to from here?" Kate asked.

He folded the map. "How about we just wander? See what we find?"

She nodded.

*　*　*

They wandered, saw their pulses spark in the giant animated heart, tried to predict where the ball would go in the world's largest pinball machine, felt the cool mist of a simulated tornado. She loved the baby chicks in the genetics section and even found the body slices interesting, although creepy. They bypassed the Farm Tech exhibit. She's already seen enough combines and corn stalks in her life.

They found themselves in the lower level of the museum, where they passed by a scrollwork sign that announced "The Wonderful Wizard of Oz."

It was her favorite book as a kid. "Go in?" she asked Peter.

He seemed hesitant. It was more of an area for kids than adults.

"Sure," he said eventually. "After you."

They walked in just as a burst of three kids ran out. Once inside, though, it was quiet.

There was a display where you could feel the beat of the Tin Man's heart, and a cutout display where you could take a photo of yourself as a Flying Monkey. Which they did.

"Here," Peter said ahead of her, "I think these are for you."

He was pointing at a giant pair of silver slippers mounted on a pink platform. A girl was standing inside them, clicking her heels together. When she did, a sign lit up in front of her in pink letters. *There's no place like home.*

She joined him. "I thought they were supposed to be ruby?" she said.

He was reading the sign next to the exhibit. "Says here they were silver in the book. They used ruby in the movie to provide contrast with the Yellow Brick Road." He looked up. "And you thought science was boring."

"Not science. Maybe scien*tists*," she teased.

"Ouch," he said, but he was smiling. The girl in the shoes had hopped down and moved on to the next exhibit. "Just for that, it's your turn," he said, pointing.

"Uh uh," she said.

"Don't think your feet will fit?"

This kidding, it was like when they were kids. "What do I do?" she asked, sliding out of her shoes.

"Hop up," he said, taking her hand. It was strong and soft at the same time. She leaned on him a little more than she needed and slid her feet into the giant shoes.

The room was empty, almost silent. A disco ball swirled mirrored stars around the darkened room.

"Now," Peter said. "Click your heels together and say, 'There's no place like home'."

Her heart bumped in her chest. The painting in front of her was of the Emerald City, a spiraling Yellow Brick Road leading up to its gates. Above it was empty blue sky.

She closed her eyes and swallowed. "There's no place like home," she said and clicked her silver shoes together three times.

She opened her eyes. The sky above the Emerald City was emblazoned in winking pink LED lights. *There's No Place Like Home.*

She swallowed again.

"Kate?" Peter said, his voice distant.

"Hmm?"

"I got a text. I've got to go."

* * *

Kate stepped out of the silver slippers, then retrieved her own shoes from the carpet. "A text? From who?"

"From Lucius," he said, his face unreadable. They began walking.

Uh oh. "Everything okay?" she asked, trying not to think the worst.

"Nothing too major," he said as he began texting back. "Water on the floor in the lab from a backed-up sink. And Barney got loose again."

"Who's Barney?"

Peter held his hands apart about two feet. "A Bearded Dragon, about so long."

"Oh, yeah. Didn't he win that beard contest in Golden Grove a few weeks ago?"

"This guy's a lizard."

She nodded. "Exactly."

A smirk. "He's gotten out before. He usually hides in the maintenance room where the heaters are."

They'd reached one of the hallways that led out into the main rotunda. The crowd noise was louder, echoing off the marble walls.

"Ah, the joys of teaching," she said, forcing a cheerful tone. "I'm glad it's not serious."

His expression hadn't changed. "No, it's just...I need to head back."

"Oh. Of course." They'd been having such a good time, joking, laughing. Flirting. She hadn't thought about the end. But here it was. Again.

"Look, Kate, I'm sorry. Even if I leave now, I won't be back in Golden Grove before eight. Between a lizard hunt and the water it might be a long night. I can't let Lucius deal with this alone."

She was waving her hands. "No, no, that's all right. You need to be there." And he did, because he was Peter, and that's where he belonged. Her heart felt dim and far away. It had been going so well. But what had she expected? He had to go back sometime.

"Where can I drop you off?" he was asking as they stopped under the planes hanging in the aviation section.

"Oh, no problem. I can catch the electric train to Millennium Station. It'll be easy to get home from there."

"You sure?"

"Hey, I'm a city girl these days." It was supposed to be a joke, but it felt flat. He smiled anyway, crooked but sad.

And then he kissed her.

He reached out with his arm, pulled her close in one smooth motion, leaned down, and kissed her.

It wasn't really sparks that were flying behind her eyes, but there were fireworks going on somewhere. The room was reverberating. He released her but kept a strong grip on her arms. She could smell him, like fresh air and peppermint, and her heart tried to recover its balance.

She could feel the stares of people around her, but she didn't care.

"What was that for?" she said finally.

"They say that if you kiss someone under the wing of the airplane, it's good luck."

She looked up, past his head. Sure enough, they were standing under the wing of the huge 727 suspended above them.

She squinted at him. "They do not."

His eyes glinted. "Well, they will now."

She might have melted, she wasn't sure.

She was here, in his arms, safe. Please, world, just go away for a few more seconds.

But, as she knew it would, it all sank. And now he had to go.

"I'll be back in Golden Grove on Sunday night," she offered.

"What a coincidence," he said. "So will I."

* * *

He was gone.

The city was big, cold, and grey. She made her way down the steps. It was a little farther to the train station than she thought but she hadn't wanted Peter to feel obligated to take her anywhere. It would be a long ride home, but she had time.

All the time in the world.

She should have been happy, right? Elated, maybe? Things were finally coming together with Nitrovex. Moving on an up.

It would have helped if she knew what she was feeling about Peter. Could have categorized her feelings, labeled them like colors on a palette. But they were too jumbled, smeared across the page in a muddy mix. Except for maybe one. The deep red of fear.

The sun was starting its dive behind the buildings in the west, although the sky was still blue, bright, and clear. It was a fleetingly familiar scene.

Except she didn't have any silver shoes to tap together. And even more disconcerting, she wasn't so sure anymore where home was.

Because the words were hanging in her heart in bright pink letters.

There's no place like home.

Chapter Twenty

Sunday's trip back the next day to Golden Grove was familiar, yet tense. Kate chalked it up to nerves. Her main proposal to Nitrovex was this Tuesday in front of their re-branding committee. If they went for it, she'd win the deal for Garman. She'd be back one more time to wrap things up, and that was it.

It was the Super Bowl and World Series in one for her. Win this, and she'd be the hero back at work, her career getting the boost it needed to move on up.

To where, exactly, she didn't know yet. That would have to come later.

Carol was out at a Community Center meeting tonight, which was good because Kate needed the time alone to work. Yesterday's jaunt in Chicago with Peter, although fun, had eaten up some clock, and she needed every slide and chart to be perfect by Tuesday. She still didn't have the main slogan or logo nailed down, which was her biggest stumbling block. Without that, her chances of getting the contract were dicey. But she had another day or so to come up with something last-minute. As long as she could keep the distractions at bay.

She found herself staring out the dining room window, past the draped lace curtains towards Peter's house. The majority of those Super Bowl and World Series distractions lived next door.

Rubbing her eyes, she checked her watch. Carol wouldn't be home for another couple of hours or so. Maybe she should take a break, a short nap, even. She felt weary. Not tired as if she'd just gotten done with a mile run. Weary, as in her bones ached. Is this what it felt like to reach thirty?

She rose, then made her way up to her room. Her old room in her old house. The stairs still creaked in all the same spots. She remembered as a girl how she used to try to see if she could make it all the way to the top without a squeak.

Practice for when she would have to come home late and not wake her parents after being out late. Something she never had to do.

Her room was at the end of the hall, at the front of the house, under the dormer and over the porch. She had picked it out when they moved in, apparently. Her parents told her that. She was too young to remember. But it was a good choice. Very artsy, she had thought, like a painter's garret in Paris.

She flopped onto the bed, calculating the familiar bounces. The ceiling angled above her where the dormer was. Once it had been loaded with posters and paintings and drawings. And, yes, her My Little Pony mural she had painted.

It had been summer. She'd spent days working on it, checking to make sure the colors matched the boxes the toys came in.

That was probably when her parents started to get worried she'd be an artist. She could tell. They were scientists. Art was something you did on the weekends or while you watched TV, as a distraction. Not for a living. Starving in some flat with dirty wallpaper in New York City, smoking clove cigarettes. She smiled, picturing Lucius smoking his clove cigarettes, grinning through his huge walrus mustache.

How we can change.

The ceiling was blank now, perfect for thinking, for leaving the past behind. But that had proven hard to do the past few weeks. She hadn't expected it to be so hard, being back. Golden Grove was just a place, like any other. But her hometown had other plans. It had leaked and spread into her like fresh watercolor paint. Or maybe it was the water washing, revealing what had been there all along. That she was home.

She shook her head, still lying on the bed. *No, home is where you make it. You make it—it doesn't make you.* This was just old memories tugging at her. What did they say? You only remember the good and forget the bad.

A thought unearthed itself from her mind. The closet?

She sat up. Pushed herself off the bed, kicking off her shoes as she went. Over to the closet door. Opened it and fumbled for the pull-cord string on the side that turned on the light. The small space still smelled like old clothes and dust with a slight tinge of mothballs. Just the way she remembered it.

Squatting down beneath some of Carol's old dresses, she moved aside a few shoeboxes on the bare pine plank floor. There. In the corner, one of the grooves of the floor was just a little wider than its neighbor, with some scratch marks near the edge.

Reaching in, she pulled the board edge with her fingernail. It slipped a few times, then slowly pulled up. She grabbed it and lifted it aside. Heart beating harder, she reached inside, feeling. Her fingers closed on a cloth bag, which she grabbed and wrested through the small opening.

She made her way back into the room and sat on the bed cross-legged, then dumped the bag out onto the quilt.

A variety of trinkets tumbled out. A few photos, some coins. An unused stamp, a rubber ball. A few colored wire bracelets she'd made with a kit she'd gotten on her third birthday. She remembered giving a silver necklace she'd made to Peter for his birthday that year. He'd been so embarrassed.

She spread them all out with her fingers. Her report card from second grade. She smiled. All "satisfactories." A photo of her in the pony Halloween costume her mom had tried to make, with her mom's old blonde wig as a tail.

A folded note on pink paper. It was worn, as if it had been carried around in a pocket for a long time. She unfolded it and read it, then sat still for a while. She began to put all the trinkets back in the bag. She paused, took the note, folded it and stuck it into her shirt pocket.

The bag went back into the secret space in the closet floorboard. It was where it belonged, back in time, back to a little girl that wasn't there anymore.

She sighed, long, as she sank back onto the bed. It was becoming too much, the pressure. Being here, this job.

Her eyes stung. How was she supposed to do this?

No, she knew what she truly meant was, how was she supposed to do this *alone*?

And that was it. Letting the word in, letting it even be possible, squeezed her heart, and she gave a short gasp. A tear trickled, and she wiped it.

Well, she didn't really have a choice, did she? In fact, the choices were made, a long time ago. She was just riding them out now.

She sniffed and sat up straight, took a chance glance out her second-story window at the house next door.

The porch light was still on, gleaming yellow. A beacon, if she wanted to be poetic. But she couldn't afford to. Not yet.

She got up and pulled the shade down, and the room went dark.

* * *

Peter thought for a moment, then rang the doorbell again. Maybe he was pushing it. Maybe Kate was inside watching him, hiding in the kitchen. Maybe it was a mistake, the kiss in Chicago yesterday. It had been spontaneous, but she hadn't pulled away. Maybe he should just...

The door opened and Kate appeared, smiling. She was barefoot in a flowered dress. Peter hadn't seen her in a dress before. At least, not since grade school. She looked good, light and airy. Her toenails were painted red.

"Peter, Peter," she said a little loudly. "Pumpkin eater."

"Can I come in?" he asked.

She bowed extravagantly. "Enter, good sir." She stumbled slightly as she stepped back.

Peter opened the screen door and let it close behind him. "Saw your car. Thought I'd stop and say hi."

Kate beamed. "Awesome! Awesome sauce." She turned and walked to a couch and flopped down, patting the seat next to her. "Come sit by me, Peter."

He glanced at the wine bottle and glass on the end table next to the couch. The glass was empty.

"Maybe I should come back later."

She shook her head. "No, no, sit down and tell me how you've been."

"Since yesterday?" He came and sat next to her. She tucked her legs under her and shifted towards him.

"You don't mind if I scooch over, do you?"

"No."

"Good. I don't like anti-scoochers."

"Me either."

"Then we are agreed. Next order of business. Getting rid of the Vipes Precipice of Operations at the place with the stinky chemicals."

"Penny?"

She put her finger to her lips. "Don't say her name or she'll appear and scratch your eyes out."

"You still have a problem with her?"

"She's trying to sabble-tage me."

"No, she's not. She's a professional."

"She's a professional...witch." She laughed in his face. "I almost said a bad word to you, Peter!" Smile vanishing, she squinted, pointing to her stomach. "My gut is telling me I need to be careful."

"I think your gut is in no shape to tell you anything right now."

She beamed. "That was a joke! Good for you, Peter. I know a joke, too."

"That's nice."

"Why is alcohol not a solution?" She leaned forward, huge grin on her face, ready to laugh.

"I already know that one," he said.

Her face scrunched in annoyance, then she seemed to think. "Okay then, how 'bout, what's the difference between a mole and a molecule?"

"I don't know, what?"

"Get ready, because this is funny." She snorted, then looked at the ceiling as if thinking hard, then recited, "A molecule is the smallest part of a chemical element that has the chemical properties of that element, and...a mole is a nasty little rodent that digs tunnels in your yard." She fell forward, snorting into his knee.

He shook his head. "C'mon, Kate, I think you need to get to bed." He stood.

Kate pasted on a stern face, then saluted. "Yes, sir, Master Chemistry Teacher of the Year." She picked up the wine bottle from the table and shook it. "Whoa...how much of this did you have?"

"Me? I didn't have any. Looks like you had a glass or three."

Kate held up two fingers. "Just three angstroms. Or two liters. Or a whole bunch of moles. Lots of moles."

Peter took her by the arm and tried to ease her to her feet. "Okay, Einstein, here we go."

Kate wagged her finger. "No, Eisenstein was a physicist, and he also directed. Movies." She giggled. "He directed Shattlebip Topemkin—I bet you didn't know that, Mister Scientist." She leaned against him, looked up, and burped in his face.

"Whew. Wow, Kate—yes, that's amazing. C'mon, up you go."

Kate's face wrinkled in a grimace. "Don't say 'up,' Peter, because it sounds like 'throw up,' and I don't want to throw up. On you." She smiled, then fell against him and threw her arms around his neck. "Y' know something, Teper? Peter?"

Peter held her waist to keep her from sliding down his chest as she leaned against him. He wished it was under different circumstances. "What's that?"

"I wrote you a note."

"Really?"

She nodded. "Yup. I wrote a note, and it was a good note, the note I wrote." She whispered in his face. "It was a love note."

"Oh?" He had her at the base of the stairs, still leaning on him.

"Yes, I wrote it to you and it was a love note in the sixth grade and it said that I loved you."

"That's very nice, Kate. Let's go up the stairs."

She shook her head vigorously. "You said 'up' again. Don't say 'up.' I don't like 'up.' "

"Sorry. Here we go."

"Wait, wait, wait, Peter. Peter, wait."

"What is it?"

"Can I tell you something?"

"Sure."

She grinned broadly. "I wrote you a note."

"You told me that already."

Her bottom lip pouted. "I did?"

"Yes."

"Well, what did the note say? Was it a good note?"

"I don't know…you never gave it to me."

The grin returned. "I know!" And she whispered again. "It was a love note." She pointed it at the ceiling. "I found it up in my room." She stopped, frowning. "Oh, no, I said 'up.' "

Peter shook his head. "Remember when I said alcohol wasn't the problem, it was the solution?"

"Yup. That was my joke."

"I was wrong." He tried lifting her by her arms. "C'mon, now, let's get to your room."

She suddenly pushed him away, stumbling slightly. "How dare you shup me to my room up there? I don't hardly know you. Varlot."

"Varlot?"

"Yeah. It's what they say in the old movies when a man was a varlot to a girl, which you are. A varlot, not a girl. I'm the girl." She pointed at herself. "I'm going to sleep on the couch if you don't mind, but I think that first I need to throw up."

She suddenly pushed past him, through the narrow bathroom door next to the staircase and slammed it shut. In seconds, Peter heard a bout of retching.

"Kate?" he called. His answer was another heave. He tried the door handle. It was locked.

"Varlot," she gagged from behind it.

A few seconds later, the toilet flushed. The door unlocked, then creaked open as a bedraggled Kate emerged, looking like a wet puppy.

Peter quickly moved to her, put his arms around her shoulders. "Hey? You okay?"

"Is okay when the room is spinning like a sideways merry-go-round?"

"No."

"Then I think I'm fine." She looked over her shoulder. "You know, I've never thrown up in that room before."

"That's great. I'm so proud of you." He reached behind her, grabbed a hand towel from a rack and bumped the cold water handle on. He wet the towel, turned off the faucet and dabbed her face. It looked so pale, like a little girl's.

One arm still around her, he guided her to the living room. Pulling a blanket off the couch and onto the floor with one hand, he gently guided her down, laid her back, then lifted her feet up onto a pillow at the other end. He grabbed a pillow from the chair nearby and tucked it under her head. "Here—here's a pillow."

She looked up at him with big brown eyes which started to fill with tears. "But I didn't get you anything."

Peter smiled, then tucked some hair from her face back behind her ear. She lay back, a smile returning, as he retrieved the blanket from the floor and gently laid it over her. He kneeled down beside her, his arm resting on the side of the couch.

"Goodnight, Kate." He thought about kissing her on the forehead.

Kate, smiling, nestled deeper into the couch and closed her eyes. In a few seconds, she was already asleep.

Peter stood, still watching her. Her chest rising and falling, he found himself seeing her as that little girl from his tree house. Wavy hair spilling around her face, a sprinkle of freckles around her eyes. Angelic and childlike at the same time. Not the sophisticated career-driven woman who felt so out of reach, but a simple small-town girl.

He knew she'd been working hard. Maybe too hard. And he felt a measure of guilt himself. Was he making her life harder? Maybe that kiss was a mistake.

He cocked his head, spying a pink piece of paper peeking out of a top pocket of her dress. Curious, he slowly removed it. It was wrinkled and old and smelled like faded strawberries. Pink paper with ruled lines from a little girl's notebook. He went to a chair, unfolded the note, and spread it on his knee. It was written in red pen, festooned with small hearts and the curlicues of a happy art-crazy girl.

Dear Peter,
I decided I Super-Love you
- Katie

P.S. I was the one who broke your favorite Star Wars guy, the gold robot.

Chapter Twenty-One

The headache hadn't been as bad as she had expected. The wine had been, though. Cheap wine, from Carol's top cupboard. Probably used for cooking years ago and left there.

She'd made it through Monday, though. Her presentation was done, double and triple checked. Still a few missing parts, but she was hoping she could fudge those well enough to make it to the final round of branding candidates next week.

She shifted her weight, standing on Peter's front porch. The sun was down, and fallen leaves rustled in the chilly shadows.

Her finger hovered over the doorbell. It was an old-fashioned one that rang an actual bell outside on the porch. She was worried it would trigger her headache again, but the hangover had finally subsided.

She'd wanted to call Peter to apologize. She was embarrassed, as if she were afraid he would call her parents or something and she'd be grounded. As if they were still back in school and she needed him to keep some deep, dark secret.

She peered through the curtains to the side of Peter's front door. The lights were on, but no one was in the living room.

Maybe he wasn't home. Maybe he was avoiding her because of last night.

She didn't know why she'd done that, drink almost a whole bottle of wine. It wasn't like her, was it?

She rang the bell again. She thought she could hear footsteps. What would she say?

Peter, I'm not really a lush. I just love cheap wine...

Peter, studies have shown that a little wine before bed helps you sleep better, until you throw up...

Peter, you should know I only drink when I'm back in my hometown dealing with a high-stress project, and a guy I can't seem to get out of my brain…

Peter, I—

The door opened.

"Hi, Kate." He didn't slam the door. Good sign. "Sorry, I was just out back on the porch."

The screen door was still there, but she didn't wait. "Peter, I just wanted to apologize for last night."

He shook his head and smiled. "No apology necessary. You're under a lot of stress."

Yes, stress. *Works for me.* "Well, I just wanted you to know I don't normally, you know, drink that much."

"Forget it." He pushed the screen door open. "Come in?"

"You're probably busy. 'A teacher's work is never done,' right?" Another flat joke.

"Actually, I'm all done for today."

"Oh. Good." She stepped through. The screen door dropped back, then settled against the jamb with a click.

She'd always liked the Clark's house, almost more than her own. It just seemed so homey for some reason. Big wrap-around front porch, two stories with lots of character. Could be a bed-and-breakfast if someone wanted to put in the work. Awfully big for one person, though.

Peter hadn't changed it much. There were a few signs a man lived alone here. A bike leaning in the corner. Running shorts draped over a dining room chair.

Music was playing in the background. She caught it from a memory. When she worked a summer at the sweet-corn stand on the edge of town. Mr. Peterson loved to listen to the oldies station. The title bounced up from her memory. "Don't Do Your Love."

"Nice song."

He seemed puzzled, then picked up on it. "Oh, that. I'm supposed to help choose music for the Homecoming Dance this Saturday. It's an eighties theme."

"I heard."

"You know how it is. Wait thirty years and everything is retro and cool again."

"Hmm." She rocked on her heels. He cleared his throat.

"Well," she said. "I guess I should be—"

"Want to see my star?" he said at the same time.

Call It Chemistry

* * *

Peter peered through the finder scope, then adjusted the focuser. He squinted through the eyepiece, which went fuzzy, then clear. In the center was a tiny, faint dot. He checked the coordinates on a small blue piece of paper again to be sure.

"There it is if you want to see it."

They were on his back porch. A ceiling fan turned slowly above them. The telescope was perched on a brass tripod near the railing, angled up past the trees. He was fortunate the star was in the right position tonight.

Kate came by his side. "I look through here?" she asked, pointing at the eyepiece.

"Yup."

She hunched over, knees bent, squinting through the eyepiece. Peter's eyes lingered on her shapely jeans.

"What's it called? Peter's Death Star?"

"Officially, it's called 6890:1457:1. But I named it Lucky."

She looked up. "You call it Lucky Star?"

"After my dog, Lucky."

"Oh, Lucky," she said, seeming to remember. "I loved Lucky, the little bugger." She returned to the eyepiece. "You know, as techie as this is, it's kind of cool," she said. "I mean, who knows if there's life on a planet revolving around that star. And it's named after Lucky."

Peter smiled, held tilted. "You know, that's probably the geekiest thing I've ever heard you say."

"Oh, I see," she said as she stood up, smiling. "Got your blood moving, huh? Well, how about I—"

She took a step forward, but her foot caught one of the legs of the telescope tripod, tripping her. Peter immediately reached for her arm, catching it as her other arm swung around and frantically grabbed his shoulder to keep from falling. Gravity did the rest. Both tumbled back into the padded wicker love seat, feet twisting, Kate landing face to face on top of Peter with an *oof!*

As quickly as it happened, they both were now frozen, arms clutching arms, staring at each other's faces, inches apart, mouths open, eyes wide. The moment of embarrassed silence broke when both burst out into simultaneous laughter. Kate rolled off Peter and slumped next to him on the padded seat.

"Nice moves, Clark," she said.

"Me? Uh-uh—you were the tripper. I was just the catcher."

"Mmm...no, I think you put that tripod thing there on purpose."

"I'm not that smooth. I'm a scientist, remember? We're only interested in cold, hard facts."

"Right. Chemical reactions in the brain."

Peter could smell her perfume. If it was just chemicals in his brain, they were certainly fizzing. He cleared his throat. "So, Kate, since you're here—"

"Yes?"

"There's something I wanted to ask you."

She turned to him, brown eyes focused. She was so close now. "What's that?"

"It's not a huge thing, really. More of a favor. You probably won't even be in town."

"Okay, then forget it." She turned away.

"No, I mean, you might be around. If you're in town."

She turned back. "I won't know unless you tell me what it is first."

"Right. So this Homecoming Dance is this week. Saturday night."

"So you said." She just looked at him, nodding once, waiting.

"And the teachers are allowed to go. With the students. Not with the students, of course, but along with the students. If they want to go. The teachers."

She was sill staring at him, nodding.

He felt like a stupid teenager. This shouldn't be that hard. *Just say it, it's not a big deal.* "So, I was wondering if you were around, of course, because I can see where you'll probably be back in Chicago by then. Most likely, right?"

More nodding, with a slight smile. She was doing this on purpose.

"Oh, geez, Kate, I'm trying to ask you to the Homecoming Dance."

She burst out laughing, clutching his knee, then looked up. "That wasn't so hard, now, was it?"

"It shouldn't have been, but it was."

"Oh, but you were so cute."

"So. You never answered my question," he said.

A smile. "You never really asked it."

Peter sighed. "Right." He got down on one knee and looked up at her, hands clasped. "Kate Brady, will you extend to me the honor of the pleasure of possibly going to the homecoming dance at Golden Grove High School, which will actually be in what is now the Community Center, next Saturday night at nine post meridiem?"

"If I'm in town."

"If you're in town," he repeated.

"Yes," she said, beaming.

"Thank you. My knee hurts." He got up and flopped back in the wicker chair next to her, rubbing his right knee.

"You're getting old."

"Not as old as you."

She swatted him. "Only by four days. We're barely thirty."

Silence came again. They rocked the wicker chair together, back and forth, as the streetlights shone through the nearly bare trees. She moved closer to him.

"Peter?" she said softly.

"Yes?"

"What does 'post meridiem' mean?"

* * *

Kate leaned on the railing overlooking Peter's back yard and gazed upward. The night was clear. The stars were huge and silent and everywhere. It was almost overwhelming. She'd forgotten how many stars there were. The city lights drowned them out in Chicago.

She shivered. "Thanks again for letting me borrow your jacket." She had his navy-blue cotton jacket wrapped around her. It was long enough that she could tuck her hands in the ends of the sleeves. She liked that.

"Certainly. Nights are getting cooler."

"They are."

She turned to face him, leaning on the wooden porch railing. "You didn't say much about the Dixon job yesterday."

He shrugged. "Not much to say. They have to review my credentials, go over the interview notes. I'm sure there a lot of other applicants."

"But you might get it?" she probed.

Another shrug. "I suppose it's possible."

He didn't seem too excited. At least, not as excited as she had hoped. "Did you like the school?"

"The school was amazing. The labs were amazing, the trees were amazing, all the students looked amazing. Everything was very…tweedy."

"What?"

"Never mind." His shoulders were slumped, his eyes looking past her.

This topic was turning into a dead end.

She laced her fingers together. "So, I've been wondering."

"Yeah?"

"What dire straits have left you Golden Grove's most eligible bachelor?"

"What?"

"Surely something's been bubbling in that lovely beaker you call a heart."

He splayed back in the love seat, arms spread on each side. "Nothing but the usual chemicals. Mostly proteins. Albumins, globulins. I had a banana today so there's probably some potassium."

She nodded. "Mmm. Albumins and globulins and potassium. Oh my." She came and sat by him. He kept his arm on the seat back behind her.

"And who's saying anything about most eligible bachelor in town?"

So, he was curious. "Oh, just about every able-bodied woman in town I meet, it seems."

He almost snorted. "They say that about anyone male under thirty with a pulse."

Kate nodded. "Mmm…I see. And what about, um…Penny Fitch?" she asked nonchalantly.

"Just a friend. If that."

She laughed. "Penny? But I thought you—I thought she was the one all the boys had the hots for."

"Yeah, maybe some of my friends. In high school. Besides, she's had a rough past few years. Got divorced a few years ago, before she moved back here."

"Really? I figured she'd have married a billionaire and be toting around five kids in a minivan by now."

He shrugged. "Things don't always go the way you think sometimes."

Kate said nothing for a moment. She was thinking of this porch. Scenes from summers years ago. "It must be hard here. Without your dad."

He looked away, pulled back his arm and ran his fingers through his hair. It fell back almost exactly into the same place.

"There are moments. But it is what it is."

Her heart tugged towards him. She felt as if what she said next would carry a huge amount of weight. Maybe enough to break whatever friendship she'd rekindled with him. Maybe enough to ruin any chances of something more. "That's one of the things I love about you, Peter."

His gaze jerked towards her. "What's that?"

"Your loyalty, your love." She looked away. "I'm not sure I could have made the same sacrifice for either of my parents." It was embarrassing to say out loud, but true.

"Well, I didn't have a lot of choice. Mom needed help, and Dad was…Dad."

"I can't imagine how tough it was for her."

"I didn't have to. I had to watch it." His face was stony for a moment, then softened. "But she was a trooper."

"I'm sorry, Peter."

"You don't have to be."

"No, I mean for everything." She reached out, touched his hand. His fingers closed around hers, and they were silent for some time.

Kate tried to find something, anything encouraging to say. "Well, you know you're doing well here, right? With teaching? It didn't turn out all that bad."

"I suppose not."

"Is it lonely?"

"Sometimes."

A slight breeze moved her hair. She could smell him on the jacket she was wearing.

He moved a little closer. "Although you never know who might turn up," he added.

Her heart bumped. "True."

"For example, say, a traveling salesman."

"Salesgirl," she corrected.

"Salesgirl. Or a new teacher at the school."

She nodded. "New schoolmarm in town? That only works in Westerns."

He nodded. "True. We're dealing with a modern chick flick here, right?"

"I'd say so, yes."

"So it would have to be someone spunky."

She shook her head. "I prefer the term highly motivated."

"Okay, so someone highly motivated, and of course she'd have to be very pretty, although she doesn't think she's very pretty."

She just nodded. Leaned closer. His arm moved around her.

"And, let's see…she'd have, what? Blue eyes?"

"Brown."

"Right, of course. Brown eyes, and wavy hair, probably reddish blonde. Something that glinted in the starlight like diamonds on spun gold."

She nodded. "Wow, that's pretty colorful for a scientist."

"Quiet, I'm on a roll. And she'd have maybe a sprinkle of freckles around her nose like a dusting from a dandelion." He traced the side of her nose with his finger. "You know. Kind of that girl-next-door look?"

"Mmm," was all she could say as she nodded.

His face was inches away. "Know anyone like that?"

"I might know someone," she whispered as she closed her eyes.

She was in a tree house, knees on the floor, leaning forward, wearing a purple dress. Yellow flower-shaped plastic barrettes from Bailey's Five and Ten in her hair. The smell of strawberries and pine boards. Please, God, don't let our braces lock together.

He kissed her, long and slow this time, his right arm reaching around her back, his left cradling her neck. She felt like she was home. Not her house, not this town, just here. With Peter, on this porch.

It was more than a kiss. It was a confirmation of what had been missing all these years. More than some fuzzy, nostalgia-fueled dream. It was real this time.

They separated, noses almost touching.

"That was much better than seventh grade," he said. "Even better than Chicago. I think we're getting the hang of this."

A dog barked, the stars silently looked on.

"Yes," she agreed wholeheartedly.

It felt right. It was right, wasn't it?

Then why was there this sinking, hard feeling in her chest?

The blanket of cool stars above her reminded her where she was. This wasn't the glow of Chicago's eternally lit sky. It was an unavoidable reminder that, even here in Peter's arms, she was still miles away.

But those thoughts could wait until later. It would all work out, somehow.

It had to, right?

Chapter Twenty-Two

Peter heard the knock on his office door frame. He knew who it was without even looking up.

"Here early?" Lucius asked.

"Apparently." He paused. "I have some labs to grade before the field trip at Nitrovex this afternoon."

Lucius nodded. "The field trip. Forgot about that. Want me to take over?"

Peter did look up now. It was tempting. Last night had been a wash after Kate showed up—a great wash, but still, he had gotten behind. But then, he might see her there. She had her presentation after lunch… "No, I can swing it. Just a few more to go." He yawned.

"Didn't get to them last night?"

"I got a little…sidetracked."

"Hmm. Been a long time since I got sidetracked."

Peter looked up. "You should try it sometime." He went back to his papers. "Maybe with Carol." He smiled. That should shut him up.

It did, for a moment. "Well, I'm very happy for you, Peter. Let me be the first to welcome you to the wonderful world of love."

Peter put up his hands. "Whoa, whoa. Slow down. No one's saying anything about love." It was just one kiss, right? Or was it three? Technically probably five…

Lucius spread his own fingers in apology. "Sorry. Didn't mean to step on your intellectual toes, Dr. Clark."

"Apology accepted."

"Just don't forget what happened to the man who suddenly got everything he wanted. He lived happily ever after."

Peter snorted. "Really? You're quoting Willy Wonka at me?"

Lucius shrugged. "I'm running out of material with you." He grabbed his jacket. "See you at lunch. Tuesday is tater tot casserole day."

"Lovely."

Peter sat back in his chair. Happily ever after? That wasn't possible. And wasn't that just for fairy tales? He'd enjoyed spending time with Kate, of course, but that wouldn't last much longer. The reality of that had hit him harder in the morning. He lived here, Kate lived in Chicago. She worked for a prestigious company in downtown Chicago. He worked—he looked around at his cramped office and sighed—in a box in Golden Grove.

The Dixon job? He almost hoped they wouldn't call. That would save him from having to make a decision. Because he wasn't sure what he would say. Take a job mostly to be near Kate?

He couldn't deny his feelings for her, even if he joked they were just chemicals shooting around his brain, playing pinball with his synapses. But he knew it was more than that. It always had been.

He closed his eyes and pressed a hand to his temple.

All he saw was her golden, fresh smiling face.

* * *

Kate had finally made it through all the suggestions from the home office she'd gotten this morning. Most were just tweaks to her proposal, but she was still worried. She'd been on this project for what? Almost four weeks? By this time she'd usually have had everything put to bed, or at least close enough to hand it off to subordinates to finish up. But this Nitrovex project had been a thorn from the start.

There had been distractions, certainly. But she should be able to handle work and a kiss-worthy chemistry teacher, shouldn't she?

She heard the stairs creak. Carol came through the door moments later, looking worried. "All set for the meeting? You've been at it all morning."

"I didn't get as much time to go over everything last night as I'd hoped."

"Oh. You got distracted?"

"You might say that."

Carol nodded. "Hmm. It's been a long time since I've been distracted." She padded to the kitchen.

"Really? You should try it sometime," Kate called out. "Maybe with Lucius," she added.

A cup clattered in the sink in the kitchen. That got her.

Carol came back a few moments later carrying two cups of coffee and sat down next to Kate.

"Here's the weekly paper." She dropped the Town Crier onto Kate's laptop.

There was a photo on the front of John Wells shaking a smiling girl's hand and giving her the Scholarship Fair plaque. *Stacy.* Kate waited for the stab of bitterness she used to feel whenever she remembered the fair, but instead she found herself smiling too. Good for her. Beneath Stacy's picture were photos of the carnival. One was Peter in mid-plunge in the dunk tank. The smile grew on her face. Nice.

She opened the paper, knocking the crease in the middle so it would lay flat. Obituaries. Mabel Webster, 96. Whoa. Birth announcements. A Tucker, a Carter, a Harper, a Hayden—she wasn't sure if that was a boy or a girl—and two Jayden's. Engagements and weddings...

More photos from the carnival. Uh, oh, one of her doing her face painting. *Chicago marketing executive Kate Brady returns to her hometown, paints a butterfly on third-grader Abby Grossman's cheek. Thanks for helping, Kate!*

Chicago executive? Wow. Was that how they saw her in Golden Grove? Was that how Peter saw her?

It made sense. She'd gotten into this business for the design work, turning a creative idea into something physical you could see. These days, though, she did more managing of projects than the actual artwork for them. Once she landed the Nitrovex account, the management part would increase. One more rung up the ladder with Garman. In Chicago.

"Any good news this week?" Carol asked.

Kate dropped the paper. "Hmm? Oh. I don't know. Usual stuff, I guess. People dying and being born, getting married."

She was relieved when Carol simply nodded and said, "Same as always."

As Carol shuffled back to the kitchen, Kate eyes wandered back to the photo of Peter on the front page. His face looked so goofy, so adorable...

She looked out the dining room window to the house across the yard. She could see the back porch, the padded wicker chair. She frowned as the word 'love seat' popped into her mind, and she quickly shoved it away.

Okay, it was just one kiss. Her forehead scrunched. Okay, two. Wait, three...

No, this wasn't like kissing some new guy she was starting to get to know. She *knew* Peter.

And that was the problem. He obviously wasn't excited about the Dixon job. On paper, there should be no comparison between backed-up sinks and loose lizards and an Ivy-League-looking private high school. But she'd said it herself. He knew what he was doing here. He loved his students, and he didn't care about the money. He'd proven that with his dad, staying here instead of running after a better job.

She massaged her temples, her head in her hands. The idea of how nice it would be for her if he lived in Chicago was selfish. Anyway, it was probably for the best. After all the work she'd done to get where she was, this wasn't the time to get distracted. She was finally succeeding. Right?

Chapter Twenty-Three

Kate jammed her car into park outside the Nitrovex offices.

Deep breath. The Super Bowl, remember? The home office had called on her way here, supportive but firm about what she needed to accomplish. Today's meeting would decide whether she'd be back in Golden Grove next week to finalize everything or in Chicago tomorrow trying to explain why she'd lost the account. Everything else needed to take a love seat—that is, a *back* seat. Right now she had a job to do.

She grabbed her briefcase and marched up the short stone steps to the Nitrovex front doors.

There was a new player today. John's grandson was here. Corey Steele, the hotshot head of Nitrovex's European division. She might have a hometown advantage with John, but Steele wasn't from here and she was going to have to win him over as well.

She'd scouted his profile on the Nitrovex website. About her age. Young for his position but with lots of credentials under his photo. Handsome, she supposed, if you weren't the kind of woman who preferred a crooked smile and twinkling blue eyes. Steele had a kind of sharp-edged face and steely-eyed expression that matched his name. Could have just been the headshot. Got to look strong when you're a corporate mover and shaker.

As she marched down the hall, she felt like she was going into battle. *Focus. You're a marketing executive.* The *Town Crier* agreed. That was who she was. Not some silly ceiling-painting art nerd, right?

The receptionist was in her spot at the front desk, smiling, hair in a bun. "Hi, Kate. You can set up in the conference room. John's just finishing up with another meeting."

Her competition?

"Thanks, Sandy." Hoisting her purse and bag on her shoulder, she headed down the hall.

She found the conference room, unpacked her laptop, and began setting up. She had about twenty minutes before her presentation, and she wanted everything to be running perfectly.

That done she had time to grab some water, which she knew they had in the break room down the hall. Not her usual Fiji, but it would do fine.

She heard her before she saw her. The musical laugh, the so-happy voice, chatting up someone in the break room. Kate stopped, then started again. She could endure a short fly-by with Penny Fitch before the meeting. Then she heard the second voice. Strong, lighthearted. The same voice that had caressed her ears last night on a cool starlit porch.

Peter. What was he doing here? And what was he doing here talking to Penny? What *was* it with these two, hanging out at every opportunity?

She ducked into the ladies room, one door away from the break room. No one in here. Good. She let the door drop to close, then caught it with her hand, listening. She frowned. Couldn't make out what they were saying, but they sure were being friendly. It was early afternoon. Shouldn't he be in class? He hadn't mentioned anything about a visit to Nitrovex last night. But then, if it was to see Penny, he wouldn't have…

Okay, this was ridiculous. There must be some reasonable—

"Okay," Peter was saying from the hallway. "See you in a bit?"

See you in a bit? See you where and why and how in a bit?

"Sure thing," Penny's voice said. "And thanks for understanding."

"I should thank you," Peter said. "This has been overdue for some time. Glad we could finally squeeze it in."

Squeeze *what* in? Kate could hear Penny's heels clacking down the hallway in the opposite direction and quickly pulled the door shut. She didn't need Peter catching her eavesdropping on his little rendezvous.

She punched on the hand drier and let it roar for a while, then poked her head out the door. All clear.

She paused, leaning against the wall next to an oil painting of a combine. She couldn't worry about some tryst between Peter and Penny. She had a presentation in a few minutes.

"Kate? You looking for something?" It was John Wells, coming down the hallway behind her.

She pushed off the wall. "Oh. No, I was just stretching my legs. Before the presentation."

He passed her, heading towards the reception area near the front of the building. She followed automatically.

"You have everything you need?" he asked.

She nodded. "Yes, thanks. You've been very helpful."

"Nothing but the best for one of our own."

She swallowed.

"Hope you're not nervous," he said. "Only the whole board is going to be there this afternoon."

It was supposed to be a joke, she knew, so she chuckled as best she could.

"I'll be fine," she said as she turned the corner into the reception area, almost running into Peter's back. She wobbled on her heel but managed to not stumble into his arms. She couldn't decide if that was good or bad.

He turned, blue eyes fixed on her.

"Well, Peter," John said, hands on his hips. "Getting ready to cart your impressionable young minds around our facility?"

What did that mean? Then she remembered. The first drive out to Nitrovex, in the Mustang. He'd mentioned a field trip he always took his students on.

Peter didn't answer at first, still staring at Kate. Then he turned to John. "We'll try not to let anyone fall into the centrifuge if we can."

John gave a laugh. "I'd appreciate it. Just had it cleaned last month." He leaned to look past Peter. "Penny."

Kate hadn't noticed Penny yet, still wobbling a little. But she was there, behind Peter, bright smile beaming.

"Say, this is old home week for you three, isn't it?" John announced.

They must have all given him the same blank stare.

He gestured. "You were all in the same high school class, weren't you?" John asked.

Penny nodded. "Yes, I guess we were. Go, Griffins," she added with a little fist swipe.

Go Griffins? Kate had to force herself not to roll her eyes.

"Peter, you were the runner, right?" John said, tapping his finger on chin. He turned to Kate. "And Kate here…I believe my wife mentioned something once about—"

"She won your Scholarship Fair," Peter blurted.

Kate's eyes grew huge. If she could have shot lasers out of them, she would have burned his blue-eyed brain out.

John was nodding, eyebrows up. "She did, did she?"

"It was a long time ago," Kate said, glancing around the room. This would be a good time for one these big storage tanks to blow up, wouldn't it? Just *foom*, and it would be all over.

John was stroking his chin, looking up. "Now, I'm trying to remember that name. Brady, Brady… My wife was a judge some years, but…"

"Mr. Wells, if I could have a word before the presentation?" Penny said, moving forward to touch John's arm. He nodded, following her to a side wall.

Kate stepped back. This was not good. The back of her neck was hot, and she rubbed it. It was like some nightmare time warp. Penny over there, flashing her perfect panther smile, blowing the whistle, whispering to the judge—to John Wells. She could almost read her lips. *She was disqualified. She's a cheater, John. She cheated then, and she's cheating now. Peter helped her. Look at them, all lovey-dovey. She used him to try to win this proposal.*

Kate ran a palm across her eye. John was saying something to Penny.

"Kate?" Peter touched her arm.

"Why did you say that?" she hissed.

He shook his head. "I'm sorry, Kate. He was going to remember, anyway. I know you're embarrassed by it, but the truth is, you did win."

"Yes, for about five minutes." She jerked her head at Penny. "Look at her. She's ratting me out."

"She's not ratting you out. She's distracting him. Don't worry."

She snorted. "Don't worry. The biggest presentation of my life is in"—she glanced at her watch—"twelve minutes. I was already worried. Now I'm just…" She wrenched out of his arm and stalked back down the hallway.

The conference room was empty, but not for long. Soon, every major board member of the company would file in. Corey Steele, stakeholders, all staring at her, wondering who this girl was, this supposed expert, the one who was going to tell them exactly what their company needed.

And there would be John Wells, sitting in the center chair, head fresh with the news from Penny Fitch that he was looking at a cheater, a woman so inept she had to rely on the help of her little high school crush—again—just to get the job done.

She took a swallow from her lukewarm bottle of water, then raised it into the air. *Here's to me.*

* * *

"Well, Kate, I think you did a great job."

"You're too kind, John." Kate was shutting down her laptop and unplugging some cables. It had gone pretty well, despite all the pre-game rattling. In some ways, it had made her throw caution to the wind. What was there to lose anymore?

There were plenty of smiles and eye contact. John never once jumped up to point a finger at her and shout "Cheater!" as two strong-armed goons grabbed her to cart her away. That would probably come during her dreams tonight. Corey Steele had done enough nodding that she felt she might have won him over. Unless he was just being polite. He had turned out to be a pretty nice guy despite his metallic name.

She couldn't help noticing that Penny, who had sat next to Mr. Steele, had done a lot of fitful glancing in his direction. Something going on there? Does she hit on every able-bodied male in the county? Or was she finally feeling some guilt in her shriveled little soul?

Whatever. Penny could take care of herself. Peter could take care of himself. She was drained, wrung out, and the week wasn't even half-over yet. Now it was back to Chicago, where she would wait for the call from Nitrovex to see if Garman had made it to the final round. It was going to be a long few days.

Most of the others had left the conference room. John stayed, sitting on the edge of the table, glancing around the room. "Still getting used to this new facility. Far cry from the dirt-floor pole barn we started out in."

Kate smiled, nodded as she kept packing. "I'm sure." Was something on his mind?

"You know, I have to confess. It's hard for an old goat like me to accept some of these changes. Websites, new logos, branding. My grandson tells me I need it, and I'm sure he's right. Just kind of hard to let go of the past sometimes."

He was watching her, something deep in his wrinkled blue eyes. He reminded her of her grandfather, a man who had died when she was ten, leaving only memories of pipe smoke, stories, and swing-set pushes.

"I suppose we all have to face the future some time," she said, forcing a half smile. "Seems to me you're doing it quite well."

He chuckled. "Some days are better than others. I've made my share of mistakes, had some missteps along the way. Some my doing, some not. Trick was to keep moving forward."

She finished sliding her laptop in its case and zipped it shut. All packed. She hoisted the strap over her shoulder. John still sat, watching, arms crossed, genial smile on his face. She felt like hugging him for some reason, not selling her down the river and all. It had already been a long day.

"We'll give you the word by Friday at the latest," he said at last, standing. "Once I have a chance to review the other three candidates' proposal with the rest of the committee, we'll narrow it down to two."

"Fair enough."

"For my part, I hope we see you again in two weeks."

"Fingers crossed," she said, smiling. Yet, part of her wished this was it. It would be easier to be done and gone for good. But wasn't it always?

"Well, I have another appointment waiting in my office." He shook her hand, gave her a couple of pats on her arm.

She only smiled, and he disappeared out the door.

"Kate?"

It was a new voice. Penny.

Kate turned. Be polite, she told herself. Only a few more minutes. "Yes?"

Penny was standing in the doorway. She had a small apologetic smile on her face, hands clasped in front of her waist. "I just wanted to say you did a great job. In there." She gestured with her head.

A compliment? From Penny Fitch? "Thanks. I'm never quite sure if John's just being nice to me."

"No, as much of a softy as he seems, John's a pretty tough customer." Penny nodded, a shy smile on her face. She looked smaller than she usually did. Or maybe just normal. "Well, for what it's worth, I'm putting my vote in to work with Garman."

Kate knew she must look surprised. "Really? Thanks." Was this guilt?

"There's something else," Penny said. "Something I'd like to say. Kind of a confession, I guess. I want to apologize. I need to apologize, actually."

Kate forced a nervous chuckle. "Apologize? Apologize for what?" she said, although she already knew the answer. *Let me get out my list…*

"It's about school. About the Scholarship Fair, and what I did. Back then." Penny paused, searching for words. "I know it was a long time ago, and we were just kids. That's not any excuse or a good reason…" She looked away, then back. "But I was desperate, Kate."

"I don't know what you mean." Kate shifted her weight, began rubbing her wrist.

"I was the new kid in school. Worse, I was the new girl in the senior class. I put on a good face, but you all had known each other since grade school, grown up together. I was the outsider, someone to be studied and categorized from the get-go. Nerd, geek, mathlete, athlete…" She ticked them off on her fingers. "After the first day, I could already tell who was going to talk to me and who was going to giggle behind my back."

Kate felt something new. A twinge of sympathy? "I suppose it's always hard coming into a new school like that."

Penny shrugged. "I'd had some practice. It was my third high school."

Kate raised an eyebrow. As much as Golden Grove had felt like an emotional jail at times, she hadn't thought of the stability it had also given. One high school had been rough enough, but having to go to three?

"So, I guess I was jealous," Penny said, looking down, then up, smiling. "Especially of you."

Me? Kate said with her eyes. "Why?"

"Because of Peter, of course." Penny said it like it was obvious. "He was the only one who was nice to me when I moved in on your street that summer. Not just like a boy trying to hit on the new girl, but genuinely nice. While everyone else was going to pool parties and having fun, he would run with me sometimes. He loved chemistry and hated Jar Jar Binks. We had a lot in common. I thought maybe this was my chance. I'd never stayed in one place long enough to have a boyfriend before."

She paused, looking away. "I should have known better, considering how much he talked about you. *Katie this and Katie that…*" She sighed and shook her head. "Girls can be so stupid. Guys too, I suppose. I knew Peter was probably just helping you with your scholarship project because he liked you, but when I had a chance to try to put you out of the picture, I took it. I told the judges you'd cheated, you'd gotten help from him when I knew you hadn't, not really." She took a deep, halting breath. "It's the one thing in my life I'm most ashamed of."

Then she looked at Kate, her blue-eyes rimmed with tears. "I know it sounds pretty desperate. Who wants to get a guy that way? But I was seventeen, and he was cute, and I was lonely and afraid. I was sure you'd want nothing to do with him after that. That part worked great. You barely spoke to him senior year. I didn't count on one little thing about Peter though."

"What's that?" Kate asked, her brain spinning.

Penny smiled, then laughed. "What do you think? He loves you, Kate."

Loves? Kate's heart buzzed an alarm. "In high school, you mean. Don't be silly."

"Then, yes, but now too."

No. Don't trust her. She's Penny Fitch, the wispy witch. She's playing an angle.

"Oh," Kate said weakly. "No, we're just friends. We *were* just friends. He's nice to everyone." Remember?

Penny reached out, touching her arm, squeezing it. "C'mon, Kate. We're not in high school anymore." She laced her fingers together in front of her. "After my divorce, when I moved back here to work for Nitrovex, I admit I gave Peter some thought. It probably seems funny, but Golden Grove was always the closest thing to home for me."

Kate realized her fingernails were biting into her palms, unclenched them.

"And, yeah, Peter and I went out for coffee a couple of times, He was always so nice," Penny said.

Yes, we've established the niceness factor, Kate thought. "Are you still in love with him?" she asked in a careful voice.

"Still? I was never in love with Peter. I liked the idea of him, sure. It's like, something can look good on paper, you know? Like it should be, right? And then it just…isn't."

Kate took a deep breath, couldn't think of anything to say. But she knew perfectly, exactly what Penny meant.

"I guess you could say there just wasn't any…chemistry?" She said it as a question, as if Kate could somehow provide the answer.

Kate nodded. Chemistry. Then her eyes narrowed. Chemistry? Moles. Angstroms. Molecules. She swallowed. Heart-melting blue eyes. Crooked, disarming smiles. Calm, smooth, small-town reassuring voices that made you feel like you were safe at home. Chemistry.

"So, I guess you're kind of mad at me, huh?"

Kate realized she'd been staring off, down the hall, into nothing. She looked at Penny. And the wispy witch was gone. Just another woman, like herself, someone who had only been trying to make her way from girl to grownup.

Kate had said it herself. *Everyone needs to grow up sooner or later.* Penny had, and maybe Kate needed to as well. She smiled, shaking her head. "No apology necessary," she said. "Actually, I'm sorry, too."

Penny cocked her head. "Sorry? For what?"

Kate smiled. "I guess for not inviting you to a pool party that summer...let's just keep it at that for now."

Penny gave her a smile and a nod. "Okay." She turned and left.

Kate stood for a moment. She felt like she had when she was eight and her mom had caught her making fun of Elizabeth, the girl in her third-grade class with the lisp. It was not a feeling she had ever wanted to repeat.

And it struck her, and she flinched inside. Take Penny the wispy witch out of the past, and Penny Finch was basically a normal, nice person doing her job. Just like Kate. Except for maybe, at the moment, the nice part.

Now she was studying the floor. *Everyone needs to grow up sooner or later.* They were her own words, and she hadn't even listened to them herself.

What else had she missed?

He loves you, Kate. She didn't dare believe that. Not now. That would mean too much. More than an impromptu kiss in a museum. Or under the stars. Or anywhere.

Too much. It didn't matter what Penny believed. Grownups had responsibilities after all.

Kate hurried back into the conference room, began unplugging and packing up her laptop. She needed to get out of here, back to Chicago. She had to finish this project, and then she could think. She needed time to think.

She stuffed some cords into her bag. *That's it,* she nodded to herself. Just some time to think.

Yet, down below, in the bedrock of her heart, she knew she didn't need more time to think. She'd never needed it, not since she'd been ambushed by his familiar crooked smile in front of Ray's Diner weeks ago.

She loved Peter. That was one thing that wasn't going to change.

* * *

She checked her watch, then hurried her pace down the hall. The sooner she got back to Chicago, the better. She'd sort out this job, her career, her life.

She stopped. Peter was standing in the main entrance, hands in his pockets. Tall and unavoidable as a roadblock. The only thing between her and escape. He was talking to a student, who nodded and headed for the front door. Field trip must be over.

She waited, half hoping, half frightened out of her mind that he would turn and see her.

She turned. No. She had work to do. And a long drive back. She couldn't deal with this right now.

Aside from her stinging eyes, she was fine. And this lead brick in her stomach. And the empty space in her chest.

She pushed through a side door that led to the visitor's lot and stood for a moment. Wiped her eyes with the back of her hand.

Maybe she could send Danni back for the final presentation if they won. She'd stay back in Chicago and…

She stiffened. No. This was her deal, her work.

Down the steps, to her car.

Back one more time if need be, then that was it. The job was done.

* * *

Peter watched from the reception area window that looked out onto the Nitrovex visitor's lot. The school bus had just chugged out of the entryway, but it wasn't what he was watching leave.

He could see her profile, standing at the top of the stairs wearing her tan double-breasted wool coat, stiff and straight, October wind ruffling her hair.

One last look, huh? a nameless voice said.

She slung her purse over her shoulder, suddenly looking all business. Her hair pulled back, her face prim. As if she were someone else.

His heart jumbled. *Go after her. Grab her. Kiss her.*

She was jogging down the steps. A hand wiped her face.

He had expected this, right? He should have. He knew she was going to go back. He had just gotten so used to having her around, even though he knew Chicago was where she belonged. It was where she'd always wanted to be.

Do something. Do something really romantic. Run after her. Tackle her. Throw roses at her. Grab her and kiss her and carry her to your car while the factory workers cheer.

Stop her.

He let her go. Down the walkway to the lot. Into her car. It backed out, paused, went forward, and she was gone.

Chapter Twenty-Four

Kate rushed to Carol's house only long enough to pick up her luggage and cram it in the back seat of her car. She wasn't sure that Carol bought her excuse when she explained that she needed to get back to Chicago tonight. Yes, the presentation had gone fine, but there was a lot of work that needed to still be done.

Her yellow VW bug floated down I-88 silently. The road was straight and smooth. Inside, she was trying to keep her mind on driving. She flipped through radio stations and iPhone playlists, but every song just seemed to annoy her.

The countryside flowed by, dull, lifeless, monotonous. She saw white farmhouses with pill-shaped propane tanks by their sides. Red combines in the fields rotating, churning chaff into the air. She saw a rusted windmill struggling to move in the breeze. She started to cry and she didn't know why, and it scared her.

Her car cruised along. Night was falling, slow and dull. Chicago crept back into her life, slowly, each building growing higher and closer to its neighbor, until all that was left was concrete, asphalt, and skyscrapers. A place that had once seemed exciting and alive now looked noisy, cheap, and lifeless. Nothing had changed, she knew, except maybe her.

A night's rest in her rumpled bed had helped some, but she was so exhausted she probably good have slept on an "L" platform.

After she parked her car in the office garage, she fixed her makeup and summoned her game face. Her office was the same. Clean, antiseptic, to the point, and ready for work. Back to work, she thought. That's what she needed. That was what got her here.

Which was where, exactly? Up this "ladder" she kept talking about? A bigger office, with better pay, longer hours, and shorter weekends? For what?

All day, she kept finding herself picturing herself in a tidy office in Golden Grove. Maybe above the bakery, with wooden floors, the smell of fresh bread drifting up, a morning croissant with a to-go cup from The Screamin' Bean sitting next to her. Working on a big-screen computer. Not crunching numbers, but design work. Nothing big, just enough to pay the bills and have some time to herself.

After her last droning meeting, she closed her computer and stared out the tall glass window. It was gray outside, no clouds, no rain, just gray. Golden Grove seemed like another world, like Narnia or Oz. Like something you needed to step through a magic wardrobe or fly in a tornado to get to.

Like the souvenir snow globe perched on the corner of her desk. She picked it up. Tiny orange and red leaves floated in slow motion past old brick houses and a church with a perfect white steeple. Just something you absentmindedly picked up and shook, then put back on the shelf before you returned to real life.

She should have known better. It was just supposed to be a job. A few weeks, maybe a month. Peter wasn't supposed to become her friend again. They weren't supposed to sit by the old treehouse or look up at the stars. He wasn't supposed to kiss her. It should have all been done by now, but instead, it was all scattered. Like fallen leaves or the past or the glass from a ruined mobile.

For an instant, she thought about going back tonight. Getting in the car and driving, all the way, back to the snow globe town, back to his house. Up his front porch and into his arms.

Then she realized why she had cried yesterday. It was loss. Loss of the past, etched forever for good or bad. Loss of the future, unknown and unknowable.

She stared at nothing out the window until the sun was far past setting. The streetlights from below cast the only light in her office, glancing pale orange light up the sides of the walls as she sat alone and silent in the dark.

* * *

The rest of the week was a blur. On Thursday, ahead of schedule even, Garman received word from Nitrovex that Kate's preliminary rebranding proposal was one of the final two candidates. The meeting with the Garman team the next afternoon was also a success. Kate breezed in, confident in her navy-blue dress, presented her designs, her plans, her new slogan.

The Art of Solutions.

It had come to her in the middle of the night, like all good ideas are supposed to, out of nowhere. She had been half asleep, thinking about the paintings at the Art Institute, as if she were in them, floating on a Monet lily pad, running through the smooth green melon-shaped hills of a Grant Wood painting. And it had come to her.

It wasn't just all chemistry. There was an art to it, even though it seemed like it was just about mixing together tanks of foaming liquid. Just like Peter had told her. *There is an art, even a beauty to chemistry.* Putting the molecules together for just the right solution. One tiny piece off and the whole thing wouldn't work. She had even remembered that Nitrovex made binding agents for paints and art supplies.

The Garman board had loved the idea and the logo she had designed. A stylized painter's palette that also looked like a beaker. It had fit perfectly into the larger proposal she had already been working on. They were just the last two pieces, the capstone that held everything together. It had finally clicked. At least something finally had in her life.

She spent Saturday at the office, surrounded by co-workers who kept congratulating her. This was the final stretch. She was due back at Nitrovex next Friday for the last presentation, then on to the next project. No more Golden Grove whether she landed the account or not. Nitrovex would be handed off to more junior staff. Onward and upward for Kate.

She should be happy. Right?

She stared out her apartment window that night, hands in her robe pocket. The view was a similar apartment building across the way, banks of rectangles, some lit, some not, staring blankly. She wondered if someone equally happy was staring back at her from the dark of their living room.

This was the part where she was supposed to be ecstatic. Her bosses were impressed, her first big project looked like it was destined for success.

She picked up her phone and popped up her music app. A variety of suggested playlists rolled through the screen, one picturing four snarling guys in eyeliner and huge blond hair.

"Pop go the eighties." She smiled sadly, thinking of the dance going on tonight, her half-promise to Peter to be there.

She thumbed a song on, and cheesy, synthesized music bounced out. She picked up her glass and sipped her wine. It was from a box left in the fridge, but it was surprisingly good. Another smile. But it was not the solution, right?

He was probably out there on the dance floor right now, with someone. Wasn't he? Getting on with his life after she left him behind again?

She grabbed her phone, heading for the couch, her fuzzy pink slippers shuffling across the wood floor of the dining area. She flipped through the playlist and found it. "Don't Do Your Love."

Don't Do Your Love... what did that even mean? How did you "do" love? Well, that was the question of the year, wasn't it? And any teacher would have failed her on that quiz. Especially Peter.

She thought about crying, but she was too tired. She'd be back in Golden Grove on Friday now since she'd done such a great job. *Yay for me.* But Peter would be busy teaching, doing what he was meant to do, where he was meant to do it.

And her? Where was she meant to be? Here? Pushing more papers, grinding out more proposals?

She stood, moving to the window, looking up at the stars. Not as many as the blanket that covered Golden Grove, but a few. Just enough, maybe. Just one, even.

Her own Lucky Star.

It was there, somewhere, shining out with blue eyes and a crooked smile. She wanted to reach out and grab it, pull it in, never let it go again.

But did she have the courage to take that chance?

* * *

The old gym at the Community Center was the way Peter remembered it from when he was in high school. A little smaller. Still the same dank, slightly musty smell every old gym has from decades of PE and sweaty basketball practices. The carnival that had been held here seemed like years ago, already.

The homecoming dance had been rolling for at least a half hour. A DJ in bright pink louvered sunglasses was pounding out eighties music from a pair of speakers set on either side of the stage, trying to get the kids excited.

And they were. A crowd of them, dressed up in what the Internet told them people in the eighties wore, were bouncing on the dance floor in the middle of the gym. Leg warmers, skinny ties, teased-out hair, humongous shoulder pads, ripped stockings. He had to smile. It was all overblown, but it was fun.

The smile faded. For the kids, anyway.

A disco ball spun up by the retracted basketball hoop, rolling out fragments of sparkly light across the gym floor. Students paired up and began slow dancing, most of them awkwardly, not looking each other in the eye.

Why were people always so afraid?

"Nice turnout."

It was Lucius who had sidled up to him, sipping from a plastic cup of pink punch.

"Not bad. I think having a theme helps."

"I didn't think you'd be here."

"Have to be. I'm one of the chaperones." He smiled and waved at another teacher walking by.

"Hmm." Lucius folded his arms, watching the students rotating in pairs on the old gym floor. The music reverberated from the concrete block walls. "Can I tell you a story?"

"Oh, geez, Lucius, I can't handle a story right now."

"It's a short one."

"Is it about how some knight saves a princess and ends up with you telling me to go after Kate on my white horse?"

"So, you've heard it before?"

"I've heard them all before."

"Well, you were pretty close. The knight is a lonely chemist and the white horse was going to be a red mustang."

"Great. Just as long as they don't fall in love and live happily ever after." He picked up a pretzel from the snack table and bit it. It was stale. He wasn't hungry anyway.

"Yes, funny thing about love."

Peter snorted. He'd never found anything funny about love in his life. "What's that?"

"It's unpredictable."

Peter pointed a finger at him. "Now *that* you got right. See, if it were an experiment, it would be quantifiable. You put two things in, you get one out. Keep the surrounding elements the same. Same heat, same oxygen. The same result every time, no matter how many times you repeat it."

Lucius chuckled. "We're talking about love here, Peter. It's not some repeatable experiment. The surrounding elements change. The heat changes. You don't just drop sodium in water and watch it go bang."

"I know that. But it would be a lot easier if you could."

"Yeah, but it wouldn't be nearly as much fun. Or real." He took a sip of his punch.

"You're a giver, Peter. That's what love does. It gives. You gave to your dad, and your mom."

"I didn't have a choice. He was my dad. My mom needed me."

Lucius shook his head, a gentle smile arcing his gray mustache. "Not just your parents. Most people would do that. Giving is your career."

Peter's look must have looked like a question because Lucius continued. "You're a teacher. You give every day. Your time, your knowledge. To your students. Not only that, you want to give where it's needed. That's why you didn't like Dixon. They don't need you there. But Golden Grove does. And the weird thing about giving is, you think you're losing something, but you're really gaining something better."

Peter was silent. He understood what Lucius was saying, but he wasn't in the mood for deep thinking right now. "And your reason for this conversation is?"

Lucius shrugged. "You stayed here because of love, once. Maybe now you should leave because of it."

He stated it matter-of-factly, but it hit Peter like a weight in his chest. Is that what this was? Love? "Aren't you putting the cart way before the horse?"

Lucius paused. "You know, the older I get, the more I think just cutting to the chase is the way to go. We dance around the issue, we think, we talk, we rehash, we wring our hands, we reconsider, we talk again, and then we go ahead and do what we knew we were eventually going to do anyway, except now it's six months later and we have acid reflux and a migraine."

You got the migraine part right, Peter thought. He must be getting old. Was thirty old? The thump of the bass was giving him a headache.

"Maybe all I'm saying is, don't regret missing out on something just because you're afraid or you think you're not worthy or something else equally stupid." He paused. "Don't find yourself twenty or thirty years down the road wondering what if."

Peter looked at his friend. There was something in his eyes he hadn't seen before. Regret? "It's not really up to me, now, is it?" He gestured with his cup. "She's there, I'm here."

Lucius shrugged. "Distance can be a problem. But some distances are measured less in miles than in attitude."

"Geez, Lucius, I know you mean well, but I can't really handle any more latent hippie platitudes tonight."

"Sorry. I'm running out of material again."

The DJ was thumping out another eighties song. This one he recognized. "Don't Do Your Love," by White…something. Tiger? Buffalo? Elephant? He couldn't remember. It was the same one that had been playing that night. With Kate. The chorus blared.

"What does that even mean, 'don't do your love'?" he muttered.

"No idea. I'm more of a Zeppelin guy myself."

Peter knew his friend was trying his best to provide moral support—Peter was supposed to be here with Kate. Tonight was supposed to be some kind of fantastic, romantic make-up-for-lost-time scene, with him and Kate whirling under the disco ball in the spotlight dance they never got in high school.

He had a sudden picture of her in leg warmers and poofy eighties hair. He wondered if he would have tripped over his own feet. He wondered why they weren't out there dancing to "Don't Do Your Love." He wondered if he'd made a huge mistake.

He'd let Kate go her way once, in high school. He thought it was for the best. Even though he'd never meant to, he'd hurt her. They were young. They'd heal, they'd move on.

But here he was, twelve years later, still alone, still acting as if he were waiting for time to reverse itself, to bring back that young love for another chance. And she had come back, and he had fallen in love with her again, and what was he doing about it?

"Tell me another story, Lucius."

His friend looked at him, then away. Then he said, "There once was a boy named Peter, who was very nice and very smart. All of the girls in Chem 2 loved him because he was such a hottie."

Peter snorted, took a drink of his punch.

"Peter lived in a huge old castle all by himself because he was too afraid to go outside where the monsters were. The meanest of the monsters was named Kate."

Peter shot a glance at his friend, then faced forward again.

"Kate was so mean that she tormented Peter day and night. During the day, she would try to hold his hand and talk about feelings. And at night she would threaten to kiss him."

"Is this going anywhere?"

"Give me break. I'm making this stuff up as I go. One day, Peter realized he was an idiot, and that if he didn't get off his butt and stop being a spineless weasel he was going to lose Kate forever. So, he drove to Chicago, stuck her in his roaring red Mustang, brought her home, and they lived happily ever after. The end. How's that?"

"You left out a few details, but…" Peter said nothing for about ten seconds, then looked at Lucius straight in the eye. "That's the best story I've ever heard. Can you watch this table of stale pretzels for me, please?"

"Sure thing."

Peter spotted Dale Schwartz, the Community Center director, milling by the double side doors, smiling, and rocking back and forth on his heels.

He had a big favor to ask him.

Chapter Twenty-Five

It was the next Friday afternoon, a little after three o'clock. The full contingent of Nitrovex board members was arrayed before Kate around the packed conference table. Garman already had the account. She'd decided to run the slogan by John Wells earlier in the week, and he'd liked the idea so much that he'd cancelled the meeting with the other company under consideration. She'd succeeded with her first big project. It should have been the highlight of her life, but she was still nervous. This wasn't just her concept. These were her actual designs. She'd spent all week creating them with the art department. It had been the most fun she'd had at Garman for a while, but she didn't have time to think about that now.

She folded her hands in front of her, making eye contact with the faces surrounding her. "Nitrovex is not only about tradition but innovation. Not just about the past but the future. Not just smelly brown chemicals swirling in a big vat but about materials and colors for the art industry." That got a few chuckles.

Kate tapped a key on her laptop. The last slide of the presentation featuring her new Nitrovex logo faded onto the screen dramatically. "So, what better way to show the industry all these components. 'Nitrovex—The Art of Solutions.'"

There were murmurs of approval and nodding heads. John grinned, and Penny even applauded. Corey Steele, smiling next to her, reached over and wordlessly gave her arm a squeeze.

She moved on to the next slide. The new logo interspersed with some stock Nitrovex materials, now in a smooth, curving layout. Clean, fresh, but not too modern. Her designs. And they liked them, judging by the approving nods.

This was supposed to be the part where her brain did cartwheels. Where she pumped her fist with a silent yes. But it all felt as flat and sterile as the blank white walls of the conference room.

The final presentation over, the Nitrovex members filed out, some shaking her hand, congratulating her as if she were now one of the team. She smiled, perfunctorily.

The last to leave was John.

"Kate, I knew from the start you had a feel for my company."

"Oh, John. I have a whole company behind me. I'm just the spokesperson."

"No, no, I was right about you." John adjusted his seed-corn hat. "I've enjoyed having you around here the past weeks. Kind of feel like I know you, you know? I mean, you are one of us."

She just smiled. And for the first time, she didn't argue that fact. It even felt true. "I appreciate that, John. Very much." She began folding her laptop, unplugging cords, now for the last time.

John checked his watch. "You leaving soon?" he asked.

She cocked her head. "Soon as I get packed up." No reason to stay, was there?

"Planning on stopping by the bakery before you leave? Might not be back this way for a while, you know? I'm partial to the bear claws, myself."

Why did he seem to be stalling? "No, think I'll just hit the road."

He nodded. "Sure. I'll leave you to it, then. And congratulations." He smiled, hand out. "You deserve it."

She returned his smile and handshake, and he left.

Did she? Maybe it was time to follow her dream, those dreams she'd left here, painted over like her mural.

Running her own design business? The idea thudded her heart, but not with fear. She had found herself already working through the details in her mind over the weekend after last weeks' session with her design department. Just for fun, right?

Start with a home office, maybe use a virtual assistant for the paperwork. The first few months might be thin, but with her experience and some jobs from Nitrovex? It might work.

The idea of it all exhilarated her. And surprised her.

Her phone rang, interrupting her thoughts. She fished it out of her purse.

"Hello, Katie? Are still you in town?" It was Carol, calling from her cell phone.

"Not for long. My meeting is over."

"Oh, dear."

Kate's brow furrowed. "Why, what's wrong?"

"Oh, nothing serious, really. Nothing too serious, anyway."

Kate heard a clanging noise in the background and some shouting. "Are you okay? What's going on?"

"Well, it's nothing really. I was just hoping you could stop by the Community Center before you leave. There's a—"

Another loud noise that sounded like a cymbal drowning in a tuba cut her off. Then more clanging and shouting.

Kate popped up out of her chair and grabbed her coat and keys. This sounded serious. "Carol, should you call nine-one-one?"

"Oh, no, dear. I'm sure we'll be able to put it out before it spreads. At the Community Center."

"Spreads? Is there a fire?" Something sounded fishy.

"And Lucius says there's always a little swelling with a broken bone. But don't worry about me here down at the Community Center. I'm sure you have a lot of important things to do."

"Carol, are you hurt? Should I call an ambulance?"

"Oh, no need for that dear," Carol said quickly. "Lucius is a qualified, um, medical helper... person. Are you on your way to the Community Center?"

Qualified medical-helper person? Okay, either Carol had double-dosed on her pills or maybe this was a repeat of her first day in town. Kate's heart thumped. "If you need help—"

"It's just we're not sure if the raccoons have rabies or not, and they look awfully hungry."

Kate's eyes narrowed, but she felt a smile tug at her mouth. "Did you say raccoons?"

"Raccoons or possums. Or bears, it's hard to tell. The lights are pretty dim here in the Community Center."

Carol was a terrible liar. But it *was* possible there was something really wrong with her. She needed to check it out, right? "Okay, Carol, I'm on my way."

Her smile kept getting wider, but her heart was racing too. Something deeper was going on, and she wasn't sure if she was ready to find out what it was.

* * *

Who was she kidding? Not ready? She'd been ready since grade school. The Community Center was about two blocks from the middle of town. Miles from the Nitrovex parking lot. She got there in ten minutes flat, grinding the Bug to a stop in front of the main doors.

The building looked quiet as she jogged up the steps. No fire trucks or police cars. No flames licking out the second-floor windows, no rabid raccoons or possums or bears bellowing as they fled out the front door. No noises, really.

She pushed through one of the thick wooden front doors.

The main hallway was quiet as well, and dark. She walked forward slowly, listening for any signs of distress.

The place was empty. She hadn't been in this section the night of the carnival when it had been lit with people and activity. She'd stayed in the gym, where there had been fewer memories.

This was like stepping back in time. She remembered it all. Old oak trophy case to the right, now filled with local art projects. Round clocks on the walls, most of them with the wrong time. Off-white ceiling tiles. The smell of must, dust, and floor cleaner. Slick, worn black-and-white-streaked linoleum floors echoed her footsteps.

"Carol? Hello?"

From down the hall, she heard something. Music. Faint but familiar. A song… *Why you got to be so cold, baby? Why you got to make me cry?*

It reflected and bounced, the delay making it hard to understand.

Why you got to hold me down, baby? When you gonna make me fly?

The chorus came on. She began singing along, softly. "Don't do your love, don't do your love, don't do your love…" She kept walking, slowly, her feet scuffing on the old linoleum. The faint music seemed to be coming from the back of the school, where the gym used to be.

Why you gotta leave me low, honey? Why you gotta steal my fun? Why you always on the run, lady? Are you gonna be the one?

It was the song from her eighties playlist. The one Peter had been playing at his house that night. *That night.* She wasn't sure if her heart was pounding from hope or fear.

She turned left at the corner and into the hallway that led down the gym. The corridor was dim where she was, just the light coming under the doors from the classrooms. But she could see flashing lights at the end of the hall by the gym entrance.

Police cars? No, these were multicolored lights, like Christmas lights but brighter and bigger.

The music grew louder the closer she walked. It was clearly coming from the gym. Still no sign of anyone. All she needed was a fog machine, and she'd be in a cheap horror movie.

She approached the doorway, saw someone silhouetted in it. They didn't have an ax or a running chainsaw, so that ruled out horror movie. And they were definitely taller than Carol.

The music was loud now, the bass thumping. She could feel it in her chest. Or was it her heart?

Why you gotta leave me low, honey? Why you gotta steal my fun?

The silhouette didn't move, just stood with his hands crossed in front of him. It was a man, she could tell now, and even though she couldn't see his face, she knew he was smiling. She wasn't sure how she knew. *Oh.* Yes, now she was sure.

Don't do your love, don't do your love, don't dooooooooooooo... your love.

The song finished, but the sound reverberated down the hall for a few moments before evaporating. A new song started, this one slower and softer, a ballad. Keyboards, lots of bass. Another eighties song?

She was about twenty feet from the figure in the doorway. She could see he was wearing a suit...no, not a suit. A tuxedo. A white tuxedo. A white tuxedo with wide black-edged lapels, black satin stripes down the pants. Hair parted in the middle and feathered to the sides. And underneath the smiling face and the crooked smile was a huge black butterfly bow tie.

It was hideous. It was the eighties. It was beautiful.

It was Peter.

Chapter Twenty-Six

The music bumped and swirled as a more upbeat part of the song kicked in. The lights behind Peter dimmed, and she could more clearly see the rest of the gym.

Twisted streamers hung from the old basketball hoops, arcing across to the rafters, where cardboard cutouts of PacMan, Rubik's cubes, and records slowly turned in the air. Multicolored lights mounted on poles randomly blinked on and off while a disco ball hanging from the old scoreboard in the center of the ceiling rotated colored squares of light around the room.

"Welcome to the Golden Grove High School Homecoming Dance," Peter said. He cocked his head. "Are you arriving without a date, miss?"

Kate had her hand on her mouth, looking left and right, still taking it all in. "I guess so," she said.

He stuck out his elbow. "Then it would be totally awesome and rad if you might extend to me the honor of the pleasure of accompanying me to the dance, which is happening now at"—he checked his watch—"three fifty-five."

"Post meridium."

"Post meridium."

She looked again at the room. There were neon-colored balloons scattered over the floor. To the side were long tables with zebra-striped tablecloths covered with trays of cupcakes and a bowl of pink punch. A huge brown-paper banner at the center of the gym floor read "Welcome to the 80's!" painted in pink, yellow, and green letters. It was all bright and garish and perfect.

"May I have this dance?" he asked.

"Okay," she said because it seemed to be the only word left in her brain.

Peter turned and shouted, "She said yes!"

A crowd of cheering people spilled out from either side of the stage where they had been hiding. Most were dressed in various eighties clothes—suits with skinny ties, piles of poofed-up hair, multicolored sweaters, jackets with giant shoulder pads, pouting girls wearing sunglasses and torn shirts that were hanging off their shoulders.

Peter came forward, elbow still extended. She kicked off her heels and slipped her arm through his as he guided her to the middle of the floor.

"What do you think?" he asked.

She couldn't think. "You did this?"

"With a lot of help from some friends." He nodded past her shoulder at someone.

Lucius was approaching from the punch bowl holding a plastic cup. Kate doubled over in laughter. He looked like he had just walked out of a Miami Vice episode. Pink pastel t-shirt under a shiny blue-gray jacket. And on his head, an incredibly fake blond mullet that coursed down his shoulders.

"I don't think she likes my outfit," he said, looking at Peter.

"You look…you look…" was all Kate could gasp, hands on her knees she was laughing so hard. "Where in the world did you get these clothes?"

"I don't know. You'll have to ask my date."

A hand squeezed her arm. She turned.

It was Carol, wearing hot pink shorts over a lime-green leotard, with purple leg warmers and black-and-white checkered tennis shoes. Her hair was teased and piled on her head, and she was wearing a t-shirt that said "SAVE FERRIS."

Kate almost fell to the floor, snorting. She thought she was going to pee her pants.

"Radical, dude," Carol said with a smile.

Kate grabbed Peter by the arm and tried to stand. When she could finally speak again, she said, "So the raccoons and the noise and the fire…it was all just to get me here, right?"

"Pretty much," said Peter. "Penny helped too. She scheduled your meeting for the afternoon so the band could be here to set up. They couldn't be here until school was out." He waved to a group of kids at the edge of the gym floor, bouncing to the music. On the stage behind them was a pile of band instruments. "We accidentally dropped a cymbal into the Sousaphone. Don't tell the band director."

"Radical, dude," Carol said again.

"Um, Lucius, now might be a good time for you and Carol go get some punch or something," Peter said.

"C'mon, baby," Lucius said, taking the hint. "Let's, like, totally go get some gnarly punch."

"Bodacious," Carol said, taking his arm. "Bye, Katie."

"Bye," Kate said and watched them go. "That has got to be the funniest thing I've ever seen." She turned back to Peter and laughed again. "I'm sorry, I don't think I'm going to be able to handle that hair."

"You don't like the hair? I spent all of two minutes working on this hair."

She reached up with both hands and tousled it. "I like the new Peter better."

He nodded. "Have it your way."

The music continued to bounce along. Students and even a few teachers were milling around. It was now officially a party. "Peter, why did you do all this?"

"It was a fair amount of work, believe me. We had to save the decorations from the dance last Saturday. I had to have Dale Schwarz convince the square dance club to practice tomorrow afternoon instead of today. Not all the students could be here, mostly just the seniors."

"No, I asked *why* did you do this?"

"You promised me a dance."

"I did no such thing."

"Well…then…you should have."

She paused, looking around. "Yes. I should have," she said.

He took her hand. "Wait a minute." He paused as if listening for something, still holding her hand. "Slow dance is coming," he said finally.

She cocked her head. As if on cue, a syrupy keyboard started to play a ballad. "How did you know that?"

He shrugged. "It's an acquired skill. Guys learn to figure out when the slow dance is coming. If there are three fast songs, then you ask the girl to dance on the fourth. You do that dance without any pressure. It's a fast dance, right? Now, the DJ usually tries to mix things up, which means the fifth song is usually a slow dance. Then you look at the girl and go, 'Hey, wow, a slow dance. Since we're already out here…' "

She nodded. "That's very scientific."

"Thank you."

"I'm not sure I meant that as a compliment."

"Well, at this point, I'll take what I can get."

She laughed. "Guys are that devious?"

"When it comes to beautiful girls, we are highly motivated. Besides, I paid the DJ ten bucks to make sure all of our songs are slow dances." He reached for her waist.

She moved closer. The song continued. They began to rotate together under the disco ball.

"You didn't have to do all this," she said, gesturing with her head.

"I really, really wanted to."

"Why?" Her heart thumped, waiting for the answer.

"Lucius told me a story."

That wasn't the answer she'd been expecting. "Really?"

"It was about Kate the Monster."

"Really." She shot a glance at Lucius, who was with Carol by the punch bowl. He raised his glass at her, grinning.

"The monster part wasn't as important as the part about me being a spineless weasel and losing you forever."

Losing me?

He drew her closer. His hand was warm and safe on her back. It carried her along as they slowly moved around the wooden floor.

She glanced around.

"They're all staring at us," she said.

"I know."

"You'll never live this down. Your students—"

"I know."

She paused, remembering. Raccoons and possums and bears. "I'm going to kill Carol."

"Oh, don't blame her. It was my idea."

"Then I'm going to kill you." But she couldn't stop smiling.

"Not until we're done dancing. It's homecoming, remember?"

The music played on, the multicolored light from the disco ball passing sleepy stars through their hair. She watched them spin away across the floor, like scattered pieces of colored glass.

The dance floor had cleared. It was just them now.

"So, I was thinking," Peter said as they turned.

"Yes?"

"I was thinking, maybe we're not as far apart from each other as we think."

She squeezed his hand, the heat from his chest warming her. "I don't see how we could get much closer."

"No, I mean, maybe it's like…a…what do you call it when two words sound the same but have two different meanings? Like 'deer' the animal and 'dear' that you start a letter with?"

"Homonyms?"

"Right. Like a homonym. There's chemistry, and then there's chemistry."

"But…those are still just the same word."

Peter scowled. "Okay, so Mrs. Harper's English Comp class was a long time ago. My point is chemistry can be chemicals and reactions and so forth but…" He took her hand. "It can also mean something intangible between two people."

"So. What's between us?"

"Right now, your extremely attractive business dress and this itchy tuxedo."

"No, Mr. Tangible, what's between us?"

He didn't say anything for a moment. "Nothing that we shouldn't have already put behind us."

A new song started. Another slow one. They were almost intertwined now.

"Peter, I don't want you to take that Chicago job. They need you here. It's where you belong." She waited, breathless.

"I've come to the same conclusion myself." His face moved closer. "Besides, it would still be too far away from you."

Kate's chest pounded. "Really?" They'd stopped moving. She lifted up slightly on her toes. "So…how far away do you want to be?"

"This far." Peter pulled her close, cupped her face, and kissed her.

The students and teachers cheered. Carol and Lucius cheered. She thought maybe even the stupid stars and birds and crickets cheered.

"Peter?" His arms were still wrapped around her. It was definitely a homecoming.

"Hmm?"

"I'm tired of being afraid. It's tiring, you know?"

"I agree."

"It's so inconvenient. I think maybe we should stop being so afraid." She twirled a lock of hair by his ear. "Maybe we should trust each other a little more. Maybe we should just throw bunches of leaves up into the air and see where they blow. Maybe we should drink some pie shakes."

"That's a lot of maybes."

She smiled as she moved towards those blue eyes again. "Maybe."

The second kiss was even more cheer-worthy, and the crowd of students obliged.

"It's getting crowded in here," she said.

"I agree. C'mon," he said. "I have something to show you."

* * *

Peter led her by the hand through the gym and to the back door of the school, the door she used to take on her way home from school. He pushed it open, and she walked through.

The day had decided to be sunny. The pea gravel she remembered was gone, replaced with wood mulch. The ground was scattered with orange and yellow leaves, a fall breeze blowing a few in tiny whirlwinds.

He passed her and took her hand again. She wanted to ask where they were going, but she just followed.

It was only a few steps until she realized he was taking her to The Tree. The Tree was their childhood rendezvous point, their secret playhouse up until third grade. She'd bring her Barbies, he'd bring his whatever robot thing he was fixated on that week. So long ago. She looked up. It was still huge, its arms stretching over almost the whole playground. Some of its leaves still clung to branches, fluttering sunlight on her face.

He walked her behind it, then stopped, turned, and took her other hand. He drew in a deep breath. She exhaled shakily.

"Katie Brady, I've decided I super-love you," he said.

Super love? Her note…

"I love that you danced with me even though everyone was watching. I love how I got my first kiss from you, and, even if it wasn't yours, it's still my best."

She leaned against the tree trunk for support, still holding his hands.

"I love how you snort when you laugh really hard, and you bend over with your hands on your knees."

"Oh, geez…"

"I love how the bridge of your nose wrinkles when you're angry, and I love your feet."

She looked down. "My feet?"

"Um, I just think you have nice feet."

"Okay…"

"I love that you've always been beautiful to me no matter how old you are or if you have braces or drive a VW Bug or slurp the bottom of your shake with your straw. I just…love you."

She stared at his face. The breeze blew a lock of his hair.

She didn't know what to say. It was what she had always wanted, wasn't it?

"Peter, I…" She sighed, dropping her hands from his, searching his eyes. "Why did you bring me here?"

He smiled. "Because I wanted to tell you something. Away from everyone else. Just us."

She swallowed. "What's that?"

"I know it was just high school. I know we were just kids. But I can't shake the feeling that we missed out on something that could have been great, that maybe should have been great. But I'm not going to miss out again. And if you do leave, if you go back to Chicago, that's fine. I'm going to follow you because that's what love does. I finally—*finally* think I learned the place just doesn't matter. I mean, it's nice if you're sitting in a fortieth-story penthouse in downtown Chicago, but you can still be just as soul-punching lonely as a guy sitting in a one-bedroom apartment with a busted air conditioner in Golden Grove."

Her eyes were hot, swimming. *Yes, keep talking. Tell me what love is, Peter, because I need to know, and I need it to be you.*

"And I'm sorry, Kate. I should have said something sooner. I should have done something sooner. I should have been braver, I guess. But you left, and then Dad died, and I was tired of people I loved leaving. And I was afraid—I knew you were going to leave, too, and the only way to keep that from happening was to follow you."

He stopped, his eyes not begging but strong, solid, a man.

She, on the other hand, had no words, and her eyes were now too wet to see anything but his blurry, beautiful face.

"So, I'm going to follow you, Kate. And if you don't want me to you're going to have to say 'Peter, don't follow me,' and slap me in the face and slash my tires or something because otherwise, I'm going to camp out on your doorstep."

"I don't have a doorstep. I live in a high-rise building."

"Fine, then I'll camp out in your lobby, or your vestibule, or whatever you have. And I'll make friends with all your neighbors and get them on my side until you see that we were meant to be together." He stopped.

She wiped tears from her smile.

"Was that too much? 'Meant to be together'?" he said.

"It was absolutely scientifically perfect," she said and launched herself at him.

Their kiss was warm and sparkly. She stood on her toes. She had a strange, fleeting thought that she was going to want to do a lot of calf exercises in the future.

They parted, still embracing. He smelled clean and bright, like sunshine. His arms were the safest, warmest place she'd ever been. She rested her head on his shoulder.

"I still don't think I'm going to take the Dixon job."

"I know," she said, still nestled.

"But I can probably find something else. Or I'll see you on weekends. Or buy a helicopter and learn how to fly, I don't know yet."

She pushed back, looked up. "You don't need to buy a helicopter, Peter. I think I'm going to quit my job."

His face was a mixture of elation and concern. "What? Why?"

"I don't love it. Not like you love teaching. Like how you give up weekends to chase lizards and mop floors just so you can help your kids learn."

"It is pretty glamorous, I admit," he said. "But I don't want you to just quit your job. What would you do?"

She shrugged, and it felt like a weight floated off her shoulders at the same time. "Not sure yet. It just came to me, this week, I think. I miss being creative. Maybe I can start my own design business. Maybe even here. In Golden Grove."

His eyes flamed. "Here? You sure?"

She chuckled. "No. But let's see what happens."

He untangled himself from her. "Almost forgot," he said. "I wanted you to have something."

"What?" She watched him, head tilted, curious, as he reached into the right pocket of his tux. He pulled out a silver strand, took her left hand, opened her fingers.

"This," he said, and placed it in her palm.

She looked down, eyes wide.

It was the necklace she had made him in third grade.

"I added a heart to it," he said. "I hope that's okay."

Her eyes shut as her hand closed around that tiny, simple, insignificant object which now meant everything in the world to her. Simple and plain. Unremarkable to anyone except them.

And she loved him. She'd always loved him, somehow. She knew because she'd never really loved anyone else. It wasn't that they were bad, or stupid. But they weren't Peter. Even when he hadn't been with her, he was there. He was her roots, like this town. This slow, desperately dopey, wonderful, lovable little town, with all its memories, good and bad, like everywhere and everything else in life. *Who we are in the present includes who we were in the past.* That's what Carol had said. But you could always change your future.

And there it was, her future, waiting, watching her with his clear blue eyes, the fall breeze ruffling his hair, late afternoon sun shining a halo behind him. She almost laughed, the angel metaphor was so corny.

"What?" he said, as always, beautifully, hopelessly oblivious.

"Nothing," she said, grinning. "Everything is fine. Everything is fine."

Epilogue

Spring was finally here to stay. The scent of fresh earth blew through town on every breeze as farmers began tilling up the dirt. Carol had no fear of leaving her marigolds out overnight in the planters on Katie's old porch. The threat of frost was gone. And the biggest wedding of the season was today.

The bride and groom dodged birdseed being flung at them from a gauntlet of friends and family lining the front steps of the church.

Peter and Kate made it down the steps, hand in hand, followed by cheering well-wishers. They stopped at the bottom, Kate brushing seeds from Peter's always unruly hair.

Students piled out of the church as well, most cheering for 'Mr. C.' School had been out a week now, and it was a perfect kickoff to summer.

Kate caught John Wells coming her way. She waved, almost laughing. He was in the first suit she'd ever seen him wear but still wearing his favorite seed corn hat.

"Kate, congratulations," he said as he shook her hand. "You too, Peter."

"Thank you, sir."

He turned back to Kate. "Thanks for the new brochures. Sandy showed them to me. They look great."

"You're welcome."

He snapped his fingers. "Oh, and remember, we've got a planning session first week after you get back. The superintendent and the representative from Arts Share will be there, too."

Kate nodded. "I'll be ready. Already have lots of ideas for the next school year."

"I bet you do. Glad you decided to come aboard."

She smiled, looking at Peter. "Me too."

"Arts Share?" Peter asked when he was gone.

"Sorry, he just sprang that on me this week. John's agreed to help fund some art tours for the students at area schools."

"Nice," Peter said, nodding. "Sure you can handle that along with your Lucky Star work?"

They'd come up with the name for her new graphic design business together. "No problem. Being self-employed gives me a ton of flexibility."

"Just remember to leave your job here while we're on the honeymoon."

"Oh, don't worry." She pecked him on the cheek. "I'm sure I'll have plenty of distractions to keep me occupied."

He grinned, that crooked, warm smile that was all hers now.

She missed Chicago a little, but she felt better leaving The Garman Group with the Nitrovex deal under their belt. They were already getting more offers from similar-sized companies. They would be fine. And they'd understood when she'd told them she was striking out on her own. Danni had even wished her luck with a surprising hug.

It was a risk, starting her own company, but the freedom was worth it. She glanced at her husband, who was busy getting congratulated. Besides, there were undeniably better fringe benefits here.

And Golden Grove? She realized a while back it had helped make her who she was. And it wasn't perfect—no place was—but it was home for her and Peter. Maybe not forever, but for now, and that was good enough.

Peter put his hand around her waist and turned to her, grinning. "I forgot to tell you how beautiful you look."

"No, you didn't. You told me once when we were up at the front of the church and twice in the hallway after we left down the aisle."

"Oh."

"But, um…you could always tell me again."

"You look beautiful."

"Thanks. And thanks for not wearing that tux you wore at homecoming last fall."

"Well, you said if I did you'd divorce me right after we said the vows."

"Correct." She brushed at his shirt collar under his tuxedo. "I see you got the stain out of your shirt."

"From the dance? Took a while. Lipstick is hard to get off. I had to use ten milliliters of hydrogen peroxide, twenty milliliters of acetic acid, and five mils of ammonia."

She leaned up and whispered in his ear. "You might want to remember that solution."

Lucius came down the steps, looking decidedly dapper in his black tux. On his arm was Carol in a light orange dress. Both were beaming.

"Okay, now you sure you two have everything under control?" Kate asked.

Carol waved her hand. "Oh, not a problem. Lucius and I will watch the house and water the plants. You two just enjoy yourselves."

"Oh, we will," Kate said, winking at Peter.

"Where are you going again?" Lucius asked.

"Chicago, then Costa Rica for a week, and from there…?" He looked at Kate expectantly.

"We're going to just take it one day at a time."

Lucius nodded. "Sound advice." He extended both arms, walked to Peter and gave him a hug accented with a few claps on the back. "All the best to you and your new bride, my friend."

Kate liked the sound of the word "bride."

He moved next to Kate, held her at arms' length for a moment, then drew her close and gave her a peck on the cheek. His mustache *did* tickle. "We wish you all the best," Lucius said.

"He said we," Peter said softly, nudging Kate.

Lucius looked lost for a moment. "What's that?"

"Nothing, nothing." Peter clapped his hand to his jacket pocket, searching. "That reminds me. We got you two a gift."

"A gift?" Carol said.

Peter pulled out a small card which he handed to Kate.

"Yes," Kate said. "A gift card we had Ray make up for us. It's good for a year's worth of free pie shakes, but only if shared by Carol Harding and Lucius Potter." She handed the card to Carol, who seemed at a loss for words.

"Bye, bye, now," Kate said as she and Peter turned to go down the front walk.

"I noticed Carol caught the bouquet," he said in Kate's ear as they made their way to the car.

"She should have. I chucked it right at her."

"Remind me to add 'devious' to my 'reasons why I love Kate' list."

"Felt kind of bad for Penny, here all alone." She nodded towards the group of laughing bridesmaids.

"When's that Remington Steele guy in town again?"

"You know it's 'Corey Steele', and from what she tells me in her not-so-casual hints, not for a few weeks."

"Then it's"—he held his fist out, which she touched with hers—"matchmaker powers activate."

"You are the biggest, most lovable nerd," she laughed, and grabbed her new husband's hand to pull him down the sidewalk. They had to get a move on if they were going to make it to their hotel in Chicago before dark.

The Mustang was waiting by the curb, gleaming, top down. Aside from the "Just Married" magnet plastered on the back and some streamers taped to the bumper it looked like it could have just rolled off the lot. The kids in the industrial arts class had done a great job adding some extra shine.

Kate nudged her new husband. "Hey. Look."

Peter turned. He smiled.

Carol and Lucius were holding hands.

Peter held Kate's door open for her, and she nestled in, smoothing her white lace dress around her.

An older couple, probably in their seventies, approached from the sidewalk.

"Hello," the woman said, smiling. "I know you don't know us, but we just wanted to say congratulations."

"We're just visiting," the man added. "You have a lovely town."

"Thank you," Kate said, and she meant it.

"We don't mean to keep you," the woman said, then gave a knowing gaze at her husband. "We're celebrating our fiftieth wedding anniversary tomorrow."

"Well, then, we should be saying congratulations to you," Kate said, instantly liking this cute couple.

The man nodded. "Thank you. Seems like just yesterday we met on a blind date. Six months later we were heading down a road, too. In a car a little older than this though." He paused, then gazed at his wife. "Fifty years."

"So, what brought you two together, then?" the woman asked.

"Oh, don't pry," the man said, putting a hand on his wife's shoulder.

Kate and Peter looked at each other, smiling. "Oh," Kate said. "The usual. We met in school."

"And we were next-door neighbors."

"Then he threw worms at me."
"Then we kissed in a tree house."
"He smashed my art project and kept me from getting into art school."
"And then she left forever, never to return."
The older couple were nodding, looking slightly confused.
"But then fate brought us together again."
"Fate and two meddling old friends."
"And timing."
"And strategically placed telescope tripods."
"But mostly timing, right?"
"Mmm...yes. Timing."
Kate nodded. "And mistakes. And braces. And...treehouses."
"A little wine also helps."
She grimaced. "Oh, and chemistry. Don't forget the chemistry."
Peter nodded. "Yup. Lots and lots of chemistry."
"Lots," she nodded, and leaned in for a kiss.

THE END

Dear reader,

We hope you enjoyed reading *Call It Chemistry*. Please take a moment to leave a review in Amazon, even if it's a short one. Your opinion is important to us.

Discover more books by D.J. Van Oss at https://www.nextchapter.pub/authors/dj-van-oss

Want to know when one of our books is free or discounted for Kindle? Join the newsletter at http://eepurl.com/bqqB3H

Best regards,
D.J. Van Oss and the Next Chapter Team

About the Author

D. J. Van Oss writes sweet and sunny romantic comedies with an emphasis on second chances; kind of like the book version of finding an extra pack of icing for your cinnamon roll.

When not writing you can find him working in the yard, walking the dog, or staying up too late watching BBC mysteries while eating honey peanut butter straight out of the jar.

He lives in the country suburbs of Iowa with his wife and three stepdaughters. His writing partner is Jack, a pretty-boy golden retriever who grunts when you rub his ears.

Books by the Author

Golden Grove Series
Call It Chemistry
Write By Your Side
D.C. Diplomats Series
Driving Miss Crazy

You might also like:

Write By Your Side by D.J. Van Oss

To read first chapter for free, head to:
https://www.nextchapter.pub/books/write-by-your-side

Lightning Source UK Ltd.
Milton Keynes UK
UKHW010719240620
365480UK00008BA/289